ZANE PR

Under WRAPPED

Dear Reader:

It is indeed a pleasure to present *Under Wrapped* by Charmaine R. Parker, my biological sister's third book, a sequel to *The Next Phase of Life*. Tai and Trista are back; two sisters separated by a horrific murder-suicide of their parents for many years. They are still trying to become reacclimated with each other but the task will not be easy. Tai has it all: a successful career, a fine husband, and a great support system. Trista has nothing to boast about except for her ability to dance. But she is trying, despite numerous challenges.

Tai has a group of friends who are also dealing with their own problems, from trying to get the proverbial ring put on their fingers to coping with relationship drama. All are right around the forty-year mark in life—slightly over or under—and that is a milestone age where things truly get real. *Under Wrapped* is full of drama, sex, intrigue, and thought-provoking scenes that will have readers yearning to turn each page to find out what happens next.

As always, thanks for the love and support shown toward myself and the authors that I publish under Strebor Books. We appreciate each and every one of you and will continue to strive to bring you cutting-edge, exciting books in the future. For more information, please join my Facebook page @AuthorZane, Twitter @AuthorZane, or Instagram@AuthorZane. You can also find my "toys" at Zanespleasureproducts.com and my main web site remains Eroticanoir.com.

Blessings,

Zane

Publisher
Strebor Books
www.simonandschuster.com

ALSO BY CHARMAINE R. PARKER

The Trophy Wives

The Next Phase of Life

ZANE PRESENTS

Under WRAPPED

CHARMAINE R. PARKER

SBI

STREBOR BOOKS

NEW YORK LONDON TORONTO SYDNEY

SBI

Strebor Books
P.O. Box 6505
Largo, MD 20792
http://www.streborbooks.com

ISBN 978-1-59309-477-5
ISBN 978-1-4516-9656-1 (ebook)
LCCN 2014936779

First Strebor Books trade paperback edition January 2015

Cover design: www.mariondesigns.com
Cover photograph: © Keith Saunders/Keith Saunders Photos

10 9 8 7 6 5 4 3 2 1

Manufactured in the United States of America

To my daughter, Jazmin

ACKNOWLEDGMENTS

I'd like to thank God for providing me with good health, mind and spirit. Through You all things are possible.

To my parents, James and Elizabeth, for emphasizing the importance of education and exposure; for being positive role models; for demonstrating the true meaning of family and friends. Your love is endless. I love you for being you. I can never thank you enough for exposing us to literacy.

To my husband, Ricardo, thank you for your love and support.

To my sister, Zane, who would've thought when you asked me to edit the manuscript for Addicted that it would become a No. 1 bestseller and a major film? Or that a decade later, you'd evolve into a nationally bestselling author of thirty-plus books? Cheers to your success.

To my sister, Carlita, a superwoman who mirrors many lifestyles as a wife and mother of four with a full-time career.

To my brother, Deotis, may you rest in peace.

To daughter Tangela and your daughter, Savannah, hugs and kisses.

To Aunt Rose, you are truly the epitome of someone with an incredibly giving nature. You have been blessed to live ninety-six years young. May you continue to experience great health.

To Aunt Margaret, you are a wonderful aunt, mother and grandmother. You and Aunt Rose represent North Carolina royally: kind spirits and good cookin'. My youth memories will always be cherished.

To Grandma Cardella, you were such a positive influence for all of your grandchildren. You were the pillar of the community and we loved you dearly.

To all of my grandparents, you were special.

To my in-laws, Richard and Pearl, thank you for treating me as your own. To brother-in-laws, David P. and Jerry. To my brother-in-law, David M.

To Sharon, since age thirteen, we have called each other "bestest" friend. Although the distance keeps us apart, the bond continues. To your sisters (and my sisters), Lisa and Gail.

To my "girls" ("Hey, girl"), Rhonda and Lena, we've celebrated years of camaraderie after meeting in elementary school and share a unique bond.

To my friends (there are so many; please forgive me if your name isn't included as it was unintentional), Donna, Susan, Mamie, Sheila, Cheryl, Teri, Tomi, Toni, George, Rico, Joyce, Yvette, Patricia, Maria, Pamela, Ardith, Deb, Noelle, Ola, Sandra, Eddie, Dwayne, Kirsten, Vicki, Reggie. Denise D., may you rest in peace, girl.

To my L.A. friends, Joyce and Curtis, China, Carolyn, Ruth, and Diane.

To my nieces and nephews, Andre R (you were like a son during childhood; thanks for being like a brother to Jazmin), Elizabeth, Jaxon, Arianna, Ashley, David, Aliya, Andre J, Jonathan, Nicolas, Zachary, Malik, Greg, Stephanie, Brandon, Danielle, Aaron and Audrey.

To my godson, Brian, and his brothers, Adam and Nicolas.

To all of my extended Sherrill family and Caldwell family.

To cousins Percy, Franklin and Alan, you are truly like brothers. Carl, you are a gem. Fidelina and Terry, Ronita, Debbie, Beverly and Nick, Francesca, Gloria Jean, Janet, Karen, Tomi, Derek and Retha, Shirl and Ed, Jackie, Tamu, Isha, Zakiya, Rashida, Rodney, Sunday, Kwesi, Dana, Jimmy, Melinda, Mercedes, Stephanie, Gregory, Courtney and many more. To the "younger cousins," Trey, Bo, Alex, Brittany, Benza, Karlan, Dean, Ray-Ray, and all of the others too numerous to name.

To all of my extended Roberts family. Lewis Brooks (you keep the family connected), Erica Robinson (much success on your Asali Yoga Studio in Harlem), Sheilah Vance (congratulations on your success as a fellow author and publisher, the Elevator Group.)

To "Aunt" Barbara Ford, you are full of advice and wisdom. To Aunt Olivia, you were a joy. You always said I'd write my own book. To Uncles T, Carl and Cecil, thanks for your kindness.

To my "new" family on the Parker and Brooks sides. Aunt Pat, you always remember the special occasions.

To Jimmy, thanks for your support.

To my sisters' friends, Destiny, Pam, Cornelia, Dawn, Pamela, Wanda, Debbie, Dionne, Tinera, Karen, Beverly and Melba.

To Yona Deshommes, my hard-working publicist at Atria/Simon & Schuster. Thanks for all you do.

To the Strebor authors. As publishing director of Strebor Books, I have enjoyed working with you. Welcome to the family. A special shoutout to Allison Hobbs, Cairo, William Fredrick Cooper, Suzetta Perkins, Lee Hayes, J. Marie Darden, Marsha D. Jenkins-Sanders, Michelle Janine Robinson, Che Parker, Curtis Bunn, Earl Sewell, Dwayne Ballen, Ahyiana Angel, Pat Tucker, B.W. Read, and Julia Blues. Thank you Marion Barry, Jr. (rest in peace, "Mayor for Life") and Mildred Muhammad for sharing your lives through your memoirs. The list of authors is numerous and continues to expand. To Nakita for assisting Zane and me at Strebor.

To Keith Saunders, your talent as a photographer and graphic artist is appreciated. You are awesome. To Deb Schuler, thank you for your efficiency and eagle eye. You are the ultimate layout designer. It has been a pleasure working with you both. I value our rapport. Strebor is blessed to have connected with such professionals.

To Johnathan Royal of Books, Beauty & Stuff for your endless support of Strebor Books.

To Lasheera Lee of Reading You Later Blogtalkradio for your support of Strebor authors.

To Imani Logan and Jackie Lawson for your love of reading and support.

To my friends from the journalism world, Toni, Denise, Cheryl, Sunni, Richard, Ita, L'Taundra, Michael and Chris.

To book clubs for showing your support to authors and appreciation for the written word. A special thank you to book clubs for inviting me to network, including the Ultimate Sistahs United Bookclub, the SCARP Book Club, Sistercircle and others. I appreciated the lively conversation and feedback. Thank you for selecting my titles.

CHAPTER 1

TAI

The sounds of Jill Scott streamed through the mini Bose speakers mounted on the walls, providing a mellow oasis as Tai melted her mind and body in her Jacuzzi. The sandalwood vanilla candles tantalized her nostrils, allowing her peace after a challenging day at the office. This was her coveted ritual.

Moments like this allowed her to meditate and reflect. She was overjoyed as her dreams had blossomed into reality. After years of waiting for her knight, it was her landscaper, Marco—eight years her junior and an unlikely candidate—who'd finally uplifted her. During two years that he'd maintained her yard, she'd never gazed past the flowers and plants to open her eyes to the man of her dreams. It wasn't until one day while working in her backyard during the searing heat, he'd removed his white tee and revealed his chiseled, dripping mocha chest. She did a double-take and thought, *Oops, no, not the landscaper…not my type. Plus, I wonder how old he is; looks like a baby.* After inviting him inside for strawberry lemonade, the sparks began. Now he was her husband, her soul mate. Tomorrow would be their first anniversary and with her enthusiasm, one would think it was their twenty-fifth.

Like other women with a similar plight, she had hit the four-decade mark with no future partner in sight. Her lover of five years, Austin, had suddenly dropped off the radar as she approached her milestone birthday, even pulling a no-show at her grand party. She'd long decided if her relationship had fizzled, she would simply take a dating hiatus. After all, she'd viewed their longtime dating as an investment—one leading down the aisle. Suddenly, when she least expected, her eyes opened to the unlikeliest prospect. Marco had been caring for her landscaping, but he was equally as capable of caring for her body and soul.

She stroked the mango-coconut gel over her body with her loofah, then closed her eyes.

"Hey, sweetheart," a soothing voice announced.

"Marco..." She exhaled, staring up at her husband. "Don't scare me like that. I didn't hear you come in and I was definitely in another place," she added with a seductive smile.

"Sorry, babe. Hmmm, that's some good-smelling stuff."

"Well, you can join me," she teased. "Plenty of room, ya know." She winked. "Plus, tomorrow's—"

"Our anniversary."

"And we can start celebrating early. Nothing wrong with that."

Marco agreed, "You bet." He slowly peeled off his shirt and then unloosened his pants, letting them and his boxers drop onto the granite floor tile.

Tai admired his muscled physique and his well-tanned skin from days in the sun. "Before you step in, why don't you pour me another glass of wine and you one, too?" He picked up her empty glass from the tub ledge and placed it atop a small cabinet. He opened the door and pulled out a wineglass. They were connoisseurs and having a stash in the bathroom was a must. He filled the glasses and carried them to the tub, setting both on the edge. He stepped inside and immersed in the soothing water, careful not to knock over the glasses.

"Hmm, feels good, doesn't it?" she asked.

"Better than good." He picked up his glass and she followed. "Let's toast."

They tapped their glasses.

"To the sexiest woman on the planet."

"Hmm, and to definitely the finest man on earth... and as you guys say, p-h-i-n-e, *phine*." She giggled and sipped the wine.

After taking a sip, Marco set his glass on the sprawling ledge, then gently took her glass from her hand and placed hers beside his.

Facing each other, he moved her in front of him, her back facing his chest. He took her loofah and dampened it, squeezing the suds over her breasts and down her back.

"Hmm, that feels soooo good, baby." She felt him rock-hard beneath her and she was overthrown with excitement, ripe and ready to make their Jacuzzi a love nest. Peering up through the skylight, she could see the raindrops that had started to pelter the glass. Luckily, it wasn't a storm or she'd have to leap out of the tub in fear of danger. Instead, the mood was ripe and sexy as she maneuvered around to face him and mount his piece, wrapping her arms around his back. She gyrated atop him as the warm, sudsy water blended with her juices, as he suckled her tender breasts.

In her head, she started singing the Dramatics' "I Wanna Go Outside in the Rain." She peeped at the wall clock over the sink and thought of the lyrics to Tony! Toni! Tone!'s "Anniversary." It was now midnight and they had survived their first year. She paused to gaze in his eyes. "Happy Anniversary, sweetie."

Marco turned toward the clock. "Oh, right, it's that time." He smiled and pecked her lips. "Happy Anniversary, sexy mama."

In his head, he was listening to Michael J's "Don't Stop 'Til You Get Enough." *Naw, ain't no stopping me now*, he thought, as he continued to thrust upward.

CHAPTER 2

CANDACE

"Hey, girls, what's happening in your worlds?" Candace beamed boldly with her usual excited disposition while Tai and Nevada watched her on the camera.

"Well, did you remember it's Tai's anniversary?" Nevada inquired.

"That's right…sorry! Happy Anniversary, Tai! Cheers to you and Marco on Year One!"

"Thanks. I couldn't be happier." Tai joined her close friends in celebration.

"My mind, as usual, has been all over the place, so forgive me."

"We know how you do, silly!" Nevada joked. "No worries. You must've forgotten why we said we'd plan the Skype date for today."

"I did, and I apologize. You're my girls and I'll never let anything change that. Nawwww."

"Well, let us guess where you are this time," Tai stated.

"Some place exotic, of course." Candace offered a tip.

"That's without saying," Nevada concurred. "I kinda get that island feel, tropical breezes and gorgeous sunsets."

"Okay, you're scaring me now. You are so close," Candace teased. "But I don't think you'd ever figure this one."

"Somewhere in the Carib—" Tai started.

"Nope, I think you should give up, Tai."

"I don't like to give up or give in, so I'mma keep brainstorming." Nevada laughed. "Never mind. Where the hell are ya?"

"Tahiti."

"Who the oops goes to Tahiti?" Nevada asked.

"Girl, ha-ha. I've been all over and we're continuing to make stops on my bucket list." She paused. "You should remember I told you Don was taking me to Tahiti."

"Naw, I've got a great memory, but hell, you've been around the world and back. My brain skills don't function to that capacity," Nevada teased. "Hey, I ain't mad at ya, though. Keep on keeping on, Candace." She added, "One of these days, I'm gonna grab Ryan, tell him to take off his cop badge and we're hitting the road. Pick out some places on the map."

"So, Tai, we should be talking about you and yours. What's up for your anniversary? You are Miss Chef-a-roo, so are you cooking a special dinner or dining out?" Candace inquired.

"We have reservations for Mandarin Oriental. I like the spa there, so we're getting massages as well."

"Well, enjoy," Candace offered.

"Where are you heading next? Can't imagine anywhere more exotic than Tahiti," Tai said dreamily.

Candace whispered, "Wish it was down the aisle."

"Say what? Don must not be around," Nevada figured.

"No, he isn't."

"So, why you whispering?" Nevada asked.

"Dunno. Maybe I'm nervous. Look, it's been a year."

"Sister, most women wouldn't have an ounce of complaint if they'd been over the world like you've been. Hanging out." Nevada was firm.

"Yeah, it's all good, but it's been such a whirlwind and now it's not dying down or anything, but I guess I'm looking for something steady. Settling, stable, whatever."

"At least you're having a blast, and you enjoy him and his company, right?" Tai asked.

"Definitely."

"I say don't rush. Keep your eyes open and let your mind be free," Nevada suggested. "Take your time."

"Again, it's been a year and look, I'm pushing over forty, up the hill and down soon."

"Okay, you lookin' good and you're in good health. What more?" Tai asked.

"I got you, but hear me out. Someday I'd still like to settle down and have a child."

"Give it time. Chill out and relax, Candace," Nevada said coolly. "I'm not tryin' to be mama or anything, but you're my girl and I must be honest. Don's in love and lust with you. I see it in his eyes. And take it from me, I see all types and can read them in a flash. I always liked him from the very first time you introduced us."

"Me too. After all these years, he was your soul mate waiting to make that connection," Tai suggested.

"Thanks to you," Candace said, referring to Tai's party where they'd met.

"Hey, but I didn't introduce you two. You met up on your own; no, I guess it was Sierra who hooked you up." Tai recalled their mutual flight attendant friend intentionally making the acquaintance.

"But if you hadn't provided the venue or the party, we never would've crossed paths."

"Maybe not. Guess it was meant to be," Tai agreed.

Tai had thrown a celebration for her employment firm, Next

Phase of Life, where Don offered to buy Candace a cocktail, and then the rest was *herstory.* Candace had a reputation for adventurous men. Her past included a scuba diving instructor. Sometimes it backfired, such as during her first date with a ventriloquist. After changing into a role-playing outfit—a lion tamer at his request—and entering his bedroom, his puppet Sammy was lying in his bed. She couldn't leave his place fast enough. She didn't mind a little freaky-deaky, but getting it in with a wooden doll watching over her was beyond bizarre.

Now, with pilot Don, she'd explored the most unusual sites.

"Well, we must celebrate when you get back on this side of the world," Nevada offered.

"Definitely. I'm so happy for our gurl," she said, referring to Tai. "Last time we had one of our ladies nights was the bridal shower." Candace smiled. "So, Nevada, I'll be in touch and we must plan something off the chain."

Nevada laughed. "Yeah, make it rain. No, maybe not; she's a married woman now."

"That don't mean a thing. Oops, it's not how it sounded. I still like how we roll out, ladies. I miss our old times. So, hurry up, Candace, and get back to D.C.," Tai demanded, laughing.

"What she means is get your shopaholic crazy ass back here." Nevada giggled.

"Can't wait."

Candace worked as a buyer for a local department store and had taken a hiatus to travel with Don. She had tried to ease up on her shopping episodes, but her wallet was like a magnet to store windows. Her unselfish nature had prompted her to buy gifts for her two closest friends during her recent journey.

"Seriously, let's make it happen." Nevada missed her friend who made up their trio.

"Well, I definitely want you both to help me plan my shower… I guess if I ever get that ring." Candace suddenly looked sad. "Sorry, Tai, not to dampen your parade—"

"Oh, no problem. It's cool. I understand totally. You do remember that I was the one worried about turning forty and no Mr. Right. My Mr. Wrong had left me hanging in the wind," Tai reminded. "If it's in the stars, your light will shine."

"You're right. I'll continue to be patient—" Candace heard the door open that led to the terrace overlooking the beach. "Well, ladies, he's back inside. Gotta go. Love ya."

"Love ya, too," they said in unison and the screen went blank.

CHAPTER 3

NEVADA

Nevada absently twirled a piece of her curly 'fro as she studied her laptop screen. She was thankful she'd decided to go natural as being a full-time detective allowed little mirror time for the glam. Her once daily flat-iron routine was often a bust if her plate was full, and it was more often than not. However, she didn't skimp on her looks and while she regularly wore comfy clothing, when she stepped out with Tai and Candace, she was on point with her attire.

Her home office was cluttered with stacks of papers and the walls showcased a zoo of photos, awards and thank-you notes. Her most prized office prop was the framed photo of her deceased grandmother, Iris, with whom she'd spent blistery Chicago summers while her father, a blues musician, sold out juke joints and toured the country. She often sensed her grandmother watching over her, carefully guarding her every move. Life as a detective could be risky and Nevada always thought Grandma was her protective angel.

Sleuths On Us was born as a result of her losing her promising newspaper career. After her success as an investigative reporter, Nevada used her creativity to launch a detective agency. She was already polished when it came to being a hawk and she was a glutton for challenge. Now she had become nationally recognized and had attracted a steady stream of clients. Nevada had discovered two bank robbers—twin brothers—after they were profiled on *America's Most Wanted.* She had shared her $50,000 reward with her live-in soul mate, Ryan, Tai and Candace. She had treated her BFFs to a weekend at Atlantis in Paradise Island, Bahamas where they celebrated Tai's engagement and partied nonstop—a surprise native dancer was even more of a treat and typical of their popular ladies nights.

Noting the time, she figured Ryan would arrive shortly. The Washington, D.C. police officer had been on the force for more than twenty years and he operated like clockwork. As their norm, he likely would bring carry-out into their noncooking household.

Their schedules rarely allowed for culinary action. Ryan often joked that Nevada needed to swap their stainless steel stove with a sofa. Nevada wasn't fazed with his comments, particularly since Tai was a sensational chef and frequently invited her to sample her dishes. Plus, she was forever trying to diet, especially as Ryan was like a drill sergeant at times, coaching her to manage her weight. His health nut status irritated her when he was overwhelming. And when it got to that point, she would simply shut him down.

She reached over and turned on Kem. The artist seemed to put her in the mood each time she needed to emerge in deep-thought mode. The private detective lifestyle was full of snags, roadblocks and twists. Sometimes she'd work crosswords or play games to strengthen her brain. Her latest case had her stumped and Nevada was driven by determination.

Seventy-one-year-old Arthur Primrose, a retired English professor who'd relocated to the D.C. area from Alabama, had hired her to investigate his lovely, Southern belle wife, Jolene. Since she'd turned seventy a year ago, Jolene was entrenched in the Christian lifestyle, obsessed with attending church services, functions, Bible study, and anything related. Her time with Arthur was mainly breakfast and lunch; otherwise, she devoted her free moments to serving the Lord. His dinners were frequently lonely several nights a week. Arthur had informed Nevada that Jolene was torn between two churches and had not settled on a permanent church home.

"Hallelujah" and "Amen" dominated her vocabulary. Now the woman who espoused nonstop praises was the focus of her husband's suspicion. Nevada had tailed her on several occasions while she entered church. Sometimes on Sundays she would assist the cooks at the smaller church to prepare and serve meals to the members at special functions.

Arthur understood his wife was wrapped up in the church community, but their love life was suffering. Whenever he took his little blue pill, he was eager to take her to paradise, but he found himself on the other side of the pillow. She'd make some excuse: she was tired or exhausted from her church activities. Sex had a permanent spot on the back burner.

The landline rang and the caller ID displayed a name unknown. Nevada picked up. "Hello, Sleuths On Us."

"Good evening, Ms.—"

"Mr. Primrose," she responded, recognizing his voice, "I told you to call me Nevada. It's fine."

"Nevada, then you must call me Arthur."

"Yes, Arthur, I will call you by your first name."

"Thank you." Arthur looked over his shoulder. "I was checking in to see if you have any news." Although he was calling from a friend's home, he instinctively was insecure about his wife suddenly appearing—even if she were miles away. He never called Nevada from his cell or his landline; it would only be guaranteed that Jolene would snoop and question the phone numbers or whom he'd called. After all, when the bills arrived to their home, she would have access.

"Not yet, Arthur. This one is tricky, but I promise you, I will figure it out." She paused. "Do you have anything new for me?"

"Nevada, it's the same; in fact, it appears to be more intense." He recalled the solitary nights when he'd often eat leftovers. "Dinner with Jolene is practically nil. I've become used to her absence."

Nevada tried to keep an objective outlook when dealing with her clients, not get involved emotionally. But it didn't mean she couldn't have compassion. As Arthur was her oldest client, she felt badly that he was suffering all around. Confident she would solve his case, she assured him that it wouldn't be long before she'd have some leads.

CHAPTER 4

TRISTA

The door slammed shut, reverberating throughout the modest studio apartment off Hollywood Boulevard. Trista stood and walked over to the window. Her boyfriend, Darren, who used the stage name, Kwik, was a backup dancer for the celebrity rap artist, Dre Dyson. Kwik had just severed their yearlong ties. Their hurricane romance had abruptly ended in a tornado of pretense and deception.

Trista's eyes became waterworks as she stared at Kwik until he disappeared around the corner, likely to his favorite hangout, where he'd down cognac until he drowned his sorrows. This time, however, she would not hit the pavement in pursuit. Often she'd run behind him and would be short of begging him to forgive her. Tonight his words, "it's over," had a finite ring. And for once, she agreed it was best to split.

She ambled to the sofa bed and sat. She picked up the remote and turned on the DVD player. Trista figured perhaps watching some of her dance performances with Kwik on Dre's videos would bring some cheer. After all, he was the only reason she was living her dream in the entertainment world.

A year earlier, when one of Dre's dancers was injured and he needed a substitute for his concert tour, Trista was a standout at an audition in D.C. She'd received the opportunity after Dre's manager contacted Next Phase of Life on a gamble, seeking a dancer. Later, she joined his entourage and became a permanent fixture in his videos, and relocated to California. It was only weeks before she and fellow dancer Kwik became romantically involved.

Equipped with one suitcase, Trista had arrived in D.C. to connect with her long-lost sister, Tai, after finding her on Facebook. The sisters had been separated as youth after losing their parents to a murder-suicide in N.C. Their grandmother, Harriet, could only afford to take in one sister, and she selected the oldest, Tai, to live with her in D.C. while Trista initially stayed with a family friend, Miss Laine, and once she passed, she entered N.C.'s foster care system. Their father, John, a vice principal, had shot their mother, Diana, a schoolteacher at a middle school, with a shotgun after discovering she'd been having an affair with the principal of her school: Then he took his own life.

Tai and Trista were becoming acclimated to each other living under the same roof and after the lengthy separation. They were true opposites, but their sisterly bond was brewing when Dre Dyson scooped up Trista and added her to his backup dancer team. She later became enwrapped with Kwik, one of the dancers.

As the videos rolled on the screen, Trista sulked, reminiscing about how she'd planned to spend her life with Kwik. Visions of her happiness dominated the screen; her dance moves seemed to be choreographed out of the name of love.

Trista yearned to mirror Tai with a new husband who adored her, but that reality proved elusive. She was sincerely in love with Kwik, but for one night, it had been challenging to be monogamous. A video producer proved to be so sexy that she couldn't resist the temptation.

Dre Dyson had just ended his rehearsal for a new single. He invited the team to a restaurant to treat them. After the last dancer had slung her backpack over her shoulder and a production staffer turned off a switch, only Trista and Todd remained in the studio. Trista realized that Todd was attracted to her; the way his piercing eyes watched her from head to toe. Trista announced that she was too sweaty to leave at the moment and needed to take a quick shower. Kwik headed on to the restaurant with the crew.

When she dressed and returned to the hallway following her shower, Todd startled her by touching her shoulder from behind. She stopped in her tracks and turned around to see a handsome face staring at her. He quickly kissed her lips fervently before lifting her petite frame and carrying her into his office.

"Oh, no, I can't do this, Todd… oh, no, don't make me say…" He kissed her intensely as he had her pinned against the wall. "No, Todd, I can't diss Kwik and neither can you—"

"Look, who says I can't..." He smiled, and then unzipped her pants and wrestled them to her ankles.

Trista was helpless. She couldn't resist the heat between her thighs and succumbed to Todd's aggressive moves. He opened his fly and entered her, pounding her against the wall and shaking up the studio while making their own music.

Suddenly, the door opened. Kwik had returned after fifteen minutes, realizing he had left something important. His mouth gaped. "Ain't this a bitch!" Trista and Todd stopped in their tracks, both looking like robots as they tried to dress in record time. Kwik slammed the door shut and walked away furiously.

Trista, disheveled and barely intact, opened the door, stepped into the hallway and yelled, "Kwik! Come back! I'm sooo sorry, babyyyyy!" He was already out of view and when she realized he wasn't returning, she stepped back inside and collapsed at the doorway. "Damn!"

As her thoughts crept back to the video pity party on the screen, she understood why Kwik was around the corner and riding solo. She'd betrayed him with one of his closest running buddies, his right-hand man who forever had his back. She thought how Todd surely could lose his steady gig over her twang as Dre was more bonded with Kwik than Todd. She pulled a tissue from a box on the end table and wiped the stream of tears. Kwik was the unforgiving type, not a believer of second chances. From this point, she would have to plot her own destiny, and this time it would be alone.

Trista tossed her head and wrestled with the sheets. Suddenly, she opened her eyes and glanced at the clock. It was 5:20 a.m. The dampness of her tear-stained pillow tickled her cheek. She finally had fallen asleep after her nightmarish episode with Kwik. She rolled over and spotted him lying next to her atop the sofa bed, fully clothed, Jordans still on his feet. *Hmmph, wonder what time he stumbled in after his cognac fest.*

Kwik had arrived with the company of his friend, Steve, after a long night of sloshing drinks and rambling about Trista's cheating. He'd thought he'd found his ride-or-die chick. He'd shared his fairy tale with Steve, who'd walked with him to ensure he'd arrived safely at his apartment.

Trista gazed and her mind played a video of her future. Kwik was pissed and she was sure he would let her leave quietly without a bunch of drama. She yearned to be in his arms, but it was the last hurrah. He'd kicked her out, but apparently he was too intoxicated to force her out last night. Later in the morning, she'd have to pack her bags and leave him and his studio apartment. Where she was headed was in the cards. She flipped over, her back facing him, and lay until she drifted to sleep.

CHAPTER 5

THE LADIES

The tray of fuchsia and canary yellow cupcakes created a tropical ambiance. Tai was proud of her latest chef treats and couldn't wait for her friends to sample and rate her creations. Her garlic lemon-pepper chicken drumettes, strawberry and mango salad, broccoli and spinach dip graced the table.

She was eager for her besties to arrive. It had been a year since she, Candace and Nevada had done damage with their ladies nights. Tonight would be no different. Candace had returned the previous week and Tai had allowed her some kickback time. Nevada had been so engrossed in her new cases, but the opportunity to see Candace made her take a much-needed break. It was nothing like good ol' girl networking—live. Not via emails, texts or Skyping.

Candace had island hopped in the Caribbean, explored French Polynesia and traveled throughout Europe for the past six months. Her welcome-home and Tai's anniversary were reasons to celebrate. Of course, it was always a no-brainer for Tai to party. She was known for cooking and entertaining in her Northwest D.C. home. Tonight, she'd ensured Marco would hang out with his buddies. He understood before their wedding vows that Tai and her friends held a strong bond; there was no need trying to break that cemented relationship. When it was girls time, ladies night, or whatever Tai would call it, he would support her wishes and go his own way.

Tai walked into the kitchen and pulled out some of her fanciest glasses. She set them on the counter and then looked at the clock. She didn't expect Candace to be on time; she was traditionally late, but Nevada, with a career where timing was crucial, would likely arrive on the minute. Soon, the doorbell rang and Tai headed to the front door.

"Hey, girl, you looking good. Taking care of yourself," Nevada complimented as Tai, wearing a black jumpsuit, opened the door.

"Yeah, I'm tryin' to get more sleep," Tai admitted.

"You'd better be. You're always on my case." Nevada reminded her of her constant push to put in more hours on the pillow. "Plus, Ryan works my nerves about sleeping."

Tai led Nevada into the sunroom. She spotted the cupcakes. "No you didn't."

"Yes, I did. You always say you're on a diet, but there's nothing wrong with a little taste. Plus, it's my first time making these and you and Candace are my guinea pigs." She laughed.

"I'll sneak one." Nevada smiled, happy not to be in the company of Ryan, who normally irked her about eating habits.

"One won't hurt," she teased.

Nevada nodded. "I like that jumpsuit."

"Thanks. So tell me, girl, what have you been up to? Any interesting cases?"

"Glad you asked." Nevada tasted the cupcake. "Hmmm, delicious."

"Thanks."

"There's this guy named Art—" She stopped midstream, with a rush that it was unethical to announce clients' names, unless related to law enforcement. "My client is the cutest older guy, very bright, retired professor from Alabama. Truly a cool dude. Well, he and his wife have been married and he's puzzled about her sudden change in attitude and habit. I don't like using this term, but he calls her a 'holy roller' 'cause she's about Jesus twenty-four-seven. Her church is not her *second* home—it's *numero uno*. Spends more time between these two churches. He says she's trying to decide which one to join. On the gut, I could say he's simply a lonely—and again, I don't like to use these words either—*old man*. But after some digging in my mind, it could be something underneath the surface."

"Hmm, interesting...how old are they?"

"He's seventy-one and she's seventy."

"Sounds like she's dedicated to the church and keeps him simmering on the back burner." She teased, "You'll get to the bottom of it, Miss Spy."

"Well, I'm damn sure trying."

Tai glanced at the wall clock. "Wonder where Miss Fashionably Late is?"

"Right," Nevada eyed the spread, her taste buds working overtime, "any longer and I'll be biting off my fingers." She laughed.

"Don't mean to torture you."

The doorbell rang. "Finally." Nevada sighed. They both were eager to see their jetsetter friend and headed toward the door.

Tai looked through the peephole and swung it open. An elated Candace stepped across the threshold and embraced Tai and then Nevada. "Ladies! I'm back!" She swirled around in her black tube-top jumpsuit and black heels, dripping in bling.

"Oh, we look like twins," she noted of them both in jumpsuits. "And we didn't plan it this way. Come on in." Tai led the way back to the sunroom and motioned for them both to sit in chairs while she sat on the sofa. She looked at Candace as if she were judging her for a fashion show. "You look fantastic! Don's treating you on the up and up, I see. You are beaming, girl."

"Yes," Candace said shyly. "My baby has come through. Let me catch my breath. Lots to share...but hey, look at you, married lady! We're here to celebrate you, not me... How's the first year?"

"Couldn't have asked for more." She gazed at the framed wedding day photo. "Truly, a gem. I feel like diamonds."

"Well, let's toast," Nevada suggested.

Tai rose and sauntered to the bar area. Nevada and Candace followed and watched Tai pour the bubbly. They raised their glasses.

"To friendship," Nevada announced.

"To love, love and more love." Tai giggled, blushing with romantic thoughts.

Candace teased, "To shoes, clothes and more shoes." She laughed, joking about her massive wardrobe she'd managed to collect during her career as a fashion buyer.

"To all of the above," Tai suggested.

They sipped and returned to their seats, setting down their glasses on the coffee table.

"Well, I've been sooo polite, Candace, but girl, I can't wait another minute to munch on these eats. Tai looks like she threw down as usual."

"Right, I spotted those lovely little cupcakes."

"Help yourselves. Besides you two, the kitchen's my best friend."

They walked over to serve plates and then relaxed on the sofa.

"So Miss Adventure Queen, tell us about all these fabulous sites," Tai suggested.

"Girl, I don't even know where to start."

"I hear ya." Nevada bit into a drummette. "Hmmm, so flavorful. Tai, I swear you really need to think about catering. You're busy and all that with running your bizness, but you could do a little sumthin-sumthin on the side." She placed the bone on her plate and sampled the dip. "Hmmm-mmm. Sorry, Candace, didn't mean to disrupt your flow."

"No problem, girl. We're some lucky chicks to have a friend like Tai who's a diva in the kitchen." Candace tasted the salad. "I've eaten in a lot of restaurants and your food..." She looked at Tai. "...is truly the bomb."

"Thanks." Tai beamed over the compliments.

"Well, let's say, I never could have imagined what I was in store for. I have tons of pictures that I plan to organize—many more than I posted online. My favorite spot, of course, was chilling on the beach with a fruity cocktail in my hand and melting in the sun."

"I see you got a decent tan going on," Nevada recognized.

"Yep. I also loved the touristy stuff like the museums in Paris and this wonderful castle we visited in Scotland. Then sailing on a gondola in Venice and skinny dipping in Barbados."

"Now that sounds like my kind of trip." Nevada was eager to someday take time off and explore the world.

"Well, look at you." Tai admired a different glow other than her skin complexion. "You shining brighter than the supermoon. We're ready to hear the good stuff. Enough of the nicey-nicey."

"You holding out, Candace. You remember we go waaay back. So give up the goodies, dear," Nevada teased. "Unless you were trying to impress your new piece, you were up to some of your old tricks." Nevada covered her lips. "Oops, sorry, not your piece, your *man*."

Candace chuckled. "No problem, Nevada, you know me, don't you?"

"Go 'head, Miss Freaky Deaky. Tell us the goodies." Nevada was feeling the full effects of her champagne, taking another sip.

Candace leaned in and set her glass on the coffee table. "Well, I have enough to put in a book. It was a whirlwind, honey. You name it, and we probably went there."

"Okay, we're waiting," Tai stated patiently.

"Got it. Listen, I think the coolest scenario was in St. Thomas. Girl, we went snorkeling in a cave and he ate me right there under the water. Honey, it was *pa-ra-*dise."

"Oohhh, that's sexy hot. Take me away," Tai teased. "You go, cave girl. Snorkeling and getting your kitty licked."

"Oh, yes, child. 'Licked' is kinda mild. It was all that." She laughed. "And the cave scene was surreal."

"Okay, so I'm dealing with the boring stuff. Ryan and I have never got down like that. But hell, I'd be his cavewoman any day. Hearing that makes me have a new fantasy," Nevada said proudly. "Speaking of fantasies, what's your desire? What didn't you get to do these six months?" She was eager to hear more tales from Candace.

"You always have questions." She giggled.

"Well, that *is* part of my duty," Nevada responded proudly in her detective/post-journalist role.

"Let's see…he was going to show me how to navigate a yacht while we were in the Caribbean."

"You like those sea adventures," Tai said. "I remember your scuba diver." She recalled Candace sharing tales of the ocean.

"And you, Mrs. Landscaper. I'm sure he plants the seeds in your garden well," Nevada teased.

"Girl, you'd better stop. Okay, if we're going there, what about your cop man Ryan handcuffing you so you can't get away," Tai rebounded.

Nevada laughed. "Well, we've gone there a few times. For me to practice. Good for my career."

"Sho' you're right." Candace smiled teasingly. "But hey, didn't know you had it in ya."

Nevada, the quiet observant link in the trio, didn't always share her innermost world. It was the detective in her to cover up, conceal by nature—even at times with the two besties whom she trusted.

"I'm sooo ready to settle down." Candace changed to a serious note.

"For you, this is tame and settled, don't you think?" Nevada referred to Candace's man adventures.

"A little, I guess. I'm talking about settle settle."

"We can relate. I didn't realize the man I was hunting was in my backyard," Tai reminded of her landscaping prospect. "Taking care of my plants and flowers. Was I in the blind! Then I had to be a cougar in order to catch the lion."

"Nothing wrong with that," Nevada interjected.

"It seems like ages and I don't want to keep dragging this out," Candace concluded.

"Well, it takes two, and he simply may not be ready," Nevada suggested.

"True, but honey, I'm not planning to hang out forever. The dating is fine, the spaces and wonderful places are fine, but I'm the impatient kind."

"I can understand to some levels. Guess I hadn't been too pressed, though. I'm actually content with our common-law thing. Ryan and I stay so busy and into our little worlds that I'm thinking, if it ain't broke..." Nevada was most interested in expanding her career as a detective than creating vows. After all, children were not seen in her future panorama vision. She enjoyed the lifestyle of a commitment but yet enough flexibility that she could come and go without feeling controlled.

"I'm not trying to tell you what to do or how, but maybe you should come out and ask him," Tai offered.

"Oh, hell no, I'm not asking Don about a proposal; he'll have to come to me." Candace was firm with her beliefs. Chivalry was alive and she preferred to play by those rules.

"So, what do you think it really is? Since you don't feel comfortable asking or being straight up, looks like you'll have to figure it out on your own," Tai concluded.

"I'm stumped. I've done everything I can do to lure him, tease him, convince him, whatever you want to call it." Candace sighed as her mind penetrated into deeper thoughts.

"Maybe there's something he's not telling you. Do you think he simply doesn't want to marry?" Nevada inquired. "Sometimes guys love to date and don't want anything permanent." She was experiencing that firsthand with Ryan. And with their busy careers, they definitely didn't see children in the forecast.

"Well, that could be the case," Candace responded sadly. "I've only been devoted to him for a year," she added sarcastically. "But my damn clock is clicking overtime. I want a little one someday."

"Girl, you could—" Nevada started.

"Have one without Don," Candace finished, projecting Nevada's next words. "I've thought about that, too. All these honeys out here, I could simply pick out a father. An adventurous, smart, intellectual one, of course."

"I'm not encouraging that," Tai disagreed. "Candace is in love with the love game, like me. She would want a permanent father, not simply a dad, but a lifelong mate." She looked at Candace. "You hear me, right?"

"You know me, but hell, I'd be willing to settle for a donor."

"But you wouldn't be too happy about that," Tai said knowingly.

"Maybe not, but I could live with it, I guess." Candace spoke sincerely, but in her mind and heart, it was so untrue. She didn't want to pull names out of a hat and end up with anyone; she lived and breathed Don.

"Hey, I've got you by a couple years, and I'm still hopeful to be a mom. We figured we'd at least give our marriage a year or two before adding a third to the family," Tai revealed.

"Cool, makes sense to me," Nevada agreed, never seeing herself as the motherly type.

Tai looked at Candace. "Don't rush. What I'm saying is we both have time. Not to put a down side on it, but the fertility rate does drop at our age, according to my ob/gyn. But Candace, I'm going to put it out there that that's not us. We're going to have faith, and soon diapers and Disney will be our best friends."

CHAPTER 6

TRISTA

The sunshine served as a wake-up call and Trista aroused lightly. She shot up and looked at the empty spot beside her. No Kwik. Last night's puddle of tears must've created a sleep haven. She had truly crashed out.

Guess he's gone for his morning run or he's at the studio. Either way I'm not hanging around for none of his mouth. He ain't listenin' to what I have to say, not acceptin' any apologies, either.

After a shower, she dressed in jeans and a T-shirt. She walked to the closet and pulled out her tattered suitcase—the same one she'd brought on her train ride to D.C. to meet up with Tai for the first time in a decade. She could've replaced it several times over, but there was sentimental value. It was the same one she'd packed when she bounced from foster home to foster home.

She proceeded to retrieve her meager belongings and tossed them into the suitcase. After packing her tote bag with toiletries, she sat on the bed and exhaled. She looked around the apartment and her mind flashed back to the good times. Kwik was her boo and maybe one day, someday, he'd have a change of heart.

When Tai's firm had received an urgent call for a backup dancer for Dre Dyson's local concert, it was a no-brainer to send Trista, who'd worked as a stripper, to audition for the spot of an injured dancer. Trista was hired immediately and her whirlwind romance started with Kwik after their first tour date in California. The two shared commonalities as dancers and he'd also grown up in a foster home in Oakland. Her modest East Coast N.C. roots and his West Coast background blended with ease as they fed off each other's cultures.

Kwik, a 170-pound chocolate chunk, had garnered the nickname "Kwik" from his fast moves. Trista soon learned it was also his rapid-fire sex, his bedroom skills offstage. During his two-year stint as a dancer, his off-and-on flings with video vixens had never amounted to a fulfilling relationship. But when he connected with Trista, he easily gave up all the cling-ons. His eyes were for her only. Trista was aware of his devotion and genuine love. That's why it was so tough for her to give up a good man. Kwik was bullheaded, though and he would not give in to her forgiveness. She couldn't blame him as having sex with their producer—and in risky territory—was the ultimate betrayal, regardless of the spontaneous move with meaningless emotions.

She walked over to the petite desk and found a notepad and pen. She scrawled a simple message: *Kwik, I will always cherish what we had. I'm sorry about my dumb fling. You will always be in my heart and mind. One Love, Trista*

Grabbing her purse, she placed the tote atop the suitcase and rolled it to the door, glancing back, leaving all her past behind and heading for her next stopover. She'd arranged via text to stay with Tara, her choreographer and dancer friend, until she could figure her next move.

CHAPTER 7

THE SISTERS

The lazy day was extremely relaxing for Tai. After topping off her lunch of fruit salad and yogurt with a Mai Tai, she'd stretched on the chaise in her sunroom. Her light snooze was suddenly disrupted when her cell phone vibrated. She reached beside her and checked the caller ID. It was Trista, a rare occasion, especially since their main communication was social media or text messages.

"Hey, sis," she answered groggily, stretching and adjusting her lounge pants.

"Hi. Catch you at a bad time?"

"No, I had dozed off. I needed some good old R and R."

"How are you and Marco?" She suddenly remembered she'd forgotten their anniversary. "Wow, Tai, apologies. Missed your one year. Congrats."

"Thank you and no problem." She gazed admiringly at her diamond ring. "Marco's well. He's out with golfing buddies." Tai yawned. "And how's it going with you and Darren, Mr. Kwik?" She smiled at his stage name, which she always found interesting.

"Well…not so good."

Tai frowned and sat up. "Sorry about that. What's up, little sis? That's not the answer I expected."

"Well—"

"Whenever I see your posts, you two are like the picture of bliss," Tai offered, referring to the photos of Trista and Kwik at the beach or in the studio.

"You're right, but we're not peachy cool anymore."

"That's sudden. Something truly funky must've gone down."

"It was all me, Tai." Trista struggled to share the facts. "I got caught in the act." She shook her head.

"Okay, go on and spill it. I can't take the suspense any longer, Trista. What happened?"

"We'd finished rehearsing at the studio. Kwik and the crew headed to a restaurant. Sometimes Dre takes a few of us out for drinks. His boy, Todd, and this is his main man, Dre's video producer, and I were the only ones left. Wasn't planned that way. I wanted to stay behind to take a shower. Well, when I stepped out, dressed and turned the corner, there was Todd in the hallway. And well, we ended up moving into the office and getting it in right there."

"Whoa. Must've been some serious attraction 'cause you and Kwik were joined at the hip."

"No doubt. Tai, this man is…hmmm. I can only say I found it hard to resist. Don't ask me why or how. It was so sudden. And I can't tell you how embarrassing it was."

Tai stood and headed to the kitchen. She needed a drink on this one. "Okay, so it was an office fling."

"A wall affair. We were bringing down the walls, but actually, I'm glad now that it never peaked. Thank goodness. I couldn't have imagined him seeing me cum with another man. Yikes."

Tai sipped on her refreshed Mai Tai. "So you apologized and now what?" she asked, presuming Trista had likely begged to be forgiven.

"He's having no parts so it's zilch, nada. It's over."

"He's pissed and I don't know Kwik like that, but seems like he'd believe in second chances. Maybe?"

"Naw, sis. He left me for the bar, then the next morning, he left before I woke up. So I packed up—I didn't have much so that was easy—and headed out. Now, I did leave him a little note, goodbye and that love stuff. That's the least I could do."

"Sis, that was the right thing to do." She paused. "So where are you?"

"You remember the sistah on my page with the dreads and we're hanging out at Venice Beach. Only the two of us in the pic?"

"Oh, yes, nice photo."

"Tara's letting me chill at her spot for a minute. She's solo and we'd connected on the set. She's a dancer, too, and I always liked her vibe."

"You've adjusted to the Hollywood style. Any prospects to continue in the music industry?" Tai asked with concern. Her sister had appeared pleased with the West Coast.

"Well, I've met some people here and there, but I haven't had a chance to even think straight. It's not going to be easy 'cause I have to heal from Kwik, too." Her voice saddened. "I definitely can't go back performing with Dre Dyson 'cause Kwik and Todd will be around." She paused. "And that's if they stay on the same team. Hope I didn't screw up that relationship."

"It could've broken their bond."

"True but I couldn't face either one of them, dancing or not. I need to be in another space…maybe another coast," she hinted.

Tai paused and waited what was to follow.

"I'm not sure how to ask this…uh, um…you think I can stay with you? Just for a minute, sis?" she asked nervously.

Tai was stunned and not sure how to respond. It was her younger sister who had experienced disadvantages compared to her own upbringing.

"I realize you're newlyweds and all that. Promise I won't be in your way or interfere in your life. I mind my biz." She added quickly, "And, oh, I can pay my own way. Saved up some funds, so you don't have to worry about flight money."

"Well..." Thoughts raced throughout Tai's mind, imagining how life would be with a new husband and a sister in the home. She would need to pick Marco's brain first. She had managed to bond with Trista when she'd allowed her to stay with her before her engagement. Trista and Marco could likely survive—at least for a short period, she thought.

Tai could relate to cheating consequences. After all, it was how her parents' lives had ended: her dad had discovered her mom was having an affair. He shot and killed her before turning the gun on himself. Her mind drifted to her own bout with dallying with her personal trainer prior to her engagement to Marco. One night at the gym, like Trista, she was left alone with the attractive and well-built Hasan. He'd captured her off guard, and she didn't fight to resist his seduction, later finding herself atop his office desk, making mad love. After a series of trysts at the gym during after-hours, she eventually never returned and walked out of his life. After her relationship with Marco intensified, she had been tempted to share her infidelity with him. Later, she decided it was better to keep it under wraps. Sometimes she wondered about Hasan and his well-being as she never had wished him any harm. She had only shared the affair with Candace and Nevada.

"Trista, I'll give it some serious thought, okay? It's not only me now, so I have to consider Marco," she responded finally after some dead-air time.

"Tara isn't kicking me out the door or anything, but I don't want to hang here any longer than I need. She's cool and I definitely value her friendship."

"I understand."

"Well, peace and thank ya, sis. Chat soon." Trista hung up.

CHAPTER 8

TAI

"Baby, you couldn't have timed it more perfectly." Tai walked out of the kitchen and greeted Marco with a hug.

"Well, I'm happy to see you, too." Marco released the embrace and pecked Tai on the lips. "Look, I'm a little grungy."

"Nope, you don't need to shower. Wash your hands." She nodded toward the powder room. "We're gonna do the Jacuzzi thingie tonight."

"Oh, I see, special plans, but I'll at least change my shirt." He entered the bathroom to freshen up. A few T-shirts were handily stacked in the linen closet.

Tai returned to the kitchen, opened the oven and pulled out her roasted chicken, surrounded by carrots and green beans. Her mashed potatoes and gravy were simmering on the stovetop. Marco returned and sat at the table, observing his chef add final touches to yet another meal. She provided extra care to her creations as if they were pieces of art.

Tai placed her dishes on the table and sat.

"Lady, you are spoiling me for real with this food." Marco rubbed his stomach. "Don't want it to go in the wrong places, though." He laughed.

"Honey, the way you work out in these yards, you are bound to keep that weight off."

"True, but remember it's a little harder, especially in the winter, which seems like it's around the corner," he reminded her. "It's all good. I appreciate the home-cooked meals." He served his plate and passed the bowls to her.

"Well, we're still celebrating our anniversary, but I guess that's a lifelong commitment. We'll always be celebrating," she teased.

"That's right, Mrs." He smiled and ate, relishing every morsel.

After dinner, Tai led Marco as they ascended the stairs. It was show time and she had to give an award-winning performance. After all, her sister's future was at stake. She needed to woo hubby into agreeing Trista could share their home—even for a brief period. The old saying was the best way to a man's heart was through the stomach—but also the vagina. She laughed internally for a moment, recalling when she and a close friend had gone out during her college years. There was a portrait on the wall, one of those classic art pieces with a nude woman. Her gay friend pointed toward it and misspoke "vaginda." She would never forget those moments and the loads of laughter they'd shared.

When they reached the bedroom, she pushed him lightly on the bed.

"I thought we were getting in the Jac—"

"Later. First things first." She proceeded to take off his shirt and then his pants, followed by his shoes. Dropping her spaghetti-strapped dress to the floor, she slowly released her bra, her perky Ds for his viewing pleasure. She stripped off her orange thong showing her ample booty. She reached over to the nightstand and picked up her latest investment, a feathered sex toy. She lay beside him and tickled his penis until it hardened like a massive boulder. Marco was gifted in that department.

"Hmmm, you treat me sooo good."

After his rock remained firm from continuous teasing, she laid the tickler on the bed and proceeded to lick his shaft as she gazed into his eyes. He closed them and smiled with delight. She released her tongue after devouring him and positioned to climb atop his tantalizing body. He reached for her breasts and massaged both simultaneously before she bent forward for his sucking pleasure. She pulled up and mounted his stiff penis and with slow, deliberate humps, she rode him like a pony, gentle and smooth.

After a hard day of landscaping, he was ready to release but wanted each moment to last forever. His thrusts intensified before she flipped over on her back and he rammed her with passionate force. They exploded, their creamy juices streaming, and collapsed.

They lay in ecstasy before Tai arose to continue her planned romantic spa night. She didn't want to lie too long and lose her steam, fizzling out her plan. She stood and went to the bathroom to run bathwater in the tub. She added lavender oil as she'd heard that it was aromatherapy for the soul. After it was prepared, she walked back to the bed and lightly kissed Marco on the forehead. He had drifted off and on the verge of a slight doze but awakened with a smile. *This must be part two*, he thought.

In silence, she helped him from the bed and led him into the Jacuzzi. The matching scent of lit candles seduced their nostrils. She turned on the jets and as they purred, she massaged his shoulders and back with gentle pressure.

"Marco, I have something to discuss with you." Tai had been awake an hour but didn't want to disturb his peaceful sleep. He'd finally caught up with her morning by stirring, basking in the excitement of the previous night.

"Baby, I first want to say last night was absolutely, absolutely a winner. Not only do you have me spoiled in the kitchen but in this bedroom, too."

That's the idea, especially with what I'm getting ready to spring on you. "Awww, sweetie, thanks and you deserve it. And you have *me* spoiled by just being you."

"Hey, the feeling's mutual." He paused and gazed in her eyes, now facing her. "What's on your mind?"

"Well, I'm a little nervous about this, but…" She hesitated. The idea of marriage had been coveted at least the past five years and when she hit forty, she'd met her king. She didn't want anything or anyone—sister or none—to disrupt her flow. With this successful relationship, it was truly mud thicker than blood, she thought.

"We have an open understanding." He reached over and stretched his arm over her shoulder. "You can always express yourself with me. I'm listening."

"Marco, I'm really not excited about this, and I hope you'll understand. Trista and Kwik have split, and it wasn't on good terms. She's out of a job and a place to stay, at least for now. She's temporarily with a friend, but that won't last. She wants to know if she can stay here a minute…with us." Tai cringed as she spoke the last words.

His mood turned serious; the satisfaction of the morning suddenly lifted. "Say what?" He frowned in her direction.

"Yes, you heard right. Baby sis called last week. It took me this long to even think of mentioning it to you."

"You threw me for a loop. I really need to think about this. We've only been married a year. You really think it's a good idea for her to move in?" Marco asked with resistance.

"It wouldn't be permanent—"

"You remember how it was before she moved to L.A. She was all over the place. It took her a while to get on her feet and then she took off in a flash."

"And that was by default, after she was hired on the spur of the moment to dance," Tai added, finding a need to defend Trista's spontaneity.

Marco had a relationship with Trista that consisted of mixed feelings. He never thought she was stable nor had Tai's best interest. Sure, she appeared to support outwardly, but he believed there was something lurking under the surface. Their dissimilar backgrounds and lifestyles had not kept her and Tai from bonding; however, he found a tinge of jealousy in the air. He'd not suggested his opinion but kept mum about what he sensed.

"Let's say it was drama and more drama," she explained, intentionally not going the gossip route and explaining the cheating scenario. "I don't want her to be in any danger," she added, realizing if Marco thought she'd be the target of some tragedy, he would show more empathy. "Well, think about it."

Tai decided to play it cool and not seem pressed, doing the reverse psychology role. *That sis of mine* would *put me in this predicament. It never fails, does it?* She had been proud that Trista had left for the opposite side of the country to pursue her own career and become independent. Now, if Marco approved of her stay, it looked like Trista would need to latch on once again. Tai only hoped it would not be an extended visit.

CHAPTER 9

NEVADA

A woman wearing an apron rushed across the parking lot, opened her car door, hopped in and pulled off. Nevada crouched farther in her seat and peeped over the window ledge of her parked black SUV as the woman turned on the street, then sped up the road, disregarding the low speed limit. The face was unfamiliar and so was the vehicle. *Hmmm.* There was only one car remaining at Beyond Horizons Church—it belonged to Jolene Primrose.

Nevada looked at her watch: 2:47 p.m. and it was the third Sunday. By four, church members would start arriving for the monthly after-service dinner. She had an hour and nothing would stop this window of opportunity. She looked in the rearview mirror and pulled down her navy cap and adjusted her shades dark as the night. She opened the door and proceeded to walk toward the church in her nondescript matching jean jacket and jeans. She treaded lightly in her comfy white tennis shoes.

Looking over her shoulder and up and down the street, all was calm. After reaching the front door, she attempted to open, but it was locked. *Okay, Plan B.* Again, she checked her surroundings and no one was in sight. She decided to go to the side door where the woman had exited in a hurry, likely planning to go home and change out of her cooking apparel and return in church attire at dinnertime. Nevada stealthily crept to the door and softly touched the knob. Bingo, it was unlocked. Perhaps Miss Apron had intended to lock up, but in her rush, she'd forgotten.

Nevada entered and admired the plush wine carpet lining the hallway as well as the religious art adorning the walls. She opted to go to her right where a dim light reflected into the hall. She felt like her snooping inside of a church was committing a devious crime. When she reached the closed door, she realized it was the kitchen. She peered through the window frame and to her right was a smorgasbord lined up on a long table. The food smell assaulted her nostrils and it was diet torture to inhale. She then looked to her left and she felt like she'd been struck by lightning.

She double blinked. Jolene, Arthur's wife, posted up on a small metal table, her pale-blue daisy print dress hiked to her waist and legs spread like the food display across the room. A man, wearing a starched white shirt with rolled-up sleeves and black slacks, had his back facing Nevada. She'd done her research to get physical descriptions of key church personnel, so it didn't take but a second to identify him. It was the pastor and while his pants were pulled up, it was evident his fly was open as he rammed her voraciously. Her salt-and-pepper flowing hair, normally pulled in a bun, was bouncing as she verbally made soft and tender "oohs" and "aahs".

I'll be da—, oops, sorry for cursing in the house of the Lord.

As she'd caught the two in action, she decided not to take her normal photo as evidence to her clients. Her word would have to be golden. She didn't have the nerve to snap a shot from her cell phone camera of a senior with all her goodies on view.

Finding not what she'd hoped to discover, Nevada dared not open the door either but turned to take tiny steps down the hall and exit. She dashed to her SUV, climbed in and made a beeline.

Jolene could recognize her, but at the rate she was being pounded, it would be a while.

Poor Arthur. Now how will I tell this sweet guy his wife is getting it in with the pastor? Jolene's been helping in the kitchen, all right. Hmmph.

She continued to zoom through the neighborhood with flashbacks of the fried chicken she'd just spotted.

Nevada clicked her garage door open and squealed inside along Ryan's patrol car. She was anxious to tell him what she had witnessed. The incident had thrown her for a major loop as the missus was not the innocent 1950s housewife image she'd portrayed. Normally, Nevada could read people through blinding rain, but Jolene had fooled her.

She eased the door open as she thought Ryan may perhaps be napping on his day off. Her kitchen was spotless, which meant he had not prepared lunch, even microwaved. Neither of them were award-winning chefs, so often the most cozy room in the house was magazine clean. As she walked into the den, she heard the vocals of a TV sports commentator and as she'd figured, Ryan was cranking out the snores as he was propped up on the sofa. She could never understand how easy it was for men to fall asleep while sitting up straight as an arrow with only their head tilted or reeled back.

Instead of waking him to share the bizarre news, she made her way into the bedroom. Jolene and Pastor had given her food for thought, and she'd sit back and contemplate how to reveal her findings to hubby Arthur. She turned on the TV and channel surfed until she found a Lifetime movie. Before fifteen minutes of watching, her eyes had journeyed to another planet.

CHAPTER 10

CANDACE

Pulling into a space at Fort Washington Park, Candace was eager to shower Don with the ultimate picnic lunch. Wearing a red halter top and cutoff jean shorts, she hopped out of her convertible and closed the door. Don followed and reached into the backseat, grabbing the huge straw basket while she unloaded a massive blanket.

"You must have the whole restaurant in here," he commented on the basket's weight. He chuckled as they walked to find a vacant spot along the banks of the Potomac River. They landed in an area that was surrounded by foliage and settled on the grassy knoll. No one was in sight and that was kismet for Candace. She was all about privacy when it came to times like this.

Candace opened the blanket and spread it, carefully maneuvering her handbag, which she could've left in the car if she hadn't left her top down. They sat on the blanket and Don laid the basket at the tip.

One of their first dates was a surprise picnic he had planned at Hains Point, another waterfront location near D.C. She had found it so romantic that she thought she'd reciprocate by planning her own. Plus, the site would allow him to experience his all-time favorite of watching planes land; this time the flight pattern was National Airport.

The fort served as a historic background for their day trip. Built in the 1800s, it was the only fort that protected D.C. Candace had never visited during her adult years but had attended family picnics there as a child. The fortress and cannons completed the classic military setting that took her back to yesteryear.

She opened the basket and pulled out a chilled bottle of Riesling and two crystal wineglasses. Don gently took the bottle and found an opener before twisting the cork and pouring the wine.

"Here's to you, my lovely," he said in his oh-so-gentlemanly manner while he raised his glass.

"And to you, my sweetie." Candace clinked hers with his. "Cheers." She sipped her wine, relishing the exquisite taste, proud of one of her selections from a local winery.

Don checked out his surroundings and basked in the late afternoon sun. "You're always full of surprises."

"I got that from you. I never know what to expect." Candace giggled, caught up in another adventurous moment with Don.

"There's much more in store," he teased, then eyed the basket. "What kind of a treat are you hiding from me?"

"True, I'm sure you're hungry." *Men can be straight no chaser when it comes to food*, she thought to herself amusingly. *He's probably thinking enough talking. Let's eat.*

Don had spent the day cleaning his plane to go with his spotless mindset. He was truly OCD when it came to his aircraft. His mechanic also had provided routine maintenance at the small airpark where he stored it. He was equally meticulous when he was scheduled to fly chartered flights. Giving him the opportunity to freshen up and change clothes, Candace later stopped by his home to whisk him away to their next adventure. He'd found that it was never a dull minute with Candace. They were definitely in sync and fed off each other's bubbly and spontaneous lifestyles.

Candace figured she'd better start her feast soon or Don would be starving. She opened the basket and pulled out glass plates and laid them on the blanket along with cloth napkins. She believed in using the real deal, even in the woods. Next she reached in and presented some wrapped chicken and cheese sandwiches on croissants made fresh from a bakery, followed by blue grain chips and organic popcorn with sea salt, and glazed carrot and broccoli slices. She pulled out two chilled bottles of orange-mango lemonade.

She handed Don a hefty plate.

"This looks delicious and healthy."

Candace smiled. "We try. Nothing too fancy."

"Looks like it to me," the bachelor said, accustomed to simple meals unless when he was wining and dining her or on business engagements.

After finishing their lunch and soaking up the now evening sun at dusk, Candace whipped out the dessert: chocolate-covered strawberries in a container with ice. She lay back and reclined on the blanket while Don followed. Facing each other, she pulled out a strawberry and placed it in his mouth. *Ooohh, those sexy lips,* she thought.

He did likewise and they alternated until the container was empty. She placed the lid on top and looked dreamily into Don's eyes. "I love you, Don."

"And I love you, Candace. What more could I ask for?"

Well, you could ask me to be permanent in your life. "Oh, I feel the same. You're all I want—and need in this world."

"Likewise," he agreed. Whenever talks became serious or mushy, he would become uneasy at some point. "So, what's on your agenda this week?" he asked, quickly changing the subject, attempting to make the mood upbeat.

"I have some appointments, the usual in-store meetings, stuff like that." Candace wished not to kill her romantic mood by discussing business. It was not the time nor place to get wrapped up in work obligations.

The planes continued to descend heading toward nearby National Airport as the sky was set to blend its colors at dusk. She closed her eyes and puckered her lips, extending them to his and tenderly locked in a kiss that she never wanted to release. He obliged and reached over to massage her breast through the opening of her halter top. While he kneaded it, she unzipped his camouflage shorts and found his member that she started to stroke gently until it became rigid.

Although it was serene with no visitors in sight, she toyed with the idea of throwing caution to the wind and going for it right there. Excited with moist panties and heated thighs, she gently pushed the closed basket off the blanket and rolled over with blanket in tow. She pulled the blanket over her, wrapping them up into the entangled fabric. She eased off her shorts and as they faced each other, they passionately grinded until their sweet juices trickled down their legs.

As the evening rolled in, she imagined the moon and stars winking at them.

CHAPTER 11

MARCO

"Man, I'm telling you. It's not a good idea. Your sister-in-law is p-h-i-n-e. What the youngbloods call a dimepiece," Steve said about Trista. "Ain't no way I could have something like that up in my house and wear blinders *all* the time." He bit into his hamburger sub while they sat in a corner booth at Ledo Pizza.

"Look, I told you she's desperate. Apparently, her boyfriend caught her cheatin'—," Marco advised to his single friend, a handsome bachelor who swore he'd never pop the question.

"Uh-hmm…there you go, she's a cheater."

"With his close buddy. May have been a case of being in the wrong place at the wrong time. I heard it was a quick office fling, a one-time situation." Tai had finally shared the details albeit with resistance.

"Still…"

Marco dipped a French fry in catsup and placed it in his mouth and chewed. "Okay, you're right about there's no excuse. Guess they got caught up in the moment. But you can relate, playa, playa."

"Hey, and that's why I remain single. 'Cause I like the different flavors of the week." He sighed and looked at him in his eyes. "I'm saying be wise and be careful." Steve thought about Trista and how easy she was on the eyes. "You have enough business with your beautiful wife to take care of." He smiled. "But hey, if sis-in-law is in the market."

"I'd never hook her up with you," Marco said frankly. "I'd be burying her alive. I know how you roll, bro."

Suddenly, a voluptuous, cocoa-skinned woman entered, wearing a tight-fitting dress and heels, her legs looking like they'd been soaked in baby oil. Steve looked at her piercingly and froze as he took a bite into his sandwich.

"Call nine-one-one and rescue me," Steve teased about the excitement of the woman who'd turned his head while his eyes followed.

"Look, all jokes aside, I wanted to see what you thought. It was truly a hard decision to let Trista stay with us."

"I understand you're a newlywed and you want to please your bride *unconditionally*."

"It's supposed to be a short period so she can get on her feet. Maybe she'll find another dancing gig…but then again, she's 'bout to hit the big four-oh. I'm surprised she held it down this long. Most of those chicks in the music biz are much younger."

"Yeah, guess it's like Derek Jeter played baseball until forty."

"And I saw on the news recently about this group of track runners and they are all over ninety." Marco sighed. "I hope it goes smooth. I don't like no drama and I can definitely do without it in my house."

"So, do you at least like her as a person, personality, etcetera?"

"She's cool, Steve. Before I came onboard, Tai had told me a few things. Strange behavior here or there. They were opposites, but before she left for Cali, I thought they'd worked out their differences. Seemed to have gelled okay."

"Well, bro, I hope it all works out. When's the lovely lady comin' through?"

"Next week, man; next week." *I love Tai or otherwise, I would've said hell to the no. Even though I'm telling Steve they're cool, it's still something about Trista I ain't feeling.*

CHAPTER 12

TAI

The rain let loose over downtown D.C. as Tai swirled in her office chair to witness the torrential downpour. Her employment firm, Next Phase of Life, was quiet today compared to the usual hump days when employers would attempt to fill temporary and permanent positions. On such a stormy day, Tai was pleased that the office atmosphere was calm. Plus, Trista was plastered all through her brain with her pending arrival in two days. She was glad it would be the end of the week and she'd have the weekend to adjust to life once again with her younger sister.

A knock on her door jolted her from her thoughts and serenity with smooth jazz streaming from her iPod. "Come in."

Felicia, her key assistant and confidante, slowly opened the door and closed it behind her. "Good afternoon. I received your voicemail to stop in. Sorry, I had taken a lunch break. Plus, I had to dry off. It's a fountain out there."

"How was it?" Tai had starved and deleted lunch from her agenda with the exception of nibbling on a granola bar.

"Tasty. I tried the new café around the corner. Crab cake platter and salad." She eased into the chair facing Tai's desk.

"Sounds tempting. Enough said." She smiled. "Well, Felicia, I'm sure you're thinking it must be something serious. Usually, that's the case when I want to talk in private."

"Yes, I figured. It's fine." She twitched in her seat and crossed her legs.

"Trista's coming back." Before Felicia could ask when, she added, "Friday."

Felicia was in shock. Last she'd heard, Trista was living splendid in Hollywood with a fantasy job and a hunk of a lifetime, who'd whisked her away for a golden opportunity. "What happened? Something had to go down for her to suddenly come back here. Not to say D.C. isn't exciting, but it can't compete with La-La Land when it comes to entertainment."

"Let's say she conducted an experiment and it exploded in the lab," Tai hinted, not wanting to divulge her sister's personal status when it involved her man trouble.

"Oh, I see." Felicia waited to hear more details but dared not pry further.

"It didn't work out, so she asked if she could stay with us a short while—let's pray it's quick—until she can stabilize."

"Certainly, she doesn't plan to sit around while you and Marco work. It's not like she's a teenager or even in her early twenties," Felicia slipped out before realizing she may have overstepped her verbal boundaries. "Sorry, Tai, I didn't mean for it to sound that way."

"Look, Felicia, you always shoot from the hip. That's what I like. I haven't shared this with a soul. It's fine 'cause you're absolutely right." Tai paused. "Please see what openings we have on file for restaurant work. Her background, as you're aware, is in the food industry. Waitress, hostess, whatever you can find."

"Maybe she can go back to Seacoast," Felicia suggested. Trista had worked tables at the seafood restaurant for eight months before she'd landed the dancing gig. She actually had become accustomed to life as a waitress and had become adept at acquiring decent tips.

"True, perhaps they have an opening. And if not, she had a great reputation there. We could simply call and see if they need help."

"I'll get on it right away." Felicia looked down, then raised her head. "How does Marco feel about it? You've made it through your first year. And having a third party around the house could disturb the flow."

"Honestly, Felicia, he's not feeling it—at all. I had to pull out some of my seductive tricks to snag him. Despite all that, he wasn't jumping for joy after reality set in." Tai sipped her water bottle, trying to substitute for her hunger urge. "It is what it is at this point. She's surely arriving on an afternoon flight at DCA. I thought I'd take her out for an early dinner, or better yet, happy hour. I'll need it."

"Best of luck. Let me know if there's anything else I can do, but I'll contact Seacoast if I don't see anything in the system."

"Thanks, Felicia. You always come through."

An hour later, Felicia knocked on Tai's door and entered without her usual "come in" greeting. Tai had been daydreaming about Trista again and turned to face her entryway.

Felicia stood before her with a wide grin. "Done deal. Seacoast manager said she'll gladly rehire Trista. Had nothing but accolades about her customer service and work ethic. I didn't even bother to look in the system."

"That was quick. Thanks, Felicia." She looked back out the window. "At least that gives me some peace of mind, knowing she already has a job before she steps off the plane." She added, "I'll wait to tell her at dinner. And I hope she doesn't take it the wrong way. After such adventures in La-La Land and traveling and being onstage, she may not want to wait tables. May find it boring in comparison, but we'll see what happens. I'm not trying to run her life or tell her how to live it."

"She'll probably appreciate you looking out for her. That's how I see it."

CHAPTER 13

NEVADA

The waitress refilled Nevada's cup of coffee. She was now on her third cup. She looked at her watch. Arthur was running late; it was unlike the older gentleman. Ready to dig in for a hearty breakfast, she dared not be rude and waited to order. She perused the menu so she'd be ready. Her conversations with Arthur were never done through their cell phones to keep their detective-client relationship on the down low. After fifteen more minutes, it was now a half-hour and she was beginning to be concerned. Perhaps he'd faced a traffic issue, although she'd conveniently set up their meeting past the rush hour.

Suddenly, Arthur pulled up slowly in his 1975 Mercedes-Benz, sputtering and sounding like it could conk out any moment. He opened the door and stepped out, Nevada watching him from the open window.

Arthur entered IHOP and strode toward her booth after spotting her immediately. "Good morning, Nevada."

"Good morning, Mr.…sorry, Arthur. You remind me of my dad, so it's hard to call you by your first name."

"But it's my wish, dear," he advised, taking a seat across from her. "I apologize." He nodded toward his car. "Ole Lucy there is on her last leg, I think. I had to stop off at a gas station to have a checkup. Turns out it needed some fluid."

"Well, I'm glad you made it safely." Nevada had surmised that Arthur seemed to take a backseat when it came to transportation. Jolene always was behind the wheel of their new luxury whip. It didn't seem fair to her, but she kept her mind and mouth out of their business. Today would be difficult enough as it was likely the most challenging report she had made during her history of five years as a detective.

Arthur picked up the menu as the waitress returned. "Can I get you some coffee?"

"Sure, thanks." She poured him a cup and he added Splenda before stirring it. "You can take our order." He already was familiar with the breakfast there. He nodded toward Nevada. "Ladies first."

"Thank you." Nevada looked at the menu. "I'll have the short stack of pancakes, egg whites and turkey bacon."

"Sounds healthy. I'll take the same," Arthur stated, diverting from his usual massive meal. The waitress wrote the order and walked away.

After a pleasant breakfast and casual conversation, the mood turned serious. Arthur looked Nevada in the eyes. "I presume you have something to report."

Nevada found it weird to stray her eyes as she was always determined—whether friends or enemies—to look a subject in the eyes. She focused intently. "Yes, I do, sir."

"No need to be formal. Call me Arthur."

"Arthur, yes, I'm not sure how to tell you this."

"I'm a big guy and wear boxers. I'm listening, all ears."

Nevada sipped her coffee. She considered another cup as she needed to feel wired. "Well, uh, uh, Arthur, your wife, Jolene, may be having an affair."

Arthur almost choked as he sipped his coffee, then set his cup on the table. "Did I hear you correctly?"

"I'm not positive you would call it an 'affair,' which usually means it's got longevity, but I am aware of at least a one-time hookup."

"*You're* saying my wife fucked someone?" Arthur said blatantly, surprising Nevada with his language, diverting from his conservative image.

"If that's how you want to put it," she responded embarrassed. She paused. "Here's the hard part—and believe me, Arthur, this is the most difficult…" *What a kind man, gentle, sweet; can I really share what I witnessed?*

His facial expression had turned sad while, at the same time, bitterness resonated. His eyes read, *come on with the info.*

"You had alerted me about her churches and how much time she spends there, and at least once a month, she stays behind at one to serve Sunday dinners. Well, Arthur, I stopped by and watched a helper, presumably a church member, leave from a side door as I was pulling up. I then figured it may be open, and bingo, she had left it unlocked. So I entered and headed down the hallway toward a light, thinking it was likely the kitchen area." She paused, lowered her head and then quickly looked in his eyes. "She and the pastor were making love." *To put it mildly. I don't want to tell him that she was actually getting her freak on atop the table.*

Arthur was speechless, his mouth agape. He finally closed it and spoke, "Well, I'll be damned. So she's been cooking in the kitchen all right. And that pastor, hmmph. Lying to me, telling me she was searching for a church home and couldn't figure out which one fit her the best." A tear trickled onto his face. "We celebrated forty-five years. She is the love of my life."

Nevada reached over and placed her hand over Arthur's, an unusual gesture for her. "I'm sorry and I understand." She paused.

"I realize you have your checkbook and want to pay me the balance for my services, but I am not going to accept it."

"I can't do that, Nevada."

"I insist, Arthur, please. I couldn't even take a photo like I usually would do. I couldn't stomach it. So I don't have proof; it's only my eyewitness account. And I see that you trust me without physical evidence. I've appreciated you hiring me and at times treating me like your own daughter."

Nevada was concerned about his physical health and driving his car.

"I think I'll go for a little ride. That's right; not in that little monster. I could break down," he added, realizing the car wasn't reliable.

"Tell you what, you leave your car here and I'll take you for some fresh air. My offer. I'm sure you can use it. Then I'll bring you back here and follow you until you're almost home. Of course, I have to stay out of sight."

"Thanks, Nevada. You are like a daughter. I appreciate your thoughtfulness," he stated solemnly.

"No problem. Detectives can have a human side." She smiled.

Nevada picked up the tab and left a decent tip. She escorted Arthur to her SUV and headed toward the Annapolis waterfront.

The IHOP meeting infiltrated Nevada's mind as she stretched across her king-sized bed in the middle of the afternoon. It was so unlike her to feel restless at this hour, but she couldn't rid her thoughts of Arthur and Jolene. It was like a recurring nightmare. Why was she so wrapped up in their lives? Detective life was complete with surprises and she'd seen and heard enough to write a horror novel. Informing Arthur had truly been one of her hardest revelations. Perhaps he reminded her of her father, a jazz musician from Chicago. They both were dedicated to their craft.

She closed her eyes, hoping to wash away her visions. She felt a peck on her cheek and promptly opened her eyes.

"Hey, babe. Can't believe you're chillin' in the middle of the day." Ryan sat on the bed. "Everything okay?"

"Naw, babe, it's not. I—"

"Gimme a sec. I don't see you like this often." He walked over to the dresser, stripped off his badge and laid it on top, then added his tie. He removed his uniform and dropped it to the floor, left wearing his boxers. He walked to the bed and lay beside Nevada, spooning her. "What's on your mind?" He affectionately wrapped his arm across her and kissed her back.

"Ooh, exactly what I needed." She exhaled and then turned over to face him, desiring to look him in the eyes. "I rarely get this involved, but you remember my elderly couple case?"

"Of course, the retired professor. Nice guy, you said."

"Yep. Ryan, I had the worst ordeal this morning. I met him to tell him his little wifey is a cheat. He was aware somethin' was up, but not that kind of flavor. He's such a sweetheart, it crushed me to deliver that news. And guess what? Missy is cheatin' with her pastor and I saw them in action."

"No way."

"I won't go any further than that." Nevada had strict morals and work ethics and kept the private parts of a case confidential.

"Well, that's sad, Nevada," Ryan stated with empathy. He would attempt to ease her mind. "Close your eyes, hun." He reached over and opened the nightstand drawer, pulling out his favorite tool.

He lifted up, removed his boxers and positioned himself on his knees, placing a leg on her right side. He pushed her hands together and placed them above her head, then locking them to the bed frame with handcuffs.

"Hmm…" Nevada already knew the scenario; it rarely changed when he was in the mood for a freaky moment. After all, as an officer, he was handy when it came to cuffing.

He moved her panties to the side, fingered her until she was moist, preparing to insert his tool, nicknamed by her as Captain Chunky, into her vagina. He entered gently and leaned over to kiss her lusciously on the lips while he stroked her vigorously until they both exploded in ecstasy. He rolled over while Nevada enjoyed the blissful orgasm. But in an unusual course of action, she had enough energy for a round two.

"That was yummy. Can I open my eyes now?"

"Of course."

"Unlock me. My turn?"

"Say what?" *Okay, I hope I can get my Johnson back up. She rarely makes a comeback. What a treat.* He unlocked the handcuffs and then positioned himself on his back.

Nevada switched positions, climbing atop him and cuffing his thick wrists to the bedframe. "Now *you* close your eyes." She loved the dominant position, going hand in hand with her detective persona. She inserted his rock-hardness in her vagina and pumped him into oblivion, collapsing on top of his hunky physique after climax. Captain Chunky was now off-duty.

CHAPTER 14

TRISTA

Tai sat in the airport cell phone lot and glanced at her car clock. She nervously anticipated any moment she would receive a text from Trista that she'd arrived from L.A. Her mixed feelings still simmered about her sister reentering her life as a housemate. She'd finally nabbed her marriage material and within a year, she now would be sharing space with a sibling who'd been away living independently. She reared her head back on the headrest and exhaled. She was torn if she were feeling selfish or simply confused.

Her cell vibrated. The screen read: *Landed. See you soon.* Tai waited before leaving the lot and heading to the terminal where she pulled up to await Trista. Shortly, she spotted her and stepped out to open the trunk. Trista rolled up with her modest suitcase and tote bag.

"Hey, sis." She reached out and embraced Tai. "Back on the East Coast."

Tai released her. "You're looking well, not like somebody who just ended a promising relationship."

"Thanks." Trista was wearing an apricot dress, a garment she used to detest, but finally she'd started to appreciate the feminine look. She hoisted her luggage into the trunk and they both hopped into the car.

"It's kinda strange being here again, although I haven't been gone that long."

"I bet." *And yes, it's strange you being here. Even stranger that it'll be three of us, but I'm glad you're safe. That cheating stuff can be dangerous. But who am I to judge after I had my little fling, but I was cool with my dirt. Didn't get caught in the act.* Her thoughts drifted to Hasan and their nights at the gym.

"So how's it going? Married life." Trista broke her concentration, thankfully, Tai thought as she reminisced about those erotic meet-ups in the past. She'd never shared those moments with her sister. She understood lust could lead to betrayal of the one you love.

"Fantastic. Loving every minute," Tai responded proudly.

"Cool. Glad to hear."

As they crossed the Fourteenth Street Bridge entering the city, Trista soaked up the tourist sights of D.C.

"Do me a favor. Drive by Seacoast. I'd like to pass by for old times' sake."

Tai had informed her the previous day that she'd arranged for her to return to her former waitress job. Trista appeared elated that she'd have income before she'd hit the tarmac.

"Sure, no problem." Tai headed to Seventh Street downtown and slowed as she passed the restaurant.

"Wow, looks like they have a crowd. Well, they always did during happy hour time on Fridays." She viewed the bustling street scene with working women who'd swapped their heels for flip-flops heading to the subway to teenagers headed to hang out at Gallery Place for an evening of movies and bowling. "Nothing's changed."

"I figured you'd be hungry, so I have reservations at Dazzle." Tai turned and drove toward where she valet parked.

Trista eyed the upscale restaurant. The good-looking, twenty-something cocoa dream winked at Trista once they stepped out before taking the keys. *I like this place already.*

Once inside, the hostess seated them near a window where they could people watch. As they perused the overwhelming menu of dozens of possibilities, a waitress stopped by. Tai ordered a bottle of Chardonnay. When she returned with the wine, Tai poured wine in the glasses, hoping the mood would become mellow and she could pick Trista's brain.

Trista scoped out the scenery inside the restaurant. She spotted a waiter who also had piercing eyes in her direction. Blushing, she quickly diverted her eyes back to the menu and sipped her wine. When she glanced back, the gorgeous chocolate M&M was still staring and then smiled. He nodded his head.

"Well, hello, Tai, good seeing you here." A tall man dressed in a dark-gray suit with a pale yellow tie approached.

"Oh, hi, Sharod. How's it going?" She smiled. Nodding toward Trista, she added, "This is my sister, Trista. She's just in from L.A."

"Nice meeting you." *Well, I'll be damned. Everywhere I look it's a fine brotha. Not sure if this is the right place for me if I ever plan to settle down. Too many boxes of chocolate.* Her eyes wandered to Mr. Candy who continued to focus in on her, not giving her panties a break from the building heat. This time his body language was definitive. He motioned slightly toward an area of the restaurant.

"Mind if I join you two for a moment?" Sharod asked, helping himself to a seat before Tai could respond. He was one of Tai's clients, and Next Phase of Life had supplied his office with competent employees.

He looked at Trista. "So, how do you like Cali—"

"Excuse me, I'm going to the ladies room." Trista pushed back her chair and stood.

"Do you know—" Tai tried to catch her to place their order. Trista was too swift. "Oh, well, I'll order when she gets back." She turned her attention to Sharod, wondering if he would be a suitable match for Trista.

Trista sailed toward the restroom, having gotten the vibe that the handsome man wanted to meet up since he'd nodded in that direction. Klymaxx's "Meeting in the Ladies Room" rang in her head. She passed him in the hallway and opened the door. Pleased to find it was a single stall, she waved him inside. She hung her purse on a ring, reached inside and pulled out a condom. He unzipped his pants and whipped out his piece, massive and thick, grabbing the protection she handed him and placed it on as she helped. She hiked up her dress, moved her panties aside and opened to allow him access. She leaned against the wall. They rocked and rolled for a true quickie. She restrained from making any verbal noise and bit her lip. Once he released, he discarded the condom, and zipped his pants. She left the stall and washed her hands before opening the door. Not seeing anyone, she motioned for him to exit. He smiled and winked, scurrying away. After the door closed, she dug inside her bag for perfume and spritzed her neck, arms and dress.

Now was that a ho move? Actually, I think it was the other "h-o" as in horny. Damn, I didn't even get his name.

She sashayed back to the table. Her body was satisfied with such a welcome-back gift, and she was now ready to please her stomach.

"Glad you're back," Tai greeted. "I'm starving. I went ahead and ordered an appetizer."

"Great." Trista concealed her ladies room adventure with a bland facial expression. She wanted to burst into a mile-wide smile. As she looked around the restaurant, her mystery man seemed to have disappeared. "So, where's the good-looking brother that was here when I left? You said his name was Sharod."

"Oh, yes, he was actually on his way out. He's one of my clients and hires us to fill positions at his firm."

The waitress arrived with Southwest spring rolls. Tai ordered a salmon Caesar salad with garlic croutons while Trista decided on pecan crusted chicken with pasta and spinach.

Tai reached to sample one and bit into the crust. "These are scrumptious. Try one."

Trista reached over and tasted the roll. "Yes, these are." She was trying to play it cool and confident, but in reality, she was nervous. Disappointed, she felt like she was back where she'd started—ground zero in her opinion. *How could I lose a* fantabulous *lover like Kwik, a dancing gig, and a comfy life—Cali style at that?*

Her thoughts drifted to the stall scenario where she'd relieved some tension before dinner. The sexy encounter in a public restroom was a first and in fact, she wasn't truly a one-night-stand kind of girl. She usually focused on one relationship at a time and worked to make the best of it. She figured the spontaneous restaurant episode with her no-name partner may have been her subconsciously trying to avenge Kwik for dropping her like a hot plate. Or perhaps her on-the-spot studio rendezvous led her to think this was the way she wanted to roll in the future. After all, she certainly had rejected flirtatious come-ons from players in the music industry. Satisfied with Kwik, she never responded positive toward any advances, even though she easily could have transformed into a gold digger on occasion.

She would have been scared crazy to stray while with Dorian, her longtime boyfriend in North Carolina locked up for embezzling money from his office job. He was an overly possessive maniac and control freak who would have gone ballistic if he'd caught her in the act like Kwik had. He didn't want her to even look at any men or communicate in any way. Having a jealous mate made it difficult when she was a waitress; she was restricted in how she behaved with customers. She often downplayed her attractiveness and how she'd learned to wear casual and loose-fitting clothes, far from the curvy wrap dress like she had on today.

"Earth to Trista," Tai teased, noticing that her sister was in a daze, barely nibbling on the appetizer.

"Oh, sorry, I zoned out a sec." Trista sighed. "My mind's everywhere."

"Well, you look great. Wearing dresses. I remember you despised those when you first came here."

"Right." She smiled. "Kwik got me to a different space."

"Speaking of—"

"Kwik. He's still on my mind, sis. Can't shake it."

"I understand. It'll improve in time. I didn't want to ask about him, but I figured no word from him."

"Nope." Trista grimaced. "And I decided I'm not callin,', textin', emailin', nothin'."

"Yes, sometimes it's best to sit back and see what happens. I did the same with Austin, never reaching out, and as you're aware, I never spoke to him again. It took me a while to get over it, though. After those long five years, he pulled that ghost act on me, standing me up and not showing for my fortieth birthday party. I was definite that we would be walking down that aisle, but hell, he faded out of my life, like that." Tai didn't like recounting the sad story, but she attempted to assuage Trista's low demeanor. She, too, had been brokenhearted after feeling she'd found her Mr. Right.

"It was only a year for me. I can't imagine *five* years," Trista acknowledged.

She sipped her wine and the tipsiness was settling in. "Sometimes I think what I did wasn't so bad. Men do it all the time. It was only one day." She giggled. "And I'm only tellin' you," she leaned in, "but it was soooo gooooood." She slapped her cheek. "I shouldn't be sayin' that. Guess I'm tryin' to justify the whole thing."

"No, if that's how you feel, no problem." *Who am I to judge, Sis? I was steady getting it in with Hasan after our training sessions in the gym. And like her, it was sooo gooood. Like Grandma always said, the pot can't call the kettle black.* Tai wanted to share her own little cheatin' past with Trista, but she never felt that she could. For now, she'd wear her innocent façade as she'd only been in her life again for a year or so. It wasn't like her girls, Nevada and Candace. The bond was forming with Trista, but it wasn't completely sealed—yet.

"And Marco was literally in my backyard. I had no idea my landscaper held the key to my heart," she shared dreamily. "All that time I was worried about Austin and I didn't realize my sweetie was right there." She lit up like a candle. "And Trista, you don't worry, there are some *fine* men in this area. In fact, you were so quick to leave, I barely got to introduce you to..."

She shook her head slowly. "Not my type, but thanks anyway."

"I'm not trying to match-make; only a thought."

"I appreciate it, Tai. I probably should focus on me for now. This entire thing with Kwik threw me for a loop. I hadn't expected to be on a plane and back on the East Coast. You've done enough. Finding out I could go back to my job at Seacoast and looking out for me. Plus, lettin' me stay with you and Marco. A lot of women—sisters or not—would've said hell to the no. Especially those who may be insecure or feel another woman in the house could be a threat."

"Well, you can count me out on that one," she spoke with confidence.

The waitress delivered their entrees.

"I still can't believe I'm back and so suddenly." Trista suddenly remembered her friend. "Oops, let me text Tara and let her know I got here okay."

"Oh, right. Thank her for me."

"Will do. She's good people and I'm blessed to have her for a friend, considering I've only known her for maybe six months."

She picked up her cell from the table and texted. *Here safe. Sorry forgot to tell u. Dazing. Hanging in there. Thanks again 4 everything. Tai thanks you too.*

Tara quickly responded. *Cool. Keep me posted. Take care.*

Trista swallowed her pride and walked across the threshold of what was now Tai and Marco's home. Her fond memories overpowered the negative feeling she felt as Tai had entered the driveway. She felt at ease with Tai but was unsure how Marco would react to her return. After all, she was elated about leaving D.C. and her sister's nest for L.A. She finally could show her sister that she was worthy, that she could be independent.

After setting her luggage in the foyer, she walked into the den. She scoped the décor and nothing had been changed since she'd left. Tai had a knack for interior design, so when Marco moved in, renting out his own home, he'd left his masculine touch behind.

Tai had gone upstairs to greet Marco. Trista sat on the sofa and picked up a magazine.

Marco descended downstairs and walked into the room and greeted Trista who stood to accept his light hug.

"Welcome back," he lied.

Trista picked up his fake smile and returned her own. "Thanks. Unexpected, of course."

"I understand. These things happen. Sorry."

"It's okay. Thanks." She offered a smug expression.

"It's an adjustment being on the East Coast. You must be disappointed at least to come back so soon."

"And you know it."

Marco felt a chilly vibe and decided he didn't want to continue the pretentious game. "Well, I'll let you ladies have your space. She'll be right down. It's good to have some sister time."

"Thanks, I appreciate it." She smiled. "Oh, let me not forget, Happy Anniversary."

Do you really mean those words? It seems like you sure got out of Dodge like a bat on wheels when we announced our engagement. "Thanks." Marco surmised that Trista had possibly been envious of Tai when she'd initially moved in. He also felt she may have been uncomfortable. He turned to head back upstairs.

I'm happy he's gone. He gives me the creeps sometimes. I know he'd better treat my sis right or he's gonna have an issue. 'Cause Tai never speaks negative doesn't mean there isn't anything wrong. She wants me to have the impression everything is always peachy cool.

Tai emerged into the room. "Well, you're all set. Towels are on the bed. Make yourself at home, but I don't have to tell you that." *Just don't interfere with me or my bizness, sweetie, and everything will be all right. Stay out of our marital affairs and we'll be cool.* Tai wasn't totally convinced that having Trista around was ideal, but she figured it was the least she could offer. She definitely didn't want to see her sister in the streets.

CHAPTER 15

THE LADIES

The light summer evening breeze tickled the senses of the sprawling crowd on the patio at National Harbor. Secret Society was in concert, their popularity appreciated by music lovers who grooved to the beats. While seated on the turf, witnessing a brilliant sunset in the backdrop and the Potomac River and Woodrow Wilson Bridge, the concertgoers relished the scene. It was Friday night and nights like this were magical for the trio, especially to mix the music with girl talk.

After the new and old fans split for the night, Nevada, Tai and Candace headed across the street to the WXYZ Lounge at the Aloft hotel to top off their ecstatic experience. They walked inside the lobby, then took an elevator to the lounge area where they found a spot.

"That was some concert. It was packed," Nevada stated.

"Definitely. I'm a fan forever," Tai stated.

"Absolutely the bomb," Candace chimed in.

The three took over a section, placing their bags on the comfortable chairs.

"What you want, Tai? You, Candace?" Nevada asked, volunteering to go to the bar. "My treat."

"Blue Hawaiian. Thanks." Candace crossed her legs, prepared

to check out any eye candy. Hell, it wouldn't hurt to look; she wasn't in the market for prospects.

"I'll go with you," Tai offered. "Think I'll get an Island Breeze."

After Nevada and Tai returned, they set their drinks on a coffee table and sat in the overstuffed chairs.

"I missed us hanging out, so glad to be back in the mix," Candace declared. "Yeah, I like this eye candy," she added, zooming her eyes around the lounge. "But I'd better be a good gurl and keep my focus."

"Especially since meeting Don, you've turned into a little lovebird." Nevada swigged her drink.

"Look, I wanted to tell you I don't know what else to do. I planned that romantic picnic thinking that would turn him out, especially since I turned him out all in the open air." She smiled mischievously. "I just knew that would seal the deal, but no such luck."

"I keep telling you to be patient. Candace, it's going to happen and catch you off guard," Nevada advised.

"I hope so. But like I keep saying, that clock is tick-ticking away. At the rate I'm going, I'm gonna have to plan to conceive on my wedding night. I'm not trying to rush and have a baby before I celebrate a year."

"Candace, plan another picnic," Nevada said blandly.

"No, I'll think of something. I'm not giving up, ladies."

"I hear you," Tai agreed.

"Well, it's no secret I'm not a fan of marriage. The arrangement I have is fine with me. Ryan and I can live together forever for all I care," Nevada stated. "Guess I'm the one who's not feeling it. I never considered myself marriage material. Nor do I think I'm cut out to be a mama," she shared, an opinion she expressed to her friends for what seemed like a thousand times.

"You keep it real, Nevada. At least you're honest," Tai complimented.

"Sometimes those marital vows can be devastating. I hadn't had the chance to update you about the cute seniors and their case," Nevada stated solemnly. "I don't like to gossip, but you won't believe I decided to go by the church one Sunday afternoon when dinner was to be served. I snuck in the side door after a member had left out. I think she forgot to lock it. I went up in that camp, and the wife and pastor were serving up dinner all right; a hot and lusty meal. They were getting it in, right there on a kitchen table."

Tai gasped. "No way. I need to drink on that one." She lifted her cocktail and sipped.

"Girl, you kidding," Candace chimed in, her eyes bulging.

"I've seen a lot in my days, but I couldn't believe it. My double-take wasn't lying to me." Nevada sighed. "It was one of the hardest cases I've had yet to deliver that news. And I didn't have the heart to take a photo. But her hubby was convinced I was telling the truth. Why the hell would I make up that kind of madness? Plus, he's the sweetest guy, such a gentleman." She shook her head.

CHAPTER 16

MARCO

Sipping on a cup of coffee and polishing off a glazed donut, Marco flipped the pages of the morning newspaper. His cell phone vibrated and he looked at the caller ID, which read *Mom*. He thought, *Hmmm. She doesn't usually call this early.* He picked up the call. "Good morning, Mom."

"Hi, Marco."

"How ya feeling? Surprised to see you calling at this hour." He glanced at the clock: 8:10 a.m.

"Not bad for a senior, I guess. Listen, I have some wonderful news. Dad and I are coming to town…if that's okay with you and of course, Tai, we'd love to stop by your place. We've didn't get to visit during the wedding weekend. He's a guest lecturer for an educators' conference so they're taking care of his hotel expenses." She paused. "Any news on your end?" Mrs. Moore asked.

"No news, Mom." Marco sighed, knowing what his mother was referring to.

"I tell ya I'm still waiting on that grandbaby." Mrs. Moore had never had a grandchild and considered her life empty without one. She consistently pressured Marco, her only son of two children, to have a child. "It's about that time—"

"It's time when *we* feel like it's time, Mom."

"I simply don't understand how you could marry someone eight years your senior. She's over the hill and may not be able to conceive. You're young and vibrant and deserve a child. And if it's a son, he'll be able to carry the Moore name. I'm telling you—"

"Mom, listen, it's the same old story. Don't you think I get tired of hearing this? I've told you, if it's meant to be, it will be. We just celebrated our first year, so give us time. Please." Marco was annoyed with his mother's steady pounding on him and Tai to enter parenthood.

"Hmmph, that woman—"

"No *that woman*. You mean to say my 'wife, Tai.' Mom, I realize you've never accepted me being with her and it's all because of her age. Do you really think that's fair to me, to us?" He sighed. "And now you're frontin' and sayin' you want to visit and play Miss Phony? No way. If you can't be for real, what's the point?"

"Hon, I understand you're touchy—"

"Touchy? It's called being respectful and cordial."

"Hmmph," she muttered under her breath. "Well, Ken and I will be in town in two weeks. I'll keep you updated, dear." She mumbled reluctantly, "And tell Tai hello for us."

"Will do. Talk with you later, Mom." Marco was a mama's boy—only from the aspect that he'd been spoiled during childhood and his teen years. Their mother-son relationship had taken a hit since his marriage to Tai.

Marjorie Moore and husband, Ken, were not ecstatic to discover their only son had selected an older bride. They had always envisioned their daughter-in-law to be a youthful twenty-something, perhaps one of the graduate students Ken taught at Savannah State University. They'd even attempted to match-make him with colleagues' daughters, only each time the blind dates were a bust.

Marco was selective and although he appreciated their efforts, he'd preferred to find his special mate on his own. He, too, never realized his landscaping customer was a potential soul mate. If he couldn't find romance in the nation's capital, he couldn't find it anywhere, he'd reasoned.

"Good morning, sweetie," Tai greeted, entering the kitchen. She reached over and planted a kiss on his lips. "I see you're up bright and early. Didn't even hear you. I think all that wine knocked me out last night. And, of course, all that good lovin' you laid on me." She smiled seductively.

"Hmmm-mmm. You mean you laid on *me*."

She swung the belt of her bathrobe teasingly. "Makes two of us, huh?"

"Mom called. She and Dad will be here later this month. He's coming for a conference and—"

"Staying here..."

"No, actually, they'll be at a hotel."

"Oh, I see, I'm surprised she didn't want to stay here. But I guess since his expenses are being taken care of, no problem." She suddenly thought, "Maybe we can take them to a nice restaurant. A lot of new ones have opened since their last visit."

"Or perhaps you can throw down in the kitchen like you usually do," Marco suggested, brainstorming that perhaps if his mother tasted her talented cooking skills, she'd open up to Tai. He figured it could be a plus.

"Of course, I'd do it for you." *And not your meddlesome mom. But I won't hold it against Pops 'cause he's a cool dude. I've always gotten a good vibe from him. But as for Moms, I'm not sure what I'm working with.*

CHAPTER 17

TRISTA

Walking briskly from the Gallery Place subway station, Trista observed the contrast of D.C. and L.A. streetwalkers. The woman breezed by her in four-inch heels headed toward her government job was unlike the woman casually strolling past shops on Melrose Boulevard or the pedestrian crossing Hollywood Boulevard among palm trees. She missed the West Coast vibe after she'd gotten a slice of life. But she had to deal with the here and now, and here she was en route to her old stomping ground, the Seacoast restaurant.

She hoped that today would rack up huge tips to start saving for her own apartment. She stopped in her tracks, finding a corner to do a spot check. She pulled out her compact from her purse, clutching it tightly for any would-be robbers, and glanced in the mirror. She had to ensure all was on point. After all, she'd left these coworkers on the fly, knowing she would never return. Her world had turned upside down once she left impromptu for California and the world of hip-hop. Now she would face some of the same ones and felt like she had reversed her good fortune. Regardless, she had experienced magical moments that were life-changing. And if life had thrown her a curve ball from the stage lights to the tabletops, so be it. After being satisfied that her looks checked out, she closed the compact and placed it inside her handbag. She held her head high and turned the corner.

Upon arrival, she opened the glass door and was in shock.

"Surprise!!!" a group of workers screamed.

"Wow!" she said with bulging eyes like she had been jolted by a bolt of electricity.

"Welcome back!" Miss Cynt, Trista's favorite coworker a la mother, was the first to offer her a warm embrace and pecked her cheek. "We missed you."

"Missed you, too, Miss Cynt. Good to see ya." Trista beamed.

Others followed suit as they surrounded Trista and offered her warm hugs.

"How did you manage this?" Trista asked, looking around and noticing there were no customers present.

"Well, we talked to boss man and asked if we could open early for a private welcome-back greeting, so he agreed. It didn't affect the lunch rush."

"Yeah, I was wondering about that. I thought ten o'clock was kinda odd to start."

"Yep, we planned it that way."

Trista looked around and spotted a huge cake with icing that read: *Welcome home, Trista*. "It's too early for cake." She laughed.

"We don't plan to cut it until lunchtime and then it'll be back in the private area," Miss Cynt alerted.

"Oh, thanks, everyone. This is so sweet." Trista believed that the surprise was genuine and she was fortunate to have such kind coworkers. *If they only knew why I was truly back here*, she thought sadly to herself. After responding to a barrage of queries about life as a dancer to shopping in California to how many celebrities she'd encountered, Trista took a mental break and walked to the bar area. She was pleased to see Miss Cynt sitting there.

"Well, sweetie, you still lookin' good and I can see life treated you well out there in that movie land," Miss Cynt complimented.

"Thanks, mama. It was a good experience. Couldn'tve asked for more. Of course, it's great being with you again."

Miss Cynt leaned in and whispered, "Can't wait to hear about you and that cute little honey you had. I saw ya'll on TV, you know. Uh-huh, yes I did." She winked.

Trista's facial expression turned sour and Miss Cynt realized she'd hit a nerve.

"Oh, sorry..."

"No, that's okay. I'll explain once we have some private time, like the old days," Trista advised.

"That's fine, sweetie. No problem. Well, we'd better start getting ready for the lunch crew. Just thought it would be nice to surprise you. After all, we were thrown for a loop when Bill told us you were coming back. Never thought I'd see you again...'specially since you'd gone off to the bright lights."

"We'll talk...later."

"Gotcha, dear." She walked off and Trista followed, prepared to restart her life as a waitress.

Trista caught the subway back to Tai and Marco's house. Her walk from the station was reminiscent about the days when she'd shared the space with only her sister. Now she had to deal with Marco and felt tiptoeing around him was not her forte. She wished it were like old times. She'd barely had enough time to truly get to know Tai again after their lengthy time apart. Even though she had abandoned her for the music world, she now had the opportunity to reconnect with her once again. Tai was happy; she could see that Marco had given her a boost and held her on the highest pedestal. It was admirable, but she had envious thoughts. Why hadn't her own relationship lasted? Even though she was caught cheating, didn't Kwik have everlasting and unconditional love? After all, she'd considered herself his ride-or-die chick.

She opened the front door and entered. The house was eerily quiet and she had to get used to adjusting to their schedules. She'd done a longer shift today and had garnered a decent tip total. Some of her old lunch customers were shocked to see her back at Seacoast. After all, she'd told everyone of her good fortune landing a dancing gig with a star and promising never to return to her waitress job. So a few had given her double what they normally did and her wallet was looking good. She climbed the steps and headed to her room on the opposite end of the hall from Tai and Marco's bedroom.

The room was unchanged and left as she'd remembered it. She turned on the flat-screen TV and flipped channels until arriving at *Martin*. She slipped off her flats and climbed onto the chaise and reclined. Thoughts of Kwik entered her mind and she realized despite her fluffing off, she truly missed her baby. She wondered if he had already hooked up with one of those ratchet video vixens that always made seductive moves toward him and gave her the evil and jealous eye. Surely they had attempted to entice him if he were alone as they definitely did when she was present. *He'd better not be with any of those hoes*, she thought. *Hey, I screwed up, but someday, maybe he will forgive me.* She pulled out her phone to check email and see if he'd possibly sent her a message since she'd not received any texts from him. As she'd suspected, there weren't any—only junk mail. *Maybe Tai's right. I need to move on.*

Trista awoke from a nightmarish slumber where she fought off ugly-looking figures that were chasing her down a winding street in San Francisco, one of the many concert stops on Dre Dyson's tour. She checked out the digital clock: it was 1:17, much too early to consider a night's sleep. She walked over to the window and peeked through the blinds overlooking the street from the second floor. Visions of her and Kwik penetrated her mind and overtook her emotions violently. She reached for a tall yellow glass statue on the dresser and slammed it on the porcelain-tiled floor. It shattered in a zillion pieces. She angrily paced the floor in a rage, placing her hands over her ears as she walked back and forth. She removed her hands and made pounding motions against the air. Suddenly, she heard her cell phone vibrate, indicating a text. She walked over to the night table and picked it up. It was Tai. *Everything OK?*

"Yes, everything is just fine, dear sister," she said aloud sarcastically. "Everything is fucking fine." She smirked as she texted, *Yes, all OK.*

I heard a loud noise. Can you please cut down the TV? It woke me but not Marco. Thanks.

"Sure, I'll cut down the damn TV all right." *OK, no prob,* she texted. Trista sat on the bed and rubbed her temple. She looked on the floor and exhaled. *That was Tai's treasured little award. Well, it's history now.* She checked the bedroom closet to see if there was a broom, then realized she would need to retrieve the one from the kitchen. She opened the bedroom door and peeked down the hallway. All was quiet. She exited the room and tiptoed down the stairs, then returned with the broom and a trash bag. She softly swept up the pieces and placed them inside the bag, then stashed it inside the closet and closed the door. Hopefully, she thought, Tai would not notice the missing statue. She hadn't been back to D.C. long, but her nemesis had returned with a vengeance.

CHAPTER 18

TAI

Having spent the full day in the kitchen, Tai was winding down from preparing her four-course meal. The influences of her Southern grandma was mixed with her taste of the North. She was confident her in-laws would relish the appetizing spread she had created especially to impress. Marco tried to conceal that his mother had specific reservations about their marriage, but she was astute about reading people and seeing through Mrs. Moore was no different. She went along with the program, particularly since they were newlyweds and determined to make their union successful.

Marco was upstairs relaxing and reading *Men's Health* magazine while sitting in the oversized chair in their bedroom. Light jazz streamed to enhance his mood. He was nervous and attempted to distract his thoughts about his parents visiting. Mom was a straight-up woman who often didn't know how to smooth out the wrinkles when she spoke inappropriately, usually not recognizing she'd said wrong words. He dreaded that she would slip and create an ugly or uncomfortable scene this evening.

Tai headed up the stairs so she could stretch out for at least a half-hour. Then she'd change into a casual outfit. She felt it was no need to dress to impress; after all, she was focused on her kitchen skills. She entered the bedroom.

Marco looked up from his magazine. "Hi, babe. You're finally done? You've been in that kitchen all day. I know you've fixed a bangin' dinner. I appreciate it and my folks will, too." He motioned to the bed. "Why don't you cool out a minute?" He looked at his watch. "I'm sure you're worn out. I don't even want to ask what you cooked; I wanna be surprised. My parents couldn't go to any restaurant here and have a better meal."

"Thanks." She sighed, stretching across the comforter. "Don't let me fall asleep. I need to change."

"No problem."

Marco and Tai greeted his parents at the door with hugs and kisses on the cheek.

Mrs. Moore stepped farther in the foyer and glanced around the area to take in the stunning décor that Tai had in place. "Lovely, Tai," she noted, aware that Tai's house was furnished and set before Marco had moved in. "Just lovely."

"Thanks," Tai offered, pleased that she'd had compliments upon entering.

Marco led his parents into the living room while Tai headed to the kitchen. She had already set the table where a bottle of red wine and pitcher of ice water awaited them.

"Well, Marco, it's good to see you again," Mrs. Moore said. "You're not losing weight, are you?" she suggested, alluding that he'd missed meals and conjuring up negative thoughts.

He touched his stomach. "Are you kidding? You're getting ready to see that I've been eatin' well," he responded to her attempt at taking a verbal jab.

"Just checking," she harrumphed, realizing she had failed.

Mr. Moore rolled his eyes. He was a man of few words and loved to smoke cigars. He'd placed a Cohiba in the corner of his mouth, aware that he couldn't light up inside the house but gaining satisfaction from the taste.

"Dad, so how did the conference go today?" Marco asked.

"Fine, Marco, fine. I was a guest lecturer for one of the workshops on the effects of social media on today's college campus."

"Great." *Even though you barely know how to use your smartphone.*

"You have a nice home here," Mr. Moore stated, absorbing Tai's decorating skills.

"Yes, I guess we'll have a tour after dinner?" Mrs. Moore gave her son an inquisitive look, eyebrow highly arched.

"Of course, Mom. I wouldn't let you come all the way to D.C. and not see the place, especially since we hung out at the hotel during the wedding."

"Speaking of hotels, who selected—?"

"Tai did. It was a fantastic choice."

"Well, I didn't particularly like that housekeeping staff. They weren't efficient enough for me." Mrs. Moore insisted on being critical.

"What about the hotel itself? It's one of the top in the city," Marco stated, realizing his mom couldn't make a comeback.

"It was okay," she responded, resisting to agree that Tai had selected a five-star property. No matter how she tried, her son would not support her beliefs. Unconsciously, she was always one to critique, and if it had anything to do with her only son, it was worse.

"Mmm, something smells good," Mr. Moore attempted to distract from his wife's ways. He'd dealt with her for thirty-four years of marriage.

Tai walked out and announced they could go into the dining room.

The table was a colorful display of Caesar salad with homemade dressing, stuffed Cornish hens with rosemary, shrimp with garlic and lime, risotto rice, yellow squash, zucchini and carrot medley, garlic mashed potatoes, and homemade wheat rolls.

They sat around the table and Mr. Moore provided the grace. "This looks delicious."

"Thanks. I love to cook and thought I'd whip up a nice dinner for you. I didn't want you to have to go to a restaurant today. Please help yourself."

"That's exactly what I plan to do." Mr. Moore spoke up, not shy about filling his plate or stomach as he initiated serving and they passed around the dishes. "I'll also do the liberty and open the wine," he offered, while standing and uncorking the bottle, then walking around the table to fill the wineglasses.

"Thanks, Dad; I was going to do that."

"No problem. My pleasure." He sat down and started to eat.

"Hmm, very good." Mrs. Moore sampled the chicken.

"Thank you." Tai was pleased she showed pride in her cooking.

"Yes, definitely," Mr. Moore agreed.

"Thank you again," Tai said, tiring of all the thank-yous. *You don't know how long I toiled in the kitchen today.*

"So, Marco told me your sister was back in town. I thought she was long gone. She was so excited at the wedding, talking about her lifestyle in Hollywood and her new man and all that good stuff." Mrs. Moore offered a phony smile. "Do you mind me asking what happened?" she asked nosily.

"Mom—"

"That's okay. Trista decided that wasn't the right place for her after all," Tai interjected, covering up the truth. Mrs. Moore seemed to always have her nostrils in someone's business. "Plus, you know our story of being separated for so long; she wanted to continue the bond we'd started once we reconnected. So, of course, I had no problem with her joining us."

"How long does she plan to stay here? Surely not long," Mrs. Moore surmised sarcastically.

Tai was beginning to get more irritated and sighed under her breath. "As long as it takes for her to get on her feet. I'm sure you would do the same if you were in the same situation. Be supportive of family."

"Well, my siblings always held their own, never needed my help. They're all college-educated and have lived a prosperous life. We have our parents to thank for that, for pushing us to be high achievers," she bragged. "Oh, I heard she's back working at that restaurant already. She didn't want to venture out a little, say, go beyond her capabilities?" she added.

Tai was tired of the insults and refused to respond. *If this bitch, excuse me, Lord, for calling my mother-in-law out of her name, doesn't tie her tongue, I'll be smashing her face with these mashed potatoes. She'd better come correct with the next thing she says out of her ugly mouth. Don't talk about my family.* She was glad that Trista was at work and didn't have to witness the foul comments. She'd created a picture-perfect relationship in Trista's eyes of her relationship with her in-laws. But her mother-in-law was a piece of work.

Marco gave his mom the disproving eye but ensured he didn't respond. The last thing he wanted was to create a scene. He witnessed that a speechless Tai was pissed. Mom always seemed to have a way of ruining anything that was positive. He looked at his dad who also was disturbed by his wife's behavior. He cleared his throat. "So what's on your agenda the rest of your visit?" he asked his parents, awkwardly making small talk.

"Well, we had thought about asking you the same thing. Ken and I talked and we wondered if you had any special plans for us. During the wedding, we didn't get a chance to do any tourist stuff since the whole weekend was centered around it. I thought we would've had some free time, but the schedule was full," Mrs. Moore said disgustingly.

"Mom, you remember I suggested you and Dad stay a couple of extra days on the back end so we could sightsee, but you said you were in a hurry to go back home."

"Did I, really?" She faked remembering her statement.

"Yes, you did. Perhaps you can visit again and this time, I'll plan something."

"Oh, you don't have to, Marco," Mrs. Moore responded. *Plus, I'd prefer to be with you alone and not have your old wifey tagging along. If we return, she surely will be some dead weight.*

"Okay, whatever works, Mom." Marco realized that difficulty and challenge followed his mother wherever she went.

"Maybe next time, we'll hear some pitter-patter in the house," she said, alluding to a toddler. While she didn't condone Marco's marriage to an older spouse, she coveted a grandchild. She would never fully accept Tai as a daughter-in-law simply because of her age, but if Tai were to bring a baby into the world, it would change her attitude.

Tai ignored her comments. Marco did likewise as he'd already argued with his mom prior to her visit. He was aware that she was faking and that she truly didn't want Tai to bear his child; she preferred someone younger, not his wife. But she desperately desired a grandchild, so perhaps if they did become parents, it would improve her actions toward Tai.

After they'd feasted on her daylong prepared meal, Tai stood and removed the plates. Marco joined her and they entered the kitchen to stack the dishes on the counter.

"Babe, I'm sorry about Mom and her little comments."

"You mean *big* comments. She really goes at it, doesn't she? I guess she's definitely not trying to win me over. Nor does she care about anyone's feelings but her own," Tai said of his mother's insensitivity.

"Mom really doesn't know what to say and when she does talk, it's always some kind of innuendo or action that turns people off. I apologize for her ways and sorry you have to be subjected to this."

"Sweetie, you don't have to apologize for how she acts. You can't pick your mother. I'm sure you've already told her to chill out, but she's the type that insists on not holding back. I get the feeling she doesn't care for me."

"No, no. She does like you, Tai. She does this with everyone," he lied. "She doesn't single anyone out. To be honest, I think Mom wants me to herself. I'm her only son, but this mother-son thing is over-the-top with her. She's never let go; she doesn't even see me as thirty-three," he tried to explain.

"Well, let's get back in there before she starts criticizing me again, saying I was rude and left them hanging or something." Tai figured she would simply have to deal with her mother-in-law for now. Their relationship was still fresh and newlywed status, but at some point, she would decide to put her in check.

She picked up the orange bundt cake with cream cheese icing and Marco grabbed the dessert plates. They returned to the dining room and set the cakes and plates on the table.

"Wow, that looks fantastic. You are quite a chef and now I see also quite a baker." Mr. Moore smiled, anxious to taste the cake that looked like it was prepared for a photo in a cooking magazine.

"Thank you. I told my friends that the kitchen is my next best friend to them," Tai said, attempting to be pleasant.

"Speaking of friends, you referring to the two bridesmaids?" Mrs. Moore asked, recalling Candace and Nevada. "Are either of them married?"

Tai presumed she'd heard some talk about both of them being single. "No, they're not, but they sure have good men in their corners." She was proud and held back no punches in defending her friends' marital status. "In fact, they have better relationships than a lot of married folks I know," she added, mentally stabbing and turning an imaginary knife in the conversation. She sliced the cake and set the dessert plates in front of her guests. "Hope you enjoy the cake." She smiled, satisfied that she'd finally rebounded.

Marco lay on his back in his king-sized bed and stared at the ceiling. "Tai, I'm sorry again for my mom and her behavior."

Lying by his side, she turned toward him. "Sweetie, you don't have to keep apologizing. It's not your fault."

"True, but I don't want it to ruin our relationship. Understand?"

"Don't worry; it won't. If anything, it could bring us closer." *I think I put her in check tonight.*

Marco reflected on his mother's iron-fisted control she attempted to use in the past. She'd always doted on her only son and never had accepted any of his previous relationships. Tai appeared to be no different, much to his dismay. He'd figured she would at least adjust her ways toward anyone he married.

"I'm glad you can deal with it. A lot of women would give me the blues, I'm sure." He reached over and caressed her cheek. "That's why I love you. You are the best." He kissed her lips.

CHAPTER 19

THE LADIES

"Well, Felicia and I were at the office the other day and I was trying to come up with a party idea. I'm always gung-ho to reach out to the community and to promote Next Phase of Life within the business arena. So I decided to host a masquerade event," Tai shared with her friends.

"You waiting till October?" Candace inquired.

"Oh, no, honey, I'm having a summer party. I thought that would be different, plus, I think people love to party in the summertime. We be lovin' cookouts, barbecues, outdoor concerts. You name it." Her eyes strayed to watch the customers who also were dining al fresco at the restaurant, enjoying the evening breeze. "Look at all the people here hanging out tonight. I love the winter holiday parties, too, but I feel like I'd be in competition. The government takes summer hiatus and schools are out, so sometimes folks are looking for something special."

"Sounds like a plan." Nevada sipped on a cocktail and dipped her shrimp in garlic sauce. "Need any help?"

"Thanks for the offer. Felicia's heading up the event and has recruited Noni and some other staff."

"Oooo, I love parties so I'm definitely down. Well, let us know how we can help." Candace leaned in. "So, I'm dying to hear how things are working out with Trista. How's it going with little sis?"

"It's going okay. It's kinda awkward sometimes, but I'm always the optimistic type."

"She's not traipsing around in her lingerie or throwing any passes at Marco, is she?" Candace inquired boldly, now that she'd downed some alcohol.

"Girl, you've got a one-track mind. You've been watching too much Lifetime, Oxygen or something," Nevada offered, being cynical.

"All of the above," Candace teased.

"No, you sound like Felicia. She wondered the same thing. Trista's cool and she's focused on her job and hoping to find another Mr. Right somewhere around here," Tai explained.

"Good luck," Nevada stated, eyeing the crowd that appeared to be mostly couples. "Only kidding. We all found love here so it's highly possible."

"True, this was the place." Candace looked at Tai. "I can never thank you enough for hooking me up with Don. If you'd never had that party, I never would've met him. It was fate."

"It was meant to be. You and Don. I only provided the space; it was the two of you who were drawn to each other."

"Yep, he asked me if I wanted a drink. The rest was magic."

"And a year later—" Tai interjected.

"I'm still trying to get him to pop that question," Candace stated.

"Not again," Nevada said.

"I can't help it. I don't mean to bring this up every single time we're together, but it's taken over my life."

"Why don't you focus on your career?" Nevada inquired about Candace's world as a fashion buyer. "You are crazy about clothes, shoes, purses, and on and on."

"And that's what I concentrate on during the day for the job. But hey, at night, it's about me," she held up her ringless finger, "and this here. I'm so ready for the diamonds, honey."

"And we know this," Nevada responded.

"I can't get it out of my mind, Nevada. I'm about to give up."

"No, I told you don't. It's gonna come…with time," Nevada advised. "You need to have patience."

"What if it doesn't happen?"

"Then it wasn't supposed to be. You've done all you can; now you need to sit back and see what's in store for the future," Tai advised.

"I'm trying. But guess what? I've got some news to share. After that picnic thingy failed, I tried another come-up." Candace smiled.

"What was your plan B?" Nevada inquired.

"Yes, give it up. What'd you stir up in your little pot this time?" Tai asked.

"Little pot, that's cute. Well, ladies—"

"You let your imagination run rampant, I'm sure," Nevada interjected and sipped on her cocktail.

Candace giggled. "You know me, Nevada." She breathed heavily eager to share what had transpired. "I've told you about Shakira, my sistergirl who I work with. She has this rich boyfriend with a yacht. She convinced him to invite us for a midnight cruise on the Bay and let's say, we did our thing right there on the deck-aroo."

"Don't tell me they joined in. That was freaky all right." Nevada was anxious to hear details.

"No, no. They stayed underneath and let us have our little privacy outside, under the moon, under the stars." She smiled. "Okay, I'll be honest. Turns out the guy's voyeuristic, so I had to agree to let him watch us."

"And Don was down with that?" Nevada asked surprisingly.

"Yep, I told you he likes it freaky. Why would he be with *moi?*" she teased.

"Girl, ya'll too much," Nevada advised. "Ain't no way no other man's gonna stand by and watch Ryan and me get busy." She smiled. "He'd have to join in," she added, bluffing. "Not." Nevada liked her privacy and one-on-one, although she'd fantasized about a threesome with another man. However, she was too much into the detective game to allow her business—or her body—to be exposed. She preferred life undercover.

"Don't put 'ya'll' into it. I never said I wanted a third wheel along with Marco and me. Hell to the no." Tai treasured her personal side and had been tempted not to share her affair with Hasan at the gym. Originally, her BFFs had thought she was simply working out overtime. Little did they know her trainer was a handsome hunk.

"Yeah, I keep trying to show him all sides of me. I'm a fun type of gal, full of adventure and game for just about anything," Candace shared.

Nevada looked at her seriously as if she'd suddenly had an epiphany. "Candace, I hope you don't take this the wrong way 'cause I know you're sensitive, but have you ever stopped to think that maybe that's the deal? You're all about excitement and fun, but maybe when Don decides to settle down, he wants to with someone who's serious. He may not see you as the wifey type, homemaker, sports mom who takes the kids to practice and helps them with homework, all that jazz."

Candace slowed her roll and her face turned sour. "Nope. I'm not offended by what you said. You always got my back so I know you're sincere. But yes, I never thought about it that way."

"That's possible, Nevada, now that you say that," Tai agreed. "Look, Candace, we're not trying to judge you, and Lord, we've always lived with fun times. You'd never given the impression you liked to settle down until you hooked up with Don."

"Honey, ain't that the truth. And believe me, I never did...until now."

Nevada chuckled. "Yeah, you little hot mamacita." She attempted to lighten the mood that she'd suddenly turned to contemplative.

Tai picked up on the vibe and suddenly brainstormed. "Well, I do think it's time for another one of our ladies nights." She looked at Nevada. "What about it?"

"I'm game." Nevada turned to Candace.

"You don't have to even ask. It's been awhile."

"Not a true one anyway. Not since my bachelorette party in the Bahamas," Tai recalled.

"Okay, you always come up with the best ideas," Candace offered.

"I'll think of something cool. We deserve to de-stress." Tai was determined not to let Trista get the best of her. She'd been acting a little strange lately and she'd found it hard to dig deeper. She figured it was partially due to her adjusting to life back on the East Coast, trying to get over Kwik, and sharing her home with Marco. She'd learned not to pursue the truth as Trista eventually might open up to her. The last thing she wanted to accomplish was to badger her sister and make her feel uneasy.

The waitress returned with the tab and Tai picked it up. "My treat."

"No you don't," Nevada stated. "It's my turn."

"I suggested we meet up so I'm going to take care of it."

"Thanks," Nevada and Candace said in unison.

"Welcome."

CHAPTER 20

TRISTA

"Okay, Trista, finally some down time." Miss Cynt motioned for Trista to take a seat across from her at the booth. "This was a helluva day, wasn't it?"

"Yes, Fridays are always busy. I should've worn skates."

"Not this granny." She laughed. "So, you've been eager to tell me what brought you back. I'm sure you love this good ol' cookin' and you missed eatin' here."

"Of course, Miss Cynt."

"Well, I'm waitin'." She looked at the clock. "In another hour, we'll be getting the happy hour crowd. So, young lady, what you got for me?"

Trista hesitated, but Miss Cynt was like a mother to her and she felt she was trustworthy. "I got kicked out. Kaboom. Kwik didn't trust me anymore… I had an affair, nope, I shouldn't call it that. It was a one-night stand."

She winked. "Honey chile, we've all had our share of those."

"True, but Miss Cynt, I did a dumb thing. I got caught. He saw me."

Her eyes bulged. "Oh, sweetie pie, that's no good. How the hell did that happen?"

"I was in the studio office and this guy came on to me and that was that. Kwik had left and I didn't realize he'd circled back around and then walked in on us. So he never forgave me and then didn't want to have anything to do with me—ever again."

"Oh, I see, well, maybe it wasn't meant to be. So stop looking all sad-faced around here. You got your whole life to live, dear. Don't let one monkey stop the show. Plenty of fishies in that big ol' sea, too. What, you got on some blinders or somethin' when you workin'? I see those young boys eyein' you."

"Yes, I play it off. I ain't interested in none of 'em."

"Well, honey, at least I know the deal now. I figured it was somethin' unusual since you had that fantasy life that so many young ladies would love. Plus, you much older than many of 'em, but you still could hang with the best of 'em."

"Yeah, that's another thing. I'm getting too old to be onstage. Probably break something one of these days if I keep it up. Shoot, I needed to find another career anyway, but I hoped to be with Kwik forever. We were good for each other. He would've helped me find something else in the industry, I'm sure."

The door opened and two handsome forty-something men dressed in business suits entered. Miss Cynt looked over at her. "See what I mean? Lots of fishies and some killer whales too." She smiled and touched Trista's hand. "Don't worry. The Lord will see you through. Think positive and focus on *you* and not who's laying in your bed."

She offered a slight smile. "Thanks, Miss Cynt, you always got my back and give me good advice. I appreciate it."

CHAPTER 21

TAI

After throwing a ladies night with a '70s theme and transforming her home into a haven of black-light posters, Afro wigs, and old school and funk music, Tai decided to move on to the next decade.

She was a Prince fanatic and she was honoring the legend on the special occasion of the thirtieth anniversary of *Purple Rain*. Dressed in a purple maxi dress and dangling purple earrings, she moved about setting up a display of '80s-themed memorabilia she'd dug from her closet. The first floor of her home was peppered with purple balloons and purple and lilac flowers.

Nevada was first to arrive and dressed in a purple, silk, short-sleeved blouse with shoulder pads atop a white tee and acid-washed jeans. "Hey, hey. Party time!" she announced as she entered. "Girl, you did your thing again. I swear you need to do this on the side." She circled the den with her eyes scoping out the scenery. "You need any help? I realize I'm a little early."

"No, thanks. I'm good. Help yourself to a drink," she said, nodding toward the bar. "I'm fixing a special one once everyone gets here."

Nevada walked to the bar. "Cool." She proceeded to mix her a Black Russian. "Who else did you invite? The usual crew?"

"Yep, Sierra, Cori and Felicia are supposed to stop by."

"Fantastic. Those are my girls and I haven't seen them since the seventies night."

Sierra, Cori and Felicia soon arrived with all three dolled up in flashy purple attire. The five of them were sharing tales of the old days and throwing back shots including grape Jell-O cups.

Tai checked the clock on the wall. "That Candace is never ever on time."

"And we know this." Nevada laughed. "My girl's gonna be late for everything but her wedding."

"She's getting married? My sister ain't tell me nothin' about it," Cori said of her younger sister, Candace.

"Oops, I was playing, nothing serious. I hadn't heard either." Nevada quickly cleaned up her statement, not wanting to spread rumors.

"Okay, I'm just saying; she'd better have me as her maid-of-honor," Cori stated matter-of-factly. "I don't know about Don, though. He seems like he's stringing her along. Damn, how long does it take for him to get on his bended knee?" she added, the effects of the shots influencing her mind. "Or do men still do that stuff?"

Tai and Nevada looked at each other in silence. They'd heard constantly about Candace waiting for a ring.

"Look, she's not here to defend herself, Cori, so let's not go there," Tai stated.

The doorbell rang and Tai headed to open the door. "Wow, look at you!" Tai exclaimed.

Candace promenaded inside and waltzed to the den area. "Hello, ladies."

"Hi!" they said in unison seated around the room.

Candace had decided to take the formal route with her '80s fashion. She wore a low-cut, tea-length, lace dress with her boobs protruding, silver bangles from her wrist to elbow and a silver tiara. Her fingers held silver rings on each except the pinkie and thumb and showed off her freshly polished purple nails. Her purple strappy sandals featured rhinestones on the thong.

"Girl, you went all out!" Tai exclaimed. "Well, we've already started so you have to catch up with us. We've been doing Jell-O shots so help yourself." She motioned toward the bar.

"You don't have to tell me twice." Candace headed to the bar and proceeded to sip from a tiny cup. "Mmmm, I'm lovin' this."

"Sis, we were just talking 'bout you," Cori alerted, giggling.

"Me, I'm sure it was good." She laughed.

"Well, I shouldn't say 'we,' as it was me. Nevada said you'd be late for your own wedding, but I went on to say I wondered when you'd be getting that ring," Cori stated curiously.

"Good question, sis."

"Hey, let's get off that subject," Tai interjected.

"Thanks. I'm here to have fun, not talk about man troubles." Candace smirked. "But leave it to big sis."

"I'm sure she's concerned and that's all," Tai advised. "In fact, speaking of sisters, I didn't even invite Trista."

"Why not?" Candace asked. "She's never going to know the true you if you keep leaving her out, right?"

"She has enough knowledge about me and now livin' here with Marco and me, I'm keeping it to a minimum. Plus, she's been acting strange and keeping her distance. She's hard to read sometimes. And she had to work tonight. She said she was going to hang out with coworkers after they got off, so that was fine by me."

"On to the fun stuff." Nevada presumed the need to turn the conversation around. She didn't like where it was headed.

"Okayyyy." Tai stood and walked to the iPod. "We're going to take turns, now that our heads are tight, and dance to these hits. We'll go around the room starting with Nevada."

"No fair. I don't wanna be first."

"Sorrryyy," Tai said, starting up the cue while Nevada stood and moved slowly to the center of the room. Tai turned on Digital Underground's "The Humpty Dance." Nevada danced doing the Humpty as best she could remember as the group cheered her on.

Next was Sierra who was delighted she'd gotten Public Enemy's "Fight the Power." She circled the room throwing imaginary punches in her off-the-shoulder top. Cori followed with House of Pain's "Jump Around." She showed off her agility from decades of gym workouts and dancing along with Candace in their parnts' basement. After the song ended, she flopped back on her chair after her vigorous performance. Although Felicia was Tai's right-hand woman at the office, she still never felt comfortable or care-free in casual, informal settings. She was pleased that her song was more subdued and bounced to De La Soul's "Me, Myself and I." Candace kicked off her heels and rocked to Tom Browne's "Funkin' for Jamaica." It was ideal for taking her mind back to the islands she adored. Tai ended the session with Wrecks'n-Effects' "New Jack Swing." Everyone joined in to sing the popular party ballad as they held up their glasses and whined the lyrics.

"So what do you think is one of the hottest songs from the eighties?" Tai asked. "I'll give you a clue. It's home-grown as in D.C."

"Must be go-go!" Candace exclaimed.

"Yeap, that's our local sound."

"What about 'Go-Go Swing.' Chuck Brown, the godfather," Nevada guessed.

"That was one of them. But here you go." Tai walked to the iPod.

"Oh, yeah, 'Da Butt.' Why didn't I think of that?" Nevada asked.

Doin' the butt, sexy, sexy. "And guess what?" Candace jumped up and started gyrating and pushing her butt in the air. "All this talk about twerkin'...hell, we were doing these kind of moves back in the day."

"I know that's right." Nevada joined in proudly with her own moves. "Ryan loves to see this booty bounce." She laughed.

Tai and the others couldn't resist dancing to E.U.'s hit. The song ended and Tai prepped her guests. "Okay, now, everyone get up! This is our anthem." Tai played Chaka Khan's "I'm Every Woman" while each danced in a *Soul Train* line.

"Well, ladies, you should know I love surprises. So please be seated." They all found a chair or spot on the sofa. She went to the CD player and put on "Purple Rain." "Drumroll..." She turned toward her staircase and an Adonis-like man strolled into the den wearing a purple mask, purple cape and black knee-high boots with a short heel.

Everyone "oohed" and "aahed." The surprise guest started working out and made his rounds, teasingly standing before each of them. The song changed to "When Doves Cry" and the Prince performer snatched off his cape to reveal a chiseled, oily chest and a to-die-for body dressed in only a purple thong.

"Hmmm-mmmm. What do we have here?" Candace licked her lips and shook her head. "I'm having flashes. Give me strength before I pass out up in here." She laughed.

"You ain't never lied," Nevada added.

Tai smiled with satisfaction. "I knew you ladies would love some eye candy." She recalled one of her past ladies nights with the group when she had three strippers, Rope, Rod, and Reel.

The "Prince" entertained them through a medley of Prince hits as they were mesmerized by his skills.

"That was some dancer," Candace stated after the stunning performance. "Where did you find him?"

Tai winked. "I'll never tell."

"You ain't right. Not wanting to share your info. But it's all good. I'm all hot and bothered now and ready to jump on Mr. Don's bones tonight." Candace was aware that Don was on a chartered trip and wouldn't be back for a few days. She was tired of her sister Cori inquiring about him and his whereabouts. Hell, he was a pilot, so it should have been obvious that he could frequently be out of town. She wanted to pretend that he would be at his place waiting for her to return from the party.

"Well, I'm glad you ladies enjoyed it." Tai loved to plan ladies nights.

"Definitely," "we loved the show" and "Hell, yes" all were comments at the same time.

Tai attempted to walk steady to the kitchen and Nevada followed to assist her to bring out trays of appetizers and plates. The treats consisted of wingettes, shrimp wraps, spinach and cheese pastries, mozzarella sticks and brownies. "We all worked up an appetite," she said, setting down the trays.

After they'd devoured the works, Tai walked over to the DVD player and popped in *Purple Rain*. "Here's one of my favorites. I loveee this movie. And if you can hang, I'll play *Krush Groove*."

She gazed at her guests and figured they'd likely not make it through the first film. Their eyelids were heavy and their energy was slowly dissipating. She walked back to her chair and sat. Maybe she'd end up having her own personal filmathon. *It's all good: me, myself and I.* They were welcome to stay as she preferred guests not to head home after a night of heavy drinking.

CHAPTER 22

TRISTA

Stretched across her bed, Trista turned the TV on low. She'd crept inside and up the stairs after observing Tai and crew lying throughout the first floor with the screensaver on the TV. She figured it must've been some party for all of them to be knocked out in such fashion. Tai already had told her they possibly could be staying overnight and that Marco had vacated to hang out with friends. He'd likely be arriving during the wee hours.

She picked up her cell to check her email. Still no word from Kwik. She truly needed to start dating to help steer her thoughts away from the failed relationship. Maybe she would accept one of the many offers from customers. So far, she wasn't feeling any of them, but it wouldn't hurt to go on a date. It had been awhile since she'd checked Facebook. In fact, she'd taken down her page after she met Kwik. She figured it was the best move for her to avoid drama from her hometown. Most of her friends were acquaintances that she personally knew. When she'd found Tai on Facebook, that had sufficed; she'd reunited with her long-lost sister and only surviving family member that she was familiar with.

She logged on and went to the group account of which she was a member. Her mouth dropped as she did a double-take. She reread and reread the top post and eyed the photo. It was Venus, her best friend from high school—and she had passed away. *Wow, what happened?* Tears started streaming from her exhausted eyes. *What the hell? Noooooooo,* she screamed inside her head. She immediately started feeling a guilt trip. She'd been out of contact since she'd first arrived in D.C. Venus may have heard through word of mouth that she was on the West Coast and performing with Dre Dyson, but she'd never told her. No one would've believed she was dancing at her age, but again, she once had worked as a stripper and had gained the reputation as one of the hottest acts in the Carolinas. Maybe they wouldn't be surprised after all. But she'd left her N.C. days behind and had moved on. She reminisced about the good times she'd shared with Venus—all the laughs, class clown antics, first boyfriends and cheerleading competitions. Tomorrow, she'd have to reach out to a mutual friend, Syndie, and find out the arrangements. She definitely felt compelled to attend any services in honor of her beloved friend.

"Hey, stranger, where you been hidin'?" Syndie was surprised to see Trista's name on her caller ID.

"Hey, Syndie, I'm in D.C. I was away for a while, but now I'm back here with my sis."

"Girl, you ain't right. You were supposed to call me and I thought you'd changed your cell number."

"Well, it was off for a while. I apologize, but after I left there, I left the life behind. So many bad memories. Of course, I'm not talking about you."

"I know, I know. It was tough on ya," Syndie recollected about Trista's foster care challenges and troubled background with her exes. "I guess you must've heard about Venus."

"Yes, I'm still in shock. I happened to go on Facebook last night. You remember I took down my page, so I went on the group page and saw the news. Not Venus! She was our girl. I can't believe it, Syndie. What's the word?"

"I heard she was found dead in her sleep one morning. She was still living in the same apartment that she was in when you moved. Her next-door neighbor got suspicious and had police go in and they discovered her."

"Wasn't foul play, was it? I hope not."

"Naw, they say she passed peacefully."

"Well, that's good. I'd hate to hear anything bad happened to her. Her parents and family must be devastated."

"Oh, definitely. I spoke to her moms and expressed my sympathy."

"Yeah, I guess I should call, but better yet, I'm planning to come down. Do you know the details?"

"I heard it was next week, Tuesday morning."

"Oh, cool, I'm off on Tuesdays and Wednesdays. I'll ask my boss to take off and maybe some extra days."

"Where you workin', girl?"

"I'm a waitress at a seafood restaurant."

"That's cool. You were a damn good one at the diner here."

"Thanks. Guess you could say I ain't doin' too bad here either." She paused. "You think I could stay with you? I promise I won't get in your way and mind my business."

Syndie found the comment strange. "Why would you say that? You're always welcome here. Plus, it'll be like old times. We can catch up. I tried to call, but must've been when your cell was off."

"Yeah, sorry about that. It's no excuse. I knew where to find you. I've been all over the place." She shared about her life as a backup dancer in L.A. "I'll explain more when I see ya."

"Okay, keep me posted on your plans. You driving, taking the train, bus or what?"

"Hmmm, I'm not sure yet, but I'll call you this weekend."

"Fine. Take care, Trista."

"You too, Syndie." They hung up.

The following week, Tai drove Trista to Union Station to take Amtrak down South. Trista had packed the same suitcase she'd brought from L.A.

Tai pulled up front and put the car in park. She popped the trunk and reached over to hug Trista. "Take care and be safe. Any idea when you plan to return?"

"No, but I'll be in touch. Keep you posted. I told boss man at work that I may need some extra time—even to mourn. I still can't believe she's gone. She was like my blood."

"I understand. Well, do what's best for you. Be safe."

"That's a bet. See ya and thanks." Trista opened the door and went to the rear to grab her suitcase and closed the trunk.

The train ride reminded her of her trip to D.C. A sea of memories floated in her mind as she passed through the backwoods. Her iPod kept her company and the girl across the aisle from her. The busybody had kept her mom occupied for hours while she fidgeted with a tablet while her mom attempted to read a novel.

Trista texted Syndie that she would arrive soon. She couldn't wait until she saw one of her besties again. She, Syndie and Venus had been an unbreakable trio—since childhood. Now a part of the link was missing with Venus' death. Even though Trista had kept her distance since leaving N.C., she had never removed them from her heart. Unfortunately, she wouldn't see Venus alive again.

"Heyyyy, Trista. Girl, you lookin' good!" a bubbly Syndie greeted her close friend in the Salisbury station. She hugged her, then pushed back while looking her up and down. "You been workin' out."

"Yeah, all that dancin' kept me goin', so I had to stay in shape to hang with the young girls. Some of 'em didn't even realize my age. They put me at ten years younger." She giggled.

"I can believe it."

"But I tell you what, I had to soak these ole bones some days."

"I heard that. You told me on the phone all about your Cali adventures. Had no idea you were on the other coast since you went ghost on us."

Trista looked down, feeling slightly guilty for being out of touch. "Yeah, I was still trying to get myself together."

"Venus and I thought you were still in D.C." Her facial expression turned sad. "I can't believe she's gon'."

"Me either."

Trista walked with Syndie through the city's train depot heading to the parking lot. Trista eyed the vending machines; her hunger pangs were working overtime. Syndie was an excellent cook and Trista had hoped she'd prepared one of her mouthwatering down-home meals. She hadn't tasted her cooking since they'd worked at the diner together.

"Well, here's Miss Ella," Syndie noted as she approached her car and then inserted the key in the lock. "It's a hoopty, but it works. Plus, it's a hand-me-down from Gram."

"No problem." Trista placed her suitcase in the backseat, then opened the passenger door and hopped in.

Syndie started the car, which made a rattling noise. "Don't worry. It's got its own soundtrack." She laughed. "But it'll get us where we gotta go." She looked at Trista. "Guess you're used to Benzes, Beemers and limos about now. All Miss Hollywood, huh?"

"Oh, no, way. I definitely wasn't pushing any of that. Sometimes we had limo rides for the concerts, yeah, but it wasn't every day." Suddenly her thoughts drifted to Kwik. She wondered how his life was going without her.

"So, I've only been in a limo once—prom night. That was sooo much fun, remember?" Syndie said, breaking Trista's trance and bringing her back to reality. "All of us piled in that baby."

"Of course, I remember. Never forget the good times." She looked out the window at the city, which, in certain parts reminded her of 1960s Mayberry, a fictional N.C. town popularized on the *The Andy Griffith Show.* Syndie continued to drive, exiting the downtown area and heading to winding country roads.

"You'll get to see everyone at the funeral. I'm sure they'll be paying their respects. Venus was so loved."

"Oh, most definitely." She paused. "It's so strange—her being found dead like that. Had she even been sick or anything?"

"Not that I know of. I'd just seen her the week before and she was fine. I ran into her at the Cookout."

"Don't mention that place. They have the best milkshakes around. I must get me one before I leave." She rubbed her stomach. "Although I don't need it."

"Speaking of food, I started dinner for us."

Oh, thank ya, Lawd. "Mmm, can't wait. I was craving your food on the train."

"Well, I don't cook as much these days. The girls are both in college now."

"Oh, cool. I was going to ask you about 'em. Where are they?"

"Tasha's at Central in Durham and Zara's started her first year at Winston-Salem State."

"That's great, Syndie. You've always been a good mom and were proud of those girls—young ladies. I'm proud of them, too."

"Thanks. They told me to tell you hello and give you a shout-out. They still call you A'nt Tris."

She smiled. "Will they be here for the funeral?"

"No, I don't think they'll make it. They both took it hard and I told them they didn't have to come. They loved her and called her auntie, too, but it's so traumatic."

"Yes, it is." Trista changed the subject so not to dwell on the loss. "Looks like nothing's changed."

"It's about the same old, same old, although we do have some new stores. It's up and coming like Charlotte, but a lot of folks like the laid-back life here."

"After living in D.C. and L.A., I can see why. It's more simple. You can find peace of mind."

Syndie pulled up to a gravel and dirt driveway and parked in front of a modest, white wooden house. She had inherited the home place from her grandmother. Trista recalled the many weekends there where she'd spent playing cards and watching movies on videotape. Syndie's spot also had been ideal for evenings after high school where she, Syndie and Venus did their homework together. Trista got out and pulled out her suitcase. After entering, she took her luggage to the guest bedroom, the daughters' former hangout. She returned to the kitchen where Syndie was washing her hands to start preparing one of Trista's favorites: potato salad.

"Something smells good." Trista inhaled the tantalizing aroma as she took a seat at the kitchen table.

"Well, I couldn't have you here without frying chicken and making greens."

"Thanks. Like old times."

"So, you haven't said much about Tai. How's she doing, the married *old* lady?" she teased about her friend's older sister. Tai used to tease her as a child before she moved to D.C. with their grandmother.

"Well, like you said, she's married now. Seems to be working out okay and happy—not sure she's feeling me being back living with her after I'd left, which we thought was for good."

"Life happens. So on to the next phase."

"That's the name of her business, Next Phase of Life, and it's going well, too."

"She's doin' good all around, huh? She always was aggressive back in the day."

"Still is. The only thing it looks like she's missing is being a mom."

"You think she still wants babies? She's forty-two, right?"

"Yeap, she doesn't talk about it much, but it's on her mind. One of the times we had some one-on-one time, chilling and having drinks, she hinted that she was hoping to start a family." She looked out the window.

"So what are they waiting on?"

"Dunno. I only know that *I* don't want any chaps, as your gram always called us." Trista laughed.

"Yeah, you chaps get on in here and wash your hands for supper," Syndie mocked her grandmother. "Ya'll chaps better be back home 'fore dark. Bless her soul. I can truly say she was my heart," she added about the woman who had raised her. She caught herself from continuing to sing praises about her family. She never wanted to rub Trista the wrong way since she'd grown up similar to Trista, without parents, but yet it seemed like worlds apart. Her parents were both in the military and decided not to uproot her and her two brothers after relocating to N.C. They'd had Syndie's maternal grandmother care for them starting in high school. Trista was opposite being raised by foster families since age twelve.

After peeling the potatoes and putting them in water to boil, along with eggs in another pot, Syndie sat across from Trista at the table. "I always thought you'd be a good mother. You've experienced so much that you'd know exactly what a child would and wouldn't like. Plus, you survived some hard times. You'd have a lot to offer."

"Girl, I'm not even settled by *myself*, so I definitely can't imagine a family."

Syndie gave her a side-eye. "But I bet if the *right* Mr. Right came along, you'd change your mind."

Trista thought about Kwik. "Well, I thought my Cali man was the one, but life dealt me a bad hand."

"You need to meet you one of these Cackalacky men."

She smiled. "Maybe I will."

"Darryl and I were doing fine, but he got that good job in New York, and he was gone. But he's a good dad and takes care of the girls. Paying their tuition and all that. I can't complain. Wished we'd eventually gotten married, though," she said of her high school sweetheart. "I didn't really want to relocate, so here I am."

"What's that saying? If it ain't broke, don't fix it? Looks like you're doing fine right where you are. Plus, you've had your hospital job for so long. You always were the stable one."

"Sometimes I wish I could've been more carefree back in my twenties. I've always admired your free spirit."

CHAPTER 23

TAI

Tai looked out proudly over a sea of costumed revelers lined up for the catered buffet in the Spy Museum. It was Nevada's suggestion to plan her fund-raiser at the D.C. venue. The event was to benefit Precious Inc., her nonprofit, which assisted needy children in the area. Beyond the city's burgeoning reputation as expensive and populated with high-income residents, there was still an excessive number living below the poverty level.

From the swashbuckling pirate dressed in all black to a woman in a slinky Cheshire cat suit to the superhero couple, her guests appeared to be entertained by the live band. Maskless and wearing a slinky, aqua mermaid dress, she sauntered across the room mingling with cheerful partygoers as she tried to guess their identities behind their masks. Pleased with the turnout, she was elated it had been a success. She maneuvered through the crowd, careful not to spill her Bikini Martini, the night's specialty drink, until she reached a corner. She stood alone to capture a bird's-eye view of the scene. A man dressed as the Hulk approached and stopped beside her, startling her when she heard his voice.

"You looking good in that outfit. I see you're still keeping in shape—like I taught you."

Tai almost choked while sipping from her glass. She froze and a chill crept up her arms. *I don't believe it.* Carefully, she turned her head to face the man behind the mask. "What are you…doing here?" she asked slowly.

"Hey, I had to come and support your efforts," he explained.

"I didn't see your name on the guest list."

"That's because I didn't use my real name."

"You've got a lot of nerve, Hasan." Tai cringed that her former lover with whom she'd had an affair while dating Marco was standing at her side. Seeing her ex-personal trainer was not what she'd planned tonight. During the time she'd dabbled, she'd kept their relationship totally secretive.

"Well, it was well publicized and open to the public and it's great that you're helping the city's children, so I figured why not. Plus, it gave me a chance to see you. Mmm-hmmm," he added lustfully.

"Hasan, I hope you didn't come here to play games. I'm happily married and—"

"I'm aware." He inspected her wedding ring. "I read in the article about this affair that you tied the knot." He looked down at her body and a bulge rose in his pants. "You sure look amazing and some kind of tasty, baby."

"I'm not your baby. Show some respect." Her eyes searched the room as she tried to locate Marco. She didn't see him, so despite being on edge, she relaxed slightly.

"I am being respectful. The way I'm feeling right now, I could ride you all night."

No he didn't go there. "Hasan, I've gotta go." She sighed. "And please, don't follow me around. I appreciate you supporting my event, but give me my space." She was uneasy about whether or not she could trust the man whose world she'd once shattered.

"Oh, I will and in fact, you've already made my night. As long as I get to see you, lovely, I'm fine." He focused on her figure, undressing her with his eyes as she strode away.

Tai steadied through the crowd, trying to pretend she'd never seen Hasan. After she'd broken up with him and never returned to the gym, she'd figured her chances of seeing him were nil. Flashbacks of their gym trysts floated in her mind. She tried to wash them away, but it wasn't easy knowing that Hasan was in the same room. She hoped that no one had picked up her mood or noticed their conversation. But Tai was unaware that her eagle-eyed friend, Nevada, had observed her engaged in the lengthy discussion. And in Nevada's keen view, Tai's body language didn't read like it was a friendly encounter.

Tai searched the large ballroom for Marco. She was feeling slightly vulnerable and wanted to be by his side, perhaps for security. Many times she'd thought she should've told Marco about their relationship, but she never wanted to hurt him. At least, she wouldn't have to be concerned with him finding out on his own. She doggedly glanced across the room and Hasan was nowhere in sight. She breathed a sigh of relief, hopeful that he had left the gala after she'd dismissed his advances. *I don't want to cross paths again. You never know what people will do, particularly trouble-makers.* She'd never pegged Hasan in that category. *I would think he has more class than try to scar my marriage...but sometimes bitterness can cause one to be vengeful.*

On Monday, staffers at Next Phase of Life gathered for a roundtable meeting. Tai sat at the end of the table while Felicia was in the chair next to hers. "I'm proud to announce our event was extremely successful, and I wanted to thank each one of you for your participation. We'll be able to provide assistance for many of the city's disadvantaged youth, so our goals were met."

"It was fun and some of those costumes were off the chain. I loved it and had some good laughs, too," Felicia noted.

Noni, the receptionist, stood in the doorway, listening to the discussion as well as keeping an eye out for visitors and the phones. She noticed a young deliveryman enter the office with a vase of brilliant colored flowers. Quietly, she headed to the front to accept the delivery, presuming it likely was a congratulatory gift from one of the guests at the fund-raiser. She placed the flowers on her desk and then signed the electronic delivery form. The carrier left and she glanced at the small white envelope attached to the vase. As she'd figured, the flowers were addressed to Tai. She sniffed the aromatic scent admiringly and then picked up the vase, heading to Tai's office to drop off the flowers.

When she returned to the doorway of the conference room, the group was adjourning to their desks and offices. Tai and Felicia remained seated.

"Well, Mrs. Moore, you have an admirer. There's a lovely gift on your desk," Noni announced.

"Really? That sounds interesting. Thanks." She stood and nodded for Felicia to follow her to her office while Noni headed back toward her front desk.

Tai walked in and immediately adored the bright arrangement on her desk. "Hmm. I bet Marco sent me these. When he remembers"—she laughed—"he knows how to surprise me. These are sweet." She sniffed the flowers. "Smell good, too."

"That was thoughtful," Felicia stated admiringly. "I can't tell you the last time I received flowers."

"To be honest, me either." She smiled. "This is a first from Marco, believe me. And he lives in the garden." She studied the flowers. "In fact, these look like some that he specializes in. Perhaps he even grew them…but they did come from a floral shop," she added, noting the logo on the gift card. She plucked the card off the vase and opened the envelope. Suddenly, her face turned into a strange look.

"Something wrong?" Felicia asked curiously.

Tai looked down at Felicia and then back to the card. "It reads: *From your secret admirer. Someday you'll know who I am.*" An inquisitive expression appeared on her face.

"That's strange—"

"Yes, it's definitely not Marco. He'd sign his name." Tai walked behind her desk and sat.

"Guess you'd better not mention to him that you received flowers from a '*secret admirer*'." She crossed her legs, leaned toward Tai and taunted her. "Hmm, sounds kind of sexy to me," she teased.

"Girl, you're letting your imagination run away. I'm sure it's one of the guests from the party. But I'm not feeling playing any games. I wished they would've said who they were." She paused. "I really don't see why they wouldn't have."

Her mind drifted to Hasan. They'd had an unsettling encounter and he had made passes at her during the event. Perhaps it was him who'd sent the flowers, she thought, careful not to share her thoughts with Felicia. *That's probably who it is: Hasan. I hope him appearing and seeing me for the first time in over a year didn't trigger some kind of craziness. I thought I made it clear that I'm not interested. Not one iota. Those days were over when I broke it off. I see now that it was a mistake to ever get involved, and I hope it won't haunt me forever. I'm happy with Marco and I don't need anyone trying to interfere.*

"Tai, you'll find out. Don't overthink it. It's probably someone who was at the party and wanted to let you know they admire you for your success. These men know you're married, but you're a good catch, so I wouldn't put it past any of them to make a move." She smiled. "Hey, you can always throw the leftovers my way," she teased. "I'm kidding."

"I won't worry about it. It was thoughtful from whoever the mystery person is. And of course, married to a gardener, I love me some flowers."

CHAPTER 24

TRISTA

The female soloist sang "His Eye is on the Sparrow" at Rolling Hill, the church filled to capacity and overflowing in a room outside the sanctuary at Venus' homegoing services. Her voice hit the rafters, transforming many to tears and stoic faces. Trista and Syndie were seated among the family in the front pews. They were like family and had been invited to join Venus' relatives.

The pastor noted that he'd never witnessed the number of flowers surrounding the cream casket. A poster-size portrait of Venus with Trista and Syndie on prom night rested against an easel next to the coffin. The program featured other photos of the trio in a collage prepared by Venus' parents.

Trista had attended a vigil the previous night at Venus' apartment complex where neighbors were disturbed of the young woman's death. They had described her as pleasant, easygoing and quiet but guarded and a loner. Other attendees included her coworkers and longtime friends.

Although the news stations had announced that foul play was not suspected, the community members were unaware that some men attending the vigil were homicide detectives with the city's police force. They were dressed down in slacks, casual shoes and collared shirts to blend in with the residents.

Friends and family gathered around the entry door of Venus'

apartment building, where they considered it an appropriate place to memorialize since she'd lived there alone for the past ten years.

Flashes of the vigil danced throughout Trista's mind as she had temporarily tuned out of the service. Focusing now on the pastor's eulogy, she attempted to find strength in his caring words: some sad, others comical as he injected humorous anecdotes in his delivery.

"Venus grew up in this church. I remember her once telling me that she didn't want to sing the solo during one of the choir practices. The director encouraged her to share her beautiful voice," the pastor stated. "There was no need for her to be shy; she had a gift from God, so she blessed us on many occasions with her talent. I can hear her singing the leading solo in heaven's choir right now. The angels are doing double-takes." He smiled at her parents seated on the first row. "Your darling is in a divine place and she's shining her spiritual graces upon you."

Trista dropped her head and then dabbed her eyes with a tissue while Syndie wrapped her arm around her shoulder and hugged. Syndie nodded her head to the pastor's consoling words. When the service ended, the congregation followed behind the pall bearers and flower girls to the rear of the church. Trista and Syndie exited with the family and suddenly, Trista felt like she was going to faint.

She spotted someone in the church whom she had least expected and almost caused her to stop in her tracks instead of continue to walk in the ceremony. She gasped, made eye contact, then looked down. It was Dorian, her ex-boyfriend, and she was in shock.

What is he doing here? I thought he was still in lockup! Of all the people for me to see…

"Are you okay?" Syndie whispered, following behind her and totally oblivious to Dorian's presence. She had noticed that Trista had stopped suddenly.

"Not at all." Trista tried to walk steady to the rear. She sighed nervously.

"It'll be okay," she suggested, unaware of what was troubling her friend.

When they reached outside, Trista turned to Syndie. "Did you see him?"

"Who? Who are you talking about?"

"*Dor*-ian."

"Dorian? I thought he was in prison."

"He is, uh, he was. You think he got out for the funeral only? Sometimes they let people out for services."

"Naw, not if you didn't see him in handcuffs or shackles."

"Oh, my, I'd better get the heck outta here." Trista was nervous seeing her former boyfriend whom she expected to be in prison.

"No, don't you run away," Syndie demanded. "No need to hide. He ain't nobody. We're staying right here. We're doing it for Venus. And we're going to the repast, too."

"Well, that's easy to say, but I don't want to see him."

"Listen, you don't have to talk to him. Ignore him, that—" Syndie wished she could call him another name but didn't due to being on church grounds.

"I know what you want to call him. Me too." Trista sighed. "I'll pretend he's not here. I don't see him; he's a stranger."

"Calm down, Trista." She looked at Venus' family and offered a faint smile, acknowledging they were preparing to trek to the cemetery behind the church for burial.

Trista opened her purse and dug inside for her sunglasses, which she mounted on her face. This way, she could shield her eyes and truly avoid eye contact with Dorian if he crossed her sight lines. She would attempt to avoid him.

After the gravesite rites, Trista and Syndie headed to the church's dining hall for the repast. The aroma of Southern cooking tantalized nostrils as attendees gathered to congregate for a traditional meal. Trista, unsure if Dorian were still present, eyed the crowd hoping not to spot him. She prayed he had left since she didn't see him in the cemetery.

She and Syndie went through the buffet line and had offered to serve plates for Venus' elder family members, but some of the church deaconesses had already started.

Trista piled her plate high with one of her favorites, macaroni and cheese, while Syndie dug into the candied yams. She always liked to sample recipes since she loved to cook. After serving their plates, they found a small table for two in a corner and sat down.

Trista relished the tasty Southern cooking. She was pleased that she and Syndie had found their own private space away from the bustle of the large group.

"It was a such a beautiful homegoing for our girl. Fabulous like she was." Trista placed a forkful of string beans in her mouth. "Hmmm. These are seasoned just right."

"Girl, you were missing this good cookin' in La-La, right? Probably turned into a tofu and hummus kind of girl, huh?"

"No, I still crave this. I tried sushi and Thai and everything else, but I still love some soul food."

"Hmm-mmm. I hear ya."

Trista tried to play it cool by not mentioning Dorian, but he was still playing on her mind. Syndie had warned her not to dwell on his presence and since they'd left the church sanctuary, neither had spotted him.

"Hey, miss lady, didn't think I'd see you again."

Trista cringed at the person mumbling behind her. She looked into Syndie's eyes and confirmed it was Dorian speaking. She hoped it was possibly a sound-alike. But no such luck, she thought.

"Dorian, you can keep on steppin'. Please don't mess with me. I'm here respectin' my friend and she's barely been six feet under for long. I have absolutely nothin' to say to you."

He walked from behind to her side and looked down. Trista avoided eye contact.

"Baby, you sure lookin' some kind of luscious. I didn't expect to see you here."

"Feeling's mutual. What are you doing here?" She eyed Syndie and still refused to look up and into Dorian's eyes. At first glance of him inside the church, she'd recognized that he had bulked up in lockup.

"Venus was a good friend, like she was to you. She was like a sis to me and never turned her back on me."

Trista refused to respond about her travel plans. She also didn't want to show any interest in his situation—whether he was simply out for the funeral or if he had finished his prison term for embezzlement. She couldn't care less and was simply visiting in honor of her best friend. She'd be heading back to D.C. as soon as she had a train ticket in hand. She'd arrived with a one-way, unsure when she would return.

"That's funny. You always had negative things to say about her when I lived here. You never liked me associating with her either."

"Oh, that was back in the day. Once we got older, I didn't have anything to say 'bout you hanging with Venus, bless her soul."

Trista continued to eat her meal. "Yeah, right. I'm not here to debate with you, Dorian. You can step away. I'm trying to reminisce with Syndie about old times with Venus—not you."

"I got you. I ain't gonna hold you, Trista. Thought I'd stop by to say hi." He added, "And you're looking edible; all I need is some honey." He unloosened his narrow black tie.

"How dare you? I hope you don't think I have any interest in you. Plus, that was totally inappropriate to say to me in a place of worship." She shook her head. *You never did have much class, did you?*

"I apologize. You're right; that wasn't cool to say here." He looked toward the ceiling. "Moms, forgive me. You taught me better."

"I'm really not feeling you standing here, Dorian. Can you please exit stage left?" Trista requested.

"Well, I'm sure it won't be the last time I see you. I'm around and ain't goin' nowhere." He hinted that he may be out of prison. "But then again, I heard you were livin' in D.C., so guess you'll be heading back soon."

Trista was curious about his prison status, but she dared not ask. She didn't want to show an iota of interest in his situation—whether he was simply out for the funeral or if he had finished his term. Dorian would take the slightest hint and read everything into it. She also didn't inquire how he knew she was in D.C.

Syndie was tiring of hearing the ex-couple's banter, so she decided she'd take her plate and drop it in the trash can, giving her a reason to leave the table. She'd let the two duke it out, and was aware that Trista would provide all the details of any actions between them. "Excuse me." She stood up and walked away.

Syndie's absence triggered Dorian to think he could now sit in her seat across from Trista. He slid into her seat, seizing the opportunity, and gazed lustfully at Trista.

"I didn't say you could join me," Trista said vehemently.

"I know you didn't. I made that decision." Dorian was always forceful and not one to easily quit if he had his eyes and mind focused.

"Look, Dorian, I'm not trying to act a fool here out of respect for Venus and her family. You plopped your you-know-what here, never asking me if it was okay. So please, go." She looked around, then whispered, "There are plenty of tables where you can sit. Are you even planning to eat or sit here and watch over me?" She sighed. "You're acting like you have brain freeze. It's nothin' new that I ain't interested. That went out the window when you closed that cell gate."

"Hey, baby—"

"Don't *baby* me. This isn't the place or the time...," Trista stated angrily through clenched teeth. She observed that Dorian's looks had turned up a notch. She could see that he had buffed up during his bid, gained some pounds that enhanced his physique, and he still had the dreamiest eyes. Those eyes were dangerous and alluring.

"You do realize you're not so squeaky-clean ya self, right? Up in here pretending—"

She refrained from cussing him out; it wasn't her way to spew foul words in the place of the Lord. "Dorian, I'm not trying to judge you. Did I even bring up the past?"

"Well, you sho' ain't talkin' 'bout the future, either. Guess I don't fit in ya game plan even though I'm outta lockup."

"So, what happened?" she decided to ask, her nosey-curious side rearing its head. Dorian's original sentence was five years.

"I was a model inmate," he whispered, scanning the room to see who may have perked ears. Perhaps it was paranoia, but he sensed some of the eyes were on them. This was his hometown and everybody's business spread like wildfire.

Across the room, Syndie continued to mingle with the crowd that felt like a high school reunion, but she'd been keeping a side-eye on Trista.

"You see what I see, and I'm sure you're thinking like me," noted

Chandra, a former classmate who had noticed Syndie constantly gazing toward Trista while they were in a huddle. "That no-good man's trying to win her back."

"Hmmm-mmm, you're right." Syndie sensed she may need to intentionally disrupt their conversation if it looked like Dorian was becoming overbearing. She'd only walked away as she despised Dorian and what he stood for; he'd been a negative influence on Trista. She'd already lost one-third of their clique with Venus, and she didn't want to lose another friend. Dorian had involved her in his scheme and she'd been fortunate that she hadn't been wrapped up in his consequences. Now he'd paid the price, but Trista could put herself in a vulnerable position. All one had to do was dial 4-1-1 and Dorian could be the connection to the dark side of her life history.

Suddenly, Syndie recognized Trista's frustrated countenance and headed back to the table on a rescue mission. She threw some shade at Dorian who picked up the negative vibe. "You doing okay, Trista?" she asked, looking out for her friend's welfare.

"I'm fine. Thanks."

"And I was just leaving." He stood and walked to Trista's side and leaned down to her ear and whispered, "Call me. I've got an opportunity for you that you can't refuse." He slickly placed his cell number written on paper into her hand. He was so adept at his Houdini-like smoothness that Syndie, who was temporarily distracted eyeing her own ex-boyfriend, didn't witness the exchange.

Trista peeped at the paper and quickly put it in her purse. Dorian walked away with an air of confidence. For a few seconds, she reminisced about their once fruitful relationship.

Lying across the sofa, Trista was zoned out after an overwhelming day: burying one of her best friends and encountering her ex unexpectedly. *A sudden death and a shocking surprise*, she thought. She picked up a Seagrams wine cooler and sipped from the bottle.

Syndie entered the room, and she'd also shed her black funeral dress for a tee and jeans. She headed to the fridge and pulled out a Coors beer and then joined Trista in the living room. "I still can't believe our girl is gone. But cheers." She held up her bottle and Trista followed. "She's in a better place, they say."

"Definitely," she said absently, then turned up her bottle for another taste.

"And she's at peace." Syndie took a swig of her beer. "I'm kinda glad the girls didn't attend. It would've been devastating." She shook her head. "Look, Trista, I'm not tryin' to get in your bizness, but what was that fool talkin' 'bout? I had to step away 'cause he was getting' on my *last* nerve. But then when I looked over, I could tell whatever he was sayin' was irkin' you, so I came back to the table." She cringed. "I swear, he gives me the creeps and I can't stand his ass, putting your life in jeopardy. Hell to the no. He needs to stay over in his part of town, wherever that is."

"Oh, nothing. It's all good. Believe me, I don't have *any* desire to hook up with Dorian. I don't believe in going backward." She paused. "It was cool of him to show his respects, though."

"Yep, but he didn't have to show in person. He was the last person I was plannin' to lay eyes on. Sorry, Trista, I guess I ain't feeling him. He turns me off completely."

"Well, he was released early, but I'm sure you won't have to worry about being in his company again. I'm nowhere near here—"

"So, when are you goin' back to D.C.?" she asked, briskly changing the subject. "Hey, don't read more into that question than I meant. I'm not trying to rush you into leavin'," she explained, "but you had started workin' at your old job and then, boom, you were here." Syndie was hopeful Trista wouldn't hang around as she feared she may hook up with Dorian, who, in her eyes, was bad news. He was known as quite the charmer who could lure women into his web of dominance and control. She wished he were still in lockup. Trista appeared vulnerable and Syndie didn't want to risk her falling for him—again. "Of course, this is your second home, and you're welcome here anytime."

"I'm supposed to be heading back in a few days. I had told them I'd be off indefinitely, and they were aware I had an one-way ticket. Look, my supervisor and boss are cool and flexible. They were so happy when I showed up. But it's been an adjustment—"

"I guess so. No comparison once you got a taste of Hollywood."

"Yeah, good old Hollywood. Hmmph, where dreams can become reality and then shattered."

"I definitely understand where you're coming from. You ever think about staying here?"

"Coming back home?"

"Yeap, North Cackalacky. You left here so quickly. You never explained it. I thought you were trying to get away from Dorian, leave the past behind."

"Well, that was part of it. I did used to visit him in lockup, if you remember. So I didn't dump him like that after he started his bid." She shrugged. "I thought I needed a change of scenery, and then when I found Tai online, I figured why not reconnect."

"I'm not sure D.C. is the place for you."

"Why you say that?"

Syndie looked at her, sizing her up.

"It's not doing you justice. I think the pace is too fast or something. You should slow your roll. Don't you think?"

"No, I've gotten used to the big city. Plus, someone may discover me."

"Trista, you sound like you're twenty years younger, trying to follow your dreams."

"Nothing wrong with that. I came to grips with the fact I can still dance and make money even at my age."

"Well, you were a hell of a dancer at Juicy. Men always be asking me 'bout you. 'Hey, where's that cute girlfriend of yours? We miss her 'round the way.' 'She could work that pole.'"

She laughed. "Oh, is that right... tell 'em they can check me out on the videos now."

"You're silly. Girl, they feenin' to see you in person. But I hate to say this, and excuse me, no harm intended, but Dorian looked like he's buffed up a little. I was checking out his swag. He strolled away like he was a king or somethin'."

"Yeah, he always had that pompous thing going on. Thought he was all that; he was invincible. That's how he got into trouble in the first place." *And my dumb ass fell in to it.* Dorian working as an accountant at a distribution plant led him into temptation. He ended up embezzling funds and was arrested.

"Well, he served his time. And, I'm not trying to encourage you, but I noticed how he was checking you out today. He had that *I'm-still-crazy-about-this-woman* look."

"Yeah, well, he can keep it, too. Syndie, I never trusted Dorian much after I fell into his trap. I hung in there with him 'cause I felt sorry for him. I was lucky I got off the hook 'cause he sure was making those deposits in my account. We were living large so I chalked it up to him having a decent salary."

"I understand the past, but maybe you should think about it. Hey, you're not with your dancer man—Kwik, right, that's his name—so what the hell? Like I said, he served his time—even got out early for good behavior—and he could deserve another chance. Lookin' back at our pasts, how many men can we say truly cared about us?" The beer was causing Syndie to become less hostile toward Dorian.

"Yeah, we were tight, but he still betrayed me, Syndie. He never told me what the real deal was and threw me for a loop—"

"But you didn't get charged. No harm done, right?"

Trista stood and headed to the fridge for another wine cooler. She walked back and sat on the sofa. She twisted off the top and sipped. "What, you on his side or something? Why are you suddenly so in favor of Dorian and me getting back together?" *Did she notice he slipped me his number? Is that why she's so encouraging? No, I doubt she saw him.*

Syndie was speechless and then said, "'Cause I believe if he hadn't gotten into trouble, the two of you would have still been together."

"In another life," she stated sarcastically. "I'm not interested. In fact, I'll likely be catching the train back to D.C. this week. So, enough, okay?" Trista was becoming pissed about Syndie drilling her.

Syndie responded by turning on the flat-screen TV and remaining silent. It was only a matter of time before the beer and coolers, along with the soft voices on screen, created a sleep haven for both of them.

Trista retreated to the bedroom that had become her oasis during her stay. Syndie had pulled out all stops to make her feel at home and not a stranger. She stretched out across the bed, lying face up, and daydreamed, feeling the effects of the Seagram's Escapes coolers. Perhaps Syndie was on to something; she could give Dorian another chance. Or was it that she was feeling lonely, after Kwik had kicked her to the curb? She couldn't determine if thoughts of reconnecting with Dorian were merely on the rebound, or if there was actually potential in rekindling a relationship. Was he worth it? What did he have to offer? Would Tai or others look down on her for forgiving him? Surely, Syndie was supportive as she seemed to be encouraging her to reestablish their once solid rock. She turned over on her side and reached for her purse on the nightstand. She pulled out the piece of paper that Dorian had given her at the repast. She gazed at it and contemplated if she should contact him. Syndie had changed her tune, gung-ho about her reaching out to him and suggesting they could jumpstart their old status. She picked up her cell and glanced at the number. She started to dial and then pushed the "end" button. She'd need to give it more thought, if she, in fact, wanted to respond to Dorian. She'd considered that the curtain had had its final close on their relationship.

CHAPTER 25

TAI

Restlessly tossing in her sleep, Tai bolted upright. She'd been seconds away from finding out who had sent her flowers. It was all in the dream. Leave it to her luck, she was left hanging, still brainstorming about the identity of her mystery admirer. She looked over and Marco was in peaceful slumber. She hadn't dared tell him about the floral arrangement or her perplexed status of the sender. The last thing she needed was to have her new hubby make accusations of any nature. Perhaps it was one of her business clients or someone who'd landed a job through her employment firm. Maybe the person simply had a crush on her, she thought. Or it could be someone who had attended the masquerade gala or who was appreciative of her community efforts. She lay back down to contemplate, even through her subconsciousness, but an identity nor any clues ever surfaced. For now, it was a guessing game.

CHAPTER 26

TAI

Felicia winked at the handsome bartender who'd delivered her and Tai another round of Cosmos. She'd decided to treat her boss after a hectic day at the office. Neither had complaints because busy meant success. Next Phase of Life had built a winning marketing campaign, and Tai's client list was expanding. Felicia also had attributed it to Tai's recognition from the community and her fund-raisers.

Felicia sipped her drink. "I think this better be the last one. Right?"

"Agreed. We must make sure we can get home safe—and sober." She tasted her cocktail. "These are good."

"I told you. And Mr. Cutie Pie..." She nodded toward the bartender. "Knows how to hook us up."

"I saw you winking. Go for it; you're single," Tai encouraged.

"You know he's too young—"

"Excuse me, you forget Marco..."

"No, I didn't. He's young, but Marco is mature."

"Yes, he is. Otherwise, I'd never have married him."

"So, I don't mean to pry, but since we're discussing age, what's it like dealing with a younger man? I'm always going for the mature, seasoned, business-natured..."

"Polished, suave and on and on. I know your type." Tai laughed as she relished her drink, looking around the bar. "Most of the men sitting at this bar are your type. So, what you doing eyeing the bartender?"

"Well, I was thinking I'd at least fantasize about something different. Sometimes it seems it's not a bad idea to think outside your comfort zone."

"It definitely worked for me."

"Oh, yes, you made out on top." She looked at her drink and then at Tai. "I'm glad that you pulled through," she added, referring to her breakup with Austin, her longtime boyfriend.

Now why is she bringing up the past? Guess it's the alcohol. She thought of "Blame It on the Alchohol," reciting Jamie Foxx's song lyrics in her head. Tai was close to Felicia, but only shared certain aspects of her life; their relationship wasn't the same as with Candace and Nevada.

Felicia grimaced, noticing Tai's expression. "Sorry, I didn't mean to allude to anything." She was well versed at recognizing her boss' moods and facial expressions. "Those flowers are lovely," she remarked, throwing attention on another subject.

"Yes, they are..."

"Did you tell Marco about your surprise delivery?"

"Oh, no, it's not a big deal. I figure it's one of our clients, Felicia—someone who wants to remain anonymous. I'm not making it out to be anything else."

"Could be. I guess I'm a little nosy. Plus, it's been ages since I received flowers." She feigned jealousy. "But I'll let it go."

Tai checked out the clientele at a popular watering hole near the office. It was bustling with the after-work crowd, so it was a collage of suit-and-ties and office dresses. They blended in ideally with their pant suits. She looked at her watch: 7:10 p.m. She motioned to the bartender, who walked toward her. "I'll take a coffee, please." She looked at Felicia. "What about you?"

"Yes, make that two. I didn't realize how those drinks snuck up on us. Even though I'm taking the subway, I still have to stand up straight." She giggled. "And you be careful on the way home."

"Oh, definitely."

After they downed their cups of coffee, Felicia closed out the tab and requested the final bill. When the bartender set it down, she was tempted to slip in her business card with a note to contact her. She decided against the flirtatious move, but did offer another wink. *Don't start nothin', won't be nothin'*, she surmised. She kept that eye candy in her memory bank; perhaps she'd get up enough nerve at another point. She was surrounded by a sea of downtown professionals, her usual bait, but this time it was the cutie bartender who'd moistened her panties.

Tai and Felicia headed out of the lounge for Tai's car. They walked a block to the parking garage and climbed inside the car. Tai drove through the garage until she reached the exit where she held up her monthly parking card for the gate to open. She turned and drove down the street to the closest subway station.

"Thanks for the ride. I'll see you first thing," Felicia noted.

"No problem. I'm planning on arriving a little early, so I can work on one of the new projects. Have a good evening, and thanks again for the Cosmos."

"You, too." Felecia hopped out and closed the door, then joined a group of riders. She alternated between driving and catching the subway to work.

Tai drove off and headed toward Connecticut Avenue where she would take the Dupont Circle route, then P Street toward Sixteenth

Street. She waited at the stoplight and observed the throngs of people heading in and out of restaurants and bars on this evening. She breezed through the streets and was pleased that the rush hour had subsided. She looked in her rearview mirror and noticed a dark car with tinted windows. When the light turned green, she turned on Sixteenth and continued up the main street. She wondered if her paranoia had set in, and in her mind, she imagined she was being followed. She then decided to turn onto a side street, after visualizing that perhaps the car was trailing her. She would intentionally take an off-the-beaten-track route instead of the main streets. She could kick herself for having the last and final drink, but she thought she'd made up for it by ordering a stimulant. She glanced at her cell phone between the front seats. Noticing in her mirror that the car also had turned on the side street, she found it a coincidence. She then found an alley and turned to take the route behind houses. The same car followed suit. Then she became extremely wary and concerned that she truly was being pursued. She took a quick turn and steered the wheel back toward Sixteenth Street, which would lead to her home. She barely whizzed through a caution light, passing a police car and breathing a sigh of relief. A glimpse in her rearview mirror showed the strange car had been forced to stop at the light; apparently, the driver was leery about crashing it with an officer in view.

Tai picked up her speed, relieved that she had made it nonstop through a series of lights. She quickly pulled through the back alley of her street and clicked open her garage door and entered, closing the door behind her. *Whew. Now that was insane. Was that car following me or was it my imagination? That was scary.*

She entered through the garage door into her kitchen. Marco

had not arrived home yet. Weighing whether to call and inform him about the incident, she decided she'd wait. It was merely speculation, she thought, that she was actually being trailed. Perhaps the drinks could have had some type of hallucinatory effect on her—although the coffee had helped her high to come down. Dropping her keys and purse on the counter, she pulled out her cell. She needed to speak to someone. Nervously, she sat at the table and dialed Trista. She hadn't heard from her since the funeral and thought it was odd, although they had a strained relationship.

After a few rings, Trista picked up.

"Hey, sis, how are you? Thought I'd check up on you. How was the homegoing for Venus?"

"It was beautiful. It was like a reunion—all my high school friends, well, acquaintances, I should say, were there. I saw some of our old neighbors."

Tai's mind drifted to the time she'd taken a solo drive to N.C. to reconnect with her past shortly after Trista had arrived in D.C. after the extended absence from each other's lives. She'd discovered that Trista was known as the best stripper at the local club, Juicy, and a popular waitress at the Fork and Spoon Diner, where she'd met gossip guru Ginger, her former coworker. Paul, the former deputy sheriff dining there that day, had offered a plethora of information into Trista's life in Salisbury. But Ginger seemed to be holding something back, stopping short while speaking of Trista. Tai's sentimental journey had taken her to their parents' gravesites where she relived the devastating murder-suicide. Thankfully, she and Trista had not witnessed the tragic incident, but their lives would be affected forever. Her first visit to her hometown in years had been an attempt at closure.

"So, how's Salisbury? Anything new?" she asked, thinking about her secretive, solo trip to their hometown—later revealed to Trista. She imagined Trista's friends bombarding her with questions about her sudden departure to head north. According to Trista, she had left without explanation.

"No, it's the same. I've only been away a couple of years. Syndie's doing good. Her girls are in college out of town, but here in state."

"Wonderful. I'm sure she's enjoying your company. I can only imagine what it's like to be an empty nester. Tell her I said hello and thanks." She wasn't sincere as she couldn't care less about Trista's friends. However, she was grateful that Syndie had welcomed her into her home.

"Will do. We've been sitting around like ol' times, having girl nights like you and your friends but only the two of us." She remembered comical moments with Venus. "The only missing link is Venus, of course."

CHAPTER 27

TAI

Curled up on the chaise lounge while flipping through a design magazine, Tai consumed her mind listening to jazz artists on Pandora radio. She totally wanted the remnants of the other night to disappear. Was her mind playing games? Had she been watching too much suspense on TV? Had those tasty drinks dazzled her brain to the point of hallucination? Maybe the driver had simply been taking the same route. The following morning at the office, she was tempted to share with Felicia about her episode but decided to store it for a rainy day. There was no need to mention if it were simply a façade.

The light shone through the blinds during the quiet Saturday afternoon. She was taking a reprieve from the kitchen and once Marco arrived, she thought perhaps they would order carryout.

Marco opened the door and heard the gentle melodies. Whenever Tai wanted to chill, he was aware that she listened to smooth jazz and neosoul artists. He didn't want to bust her groove with a sudden interruption, so he strolled casually toward the sunroom, his hands planted behind his back. He walked inside while Tai's mood created the mellow ambiance.

"Hi, sweetie. I didn't want to disrupt your flow…"

"Oh, no problem. I was taking some me time for a change—not to say I wouldn't share it with you."

Marco whipped out a bouquet of flowers from behind him, walked closer and handed them to her. She gracefully accepted them and he kissed her forehead.

She smiled with surprise. "These are gorgeous, Marco. How sweet." She sniffed the bouquet. *Hmmm, what's he up to? He hasn't given me flowers since we first dated and he arranged those roses from his own garden.* Suddenly, she recalled the mystery flowers and how she never determined the sender. *What a coincidence—flowers twice.*

"Glad you like them. Be right back." He headed to the kitchen and selected a crystal vase from a cabinet. He filled it with water, removed the plastic from the flowers and then placed them inside before going back to the sunroom. He set the vase on an end table and then joined her on the chaise. He grabbed her chin and pulled her face to look into her eyes. "Tai, I love you and there's nothing wrong with showing a lady in more ways than in the bedroom." He teased, "Although I know I have some mean skills."

"Now that's for sure." She smiled, cuddling closer and gazing at the flowers admiringly.

"And I'm still feeling..." *Bad about the negative BS that Mom dished during her visit. No, I don't wanna go there.* "...so good about finding my true soul mate," he added, cleaning up his original thought. He wrapped his arm around her and affectionately squeezed her shoulder. He turned and they locked lips. As their kiss grew more intense, he seductively lured her toward the stairs and they slowly ascended. After reaching the landing, they tangoed toward the bed before they plopped onto the comforter together. They stripped each other out of their clothes, a task that they couldn't complete fast enough.

Marco tickled her neck with his tongue and then moved toward her breasts, nibbling and sucking tenderly. His tongue slid down her navel toward her love nest, where he lavished her juices. Tai was so enthralled in heated passion that she gripped his rock-hard penis and massaged it briskly to amp up the excitement. She inserted it into her vagina and he plunged with rapid-fire precision while she squeezed tightly. She wrapped her legs around his back and lifted her hips high for maximum fulfillment to intake his full girth. Marco thrust as if with erotic vengeance, seeking the ultimate cum bath. Neither could hold their peak any longer and exploded into a warm pool of oblivion.

CHAPTER 28

CANDACE

The cell phone continued to ring before Candace was stunned by a voicemail. Don consistently would accept her calls. She was aware of his schedule and presumed that he would be available despite him being in Chicago for the weekend. According to Don, his chartered flight would be on the ground until Monday. She didn't leave a message but instead redialed, convinced that Don would pick up on the second go-round. Once again, his voicemail message kicked in. She hung up.

Now this is a first, she thought. She checked her cell and it was 10:24 p.m., still considered early for a Saturday night. *Hmmm, maybe he's tired and fell asleep. But it is an hour earlier there, so doubt he's turned in for the night.* She suddenly remembered that he had an uncle in the area; he was his father's younger brother. She thought Don possibly could be hanging out with him. Chi-town was Nevada's hometown and while she'd never visited, Nevada had frequently shared that the music scene was popular—especially blues. She figured maybe Don and his uncle were spending a night on the town. She dared not call him a third time. She could envision him in heaven surrounded by talented musicians known to blanket the city.

She plugged her phone into the charger—a sure sign that she

was giving up for the night. She adored Don, but she had slowed on her chase. If he couldn't see that she held over-the-top love for him, then why would she continue to pursue him as if it were some game of cat and mouse? She figured she'd truly given him her all and it was beginning to be tiresome at the guessing game. *Will he ask me to marry or will he not?* She'd downed several Tequila shots, so she wasn't sure if it were her or the alcohol twisting her thoughts.

CHAPTER 29

NEVADA

"Good afternoon. Sleuths On Us."

"Well, well, if it isn't my baby. You awake, answering Sleuths?"

Nevada yawned. "Oh, Dad, you woke me up. Crazy I answered like it was a business call." She exhaled. "Let me sit up so I can talk to you straight." She laughed.

"You always did like those midday naps."

"Yep, how are you? So good to hear from you."

"Good to hear your voice, daughter. I'm sure you've been busy as hell."

"Dad, I can hardly keep it all together. But guess that's a good thing, especially when you're in business," she admitted. "How's Mom?"

"Oh, she's fine; just fine as wine," he teased. "Right now, she's out with Marie and Danna."

"Great. She doesn't let no grass grow under those footies. I'm glad she's able to hook up with her longtime friends."

"You got it, baby."

"So how's the gig at the Back Room? I'm sure you are rockin' Chicago crazy."

Roderick, better known as "Rockin' Roderick," was a self-taught harmonica and banjo artist who'd spent many a day performing at the famous club in the city's blues district along Rush Street. Nevada had made his dressing room her palace on many occasions during her teen years as she was too young to sit in the club. The family had moved to D.C. when he'd been offered a position to teach music at Howard University. He had been invited back for several months to perform at the Back Room during one of its throwback seasons. Her Aunt Roz had welcomed her parents to stay at her place during his gig.

"This experience has reminded me how much I loved the performance part of being an artist. Since teaching, it's been rare for me to be onstage. So I'm actually lovin' it, baby."

"Wonderful. Sorry you caught me off guard. I wished I wasn't so drained."

"Not a problem, baby." He cleared his throat. "Listen, I want to ask you somethin', or rather share somethin' wit' you."

"Okay, I'm listening, Dad. But don't scare me like this; setting it up like it's serious. I hope it's not..."

"Well, depends on how you look at it."

Nevada grimaced.

"Your friend, one of your best friends, Candace—"

"What about her? Is she okay?" she asked breathily.

"Oh, sorry, maybe that was the wrong intro." He sighed. "Candace, is she married?"

"Dad, no, you would be one of the first to know. She definitely wants you to perform at her reception."

"Okay, well, maybe I recall you saying she was close to it."

"You probably heard me say she's been dying to get the question popped to her, but it's been slowwww."

"Oh, my bad, it was something like that."

"Dad, what are you getting at? I'm a detective and all, but I still like clues or at least come out with it," she teased.

"You remember you texted me a photo of her and her boyfriend, fiancé, or whatever he's supposed to be?"

"Of course, they were on vacation and she sent me a selfie. I thought it was so cute that I sent it to you and asked you to show Mom. She adores Candace."

"We both do, baby...I don't know how to say this, but I've been seeing this man at my shows lately; in fact, every Friday night. He looked familiar and I couldn't figure out where I knew him from. Like you, I've gotten so I observe folks and it's so important when you have fans. You want to be sure you remember their faces, even if you never know their names."

"Oh, how cool. Candace told me recently that he was in Chicago. What a small world. I'll have to tell—"

"No you don't. He's been at the shows...but he's not alone. He's had the same woman with him each time."

"Oops...woman, huh? No, I guess I'd better not give her the four-one-one."

"Yeah, it's none of our business—"

"It's my business if I think my girl is being played, Dad," she stated defensively.

"I figured you'd say that and maybe I shouldn't have meddled, but I thought it was ironic after I realized I recognized him from the photo. I even went back on my cell and double-checked it from the stage while he was in the audience. And yep, that's him."

"I believe you. You always made a point of audience recognition. Where you think I got my memory skills from? Chip off the block," she complimented proudly. "If you say it's definitely Don, it's Don. He's a pilot so he's all over the place all the time. Wouldn't be surprised he has some other chicks on the side. But girlfriend will be devastated...she thinks she's the only one and playing the waiting game for that ring."

"I can relate from days on the road; you always had your groupies. And he travels a lot, so I'm sure he has his pick."

"Well, Dad, thanks for the info. The detective in me won't let this slide. But I won't say a word to Candace—yet."

"Please don't. And promise me, when you do, be easy."

"I will, Dad, no worries," she promised. Candace already was a basket case and overly sensitive when it came to Don. It was fresh for her to be so wrapped up in anyone as she usually treated men as simply fickle play toys. For once, she was serious about romancing.

"Anyway, how's Ryan? You two ever plan on tying the knot?"

"Okay, Dad, that's enough. Think that's my 'exit stage right' alert." She laughed.

"Nothin' wrong with checkin', baby. I hear you on the staying single frame of mind. So many folks in my line of work don't do the marriage thing 'cause there's a lot of instability involved, especially when you're on the road a lot. I thought I'd ask. But take care, baby, and speak with you real soon. We'll be back to D.C. after my gig is up."

"Cool and Dad, love ya."

"Love ya, too, baby." He hung up.

Well, I'll be damned. What the hell is going on up there in Chicago with Don? Let me not be a gossip guru but be professional about how to handle. Mum's the word until I investigate. She looked at her cell phone. *Damn, Dad, you really threw me for a loop. Candace is my girl, so I must tread lightly.*

CHAPTER 30

TRISTA

Syndie pulled her prized hoopty into the station lot and parked. Trista had decided to return to D.C. and contacted her boss at Seacoast to alert she wasn't extending her stay in N.C. after all.

She looked over at Trista and smiled. "Well, girl, it was fun while it lasted. You be sure and take care of yo'self."

Trista smiled in return. "And you take care of my little ladies. So proud of them being in school. Tell them Auntie Tris wishes them the best of success."

"I will." She opened the door and headed to the trunk where she reached in and pulled out Trista's suitcase, placing it on the ground.

Trista hopped out of the car and walked toward the trunk. "Funny I feel like I'm living out of this suitcase. Shows I've been a gypsy for a minute. Some kind of drifter or something." She shook her head. "I'm getting too old for this, almost forty and still all over the place."

"Look, don't be down on yo'self, Tris. You should be proud that you were in L.A. doing your thing. How many forty-somethings can still command the stage? You would still be there—"

"If Kwik hadn't shut me out of his life. Oh, well, guess looking back, I can't blame him. Maybe it was never meant to be; we were never meant to be."

"Never say never. And like you told me your sis says..."

"Forty is the new twenty," they both recited in unison.

"And in that case, we have nothin' but time," Syndie advised.

Hmmph, if you think so... "Yeah, I need to look at the brighter side." She paused, reached into her purse, pulled out her sunglasses and placed them on. "Syndie, thanks for everything. I value your friendship and as soon as I can get settled, I'll invite you and the girls for a visit."

"They would love it. Unfortunately, they both missed their high school class trips to D.C., so this would give them a chance to do the tourist thing."

"Right. I've yet to do much of that myself."

They hugged and Trista grabbed her suitcase and walked toward the Amtrak depot.

Trista peered out the station window and watched Syndie drive off the lot. She nervously looked at the clock. *I feel like I'm a kid, trying to hide from my parents while sneaking out the house or sneaking in past my curfew. But I'm fricking forty—well, almost—that's right, I'm twenty.* "Where is he?" she mumbled softly to herself. *I told him I didn't want to hang around this place 'cause someone might see me.* She adjusted her sunglasses and continued to stare out the window, her back turned to the patrons inside the station. He'd described that he would borrow a friend's car.

After patiently waiting fifteen minutes, she noticed a black Malibu slowly crawl onto the lot. She piercingly looked at the car before recognizing it was her ride. She picked up the suitcase and walked out the door, then toward the car. She opened the back door and tossed her suitcase on the backseat before opening the passenger door and jumping inside.

"Hey, what's up? You sho' lookin' lovely."

"Thanks, but Dorian, you are simply runnin' game. I'm in my usual jeans and tee, so it's nothing fancy."

"Are you okay? You look a little uneasy."

"Of course, I'm jittery 'cause I just lied to my best friend. She thinks I'm heading back to D.C. and here I'm in the car with you." She sighed.

"I'm sure if she knew, she'd think you were in good hands."

Don't be sweet on yourself. She would kill me if she was aware I wasn't on the train but with you instead. "Please drive away from here."

"Okay, okay, just chill." He pulled off the lot onto the street. "What's up with Syndie anyway?" He gave her the side-eye. "She was grittin' on me at the repast. I wasn't doin' nothin' but reconnectin' with you."

Trista sighed. "No comment." She gazed out the window soaking in the picturesque setting. "Remember, I only agreed to stay until the next train so I can hear this proposition you're talking about. You practically begged me with your texting."

He reached over and rubbed her thigh. She smacked his hand and he jerked it away despite the temptation.

"Don't start; we're not going there. I told you, strictly business." She clarified their previous text discussion they'd had earlier.

If you say so…but once you see this bod that got buff while I was away, you won't be able to resist.

"Oooh, baby, baby, baby," she moaned, biting her tongue to keep from exploding. "You sure didn't lose your mojo." Trista panted as she worked hard to match Dorian's energy, going toe to toe as he rammed deep inside her walls.

I was right. It only took seconds for you to give it up. You couldn't say no to all this.

"Hey, Dor, I think you got better," she complimented. "What went down in the slammer? They offer you screw classes or something? I don't remember all these skills."

"Tris, nothing's changed. Maybe I'm more on point, but I'm also not selfish anymore. I aim to please you—not only me."

"Oh, I can see that." She gripped his back tighter as they rolled over on the sofa bed. "This feels sooo good." She'd tried hard not to get locked into anything sexual, but she couldn't help it. *Dor still has the charm and could seduce the panties off an alligator. I'm such a weakling and never should've let him have the upper hand this time around. We barely had a chance to breathe.*

Once they had arrived at his temporary living space, his friend Craig's apartment, Dorian had not wasted any minutes before going in for the booty kill. He was aware that Trista had been faking rejection as he could skillfully read her body language. He hadn't pried but could tell she was beyond horny despite her pushing his hands aside in the car and then objecting to his hand gropes at the house. As soon as they'd arrived, he mixed her one of his specialty drinks and Trista became weak at the knees, falling into his preyful trap.

Her last tango had been with the fling in the restroom. As long as Dorian put on his protective glove, which she insisted, she was prime for an evening of sex and seduction. Guiltily, she thought about how she'd fooled Syndie into thinking she was heading to D.C. on the train. *She'd be all on my case if she realized I was here with Dorian instead of riding on that train. She even said I might meet me a cutie pie and look for a seat near one.* She attempted to play it off, but it didn't take much to sway her to drop her panties. She was in lust with Dorian—especially after he'd exposed his M&M body.

"Dor, oh, Dor, why you do this to me? I'm supposed…to be…on the…train." Her plan was to catch the next daily train going North. Now, she'd missed the evening ride and would need to text Tai again to alert her that she would not be arriving.

Dorian plunged harder and quicker, maneuvering his powerful tool while she absorbed each and every sensual thrust. He remained quiet as he concentrated on the ultimate peak. Trista matched his focus and rocked to his rhythm intensely. They exploded in ignited passion.

Trista rolled over and immediately felt guilty about giving in to the lust. Thoughts of Kwik infiltrated her mind and while they no longer were a team, she still yearned for his touch and to hear his voice. Dorian had simply been a replacement for the moment. She wished the temptation had not been overwhelming as she had vowed to herself that she would not hop in bed. She was supposed to be there on business and now she'd broken her own promise. She jumped up from the bed and grabbed her clothes, clinging on to them and covering her body as she walked toward the bathroom.

"You can't be actin' shy after that sweet luvin'. Why you tryin' to hide your body? Didn't I just see every *inch* of you?"

Trista remained silent and continued inside the bathroom and closed the door.

"Okay, guess you have nothing to say. I'm sure you haven't been that satisfied since our last hookup."

Hmmph, that's what you think, she thought while looking into the mirror and despising what was staring back at her. She envisioned a contorted face and was about to slam the mirror with her fist before recognizing it was an illusion. Trista reached inside the linen closet and found a towel. She prepared to wash up, then get dressed.

"I told you this is my brothaman's place," Dorian yelled from the living room. "I'm chillin' here only for a minute till I can get myself situated. So feel free to shower if you like." Craig was at work and Dorian realized there was no chance he'd walk in on them.

Fuck that bastard. He ain't shit and never cared an iota about you. So what you doing here sharing your body with that fool? Him getting you caught up in that scam he was running at work wasn't enough, huh? Why'd you even give him the time of day going to visit his ass in jail? Look at yourself in the mirror and see how stupid you are! Voices penetrated Trista's mind as she gritted and smashed her fist on the mirror, bouncing back as her hand pulsed achingly.

"Arrrrrghhhhh!" she yelled as she stomped on the floor, jumped in the tub, turning the shower to the maximum hot temperature. She screamed as the fiery stream scorched her body. "Ahhhhh!"

Dorian dashed to the bathroom and twisted the knob. The door was locked. He pounded on it. "Trista, what's going on? Open the damn door!"

She turned the water to cold and danced around in the tub as the burning sensations intensified.

Dorian continued hitting the door. "I said open the door!" he repeated.

"No!" she yelled as she grabbed a bath towel, wrapped it around her and stepped out of the shower.

He gave up, slowly walked away and returned to the bedroom where he sat on the edge of a chair. He put his forehead into his hand as a headache started to form. *Looks like she just had one of those moments. I guess I must've set her off. Glad my man and his neighbors are at work this time of day. I hope I can convince her to stay, but I'd better be ready for the flip side.*

More than an hour passed and Trista emerged dressed from the bathroom, where she'd been hallucinating. Self-described weird images had dance throughout her mind until she became focused on the present situation. She was headed to D.C. and had taken a detour by way of Dorian. She walked toward the bedroom and spotted him seated. "You have anything good to eat in this place? I'm starving."

He was startled and looked up to lock his eyes on hers. He watched like he was staring at a zombie. *No she didn't ask me about food after actin' like a madwoman...* "Tris, sit down." He motioned to another chair. "You been takin' your meds?"

She looked down in her lap and twiddled her fingers. "What meds?"

Well, I'll be damned. She's acting like she's never heard of the meds and like nothing happened in there.

"Tris, this is me. I know you got issues, so you don't have to play games with me," he stressed.

"I don't under—"

"Oh, yes you do. Look, you need some help. It's been years and I thought all that had disappeared once you left here."

"What are you talkin' about?"

"Never mind..." He grimaced, realizing she didn't comprehend.

"You're being rude. I asked if you had something around here to eat."

He exhaled. "Hang tight. Let's see what I can find. I'm not a cook, but I don't have to tell you that." He left for the kitchen, then stopped in the hallway and listened to hear if she would talk to herself. It was silence and he proceeded toward the fridge. *That was some scary shit. Whew. Maybe I'd better rethink this 'cause I'm not 'bout to be up in this camp with a looney tune. Won't know which Tris will show up.*

The first time Dorian had experienced one of Trista's outbreaks was when they'd shared an apartment. They'd been dating a year and one night they passed through a neighborhood where she'd lived as a foster teen. He was driving and suddenly she grasped the wheel and tried to steer the car in the opposite direction. He was able to maneuver and bring the car to a halt. She spoke some unintelligible words and appeared to have a conversation with someone. He'd written off her behavior as some knee-jerk reaction to a negative flashback. Perhaps he should have taken another route although she'd never expressed any disdain for the specific area. Suddenly, she transformed from her berserk zone to a neutral one.

While incarcerated, she'd had another attack while working at the Fork and Spoon Diner. Ginger had visited him to share her outburst after a customer complained about his order mix-up and he refused to offer her a tip. The diner had closed and the last patrons had left. She entered the kitchen and began to toss pots and pans, crashing them on the floor and yelling in a rage. Ginger, always the empathetic one, took up for her behavior and suggested it was a relapse from her past. As supervisor, she had talked the owner out of firing Trista, stating she was one of the most likable servers. Ginger had blamed it on her parents' murder-suicide and that perhaps she'd never overcome the tragedy. She had taken Trista under her motherly wing and recognized that despite her thirty-something age, she needed as much support as a child. She was familiar with her family history and that she was without relatives in the area.

Dorian opened the fridge door and surveyed the choices. He thought perhaps he'd made the mistake of inviting Trista over to discuss his latest scheme. He'd yet had the chance to divulge what he considered an ideal option. He'd need the bold but vulnerable Trista to enrapture her in his plan of action.

She had an eerie feeling and while she preferred to take a shower, she didn't feel comfortable in this stranger's apartment nor with Dorian. *He already got me into his trick bag. I could kick myself for falling for him, horny or not. He's not my cup of tea anymore. I'd do anything to have Kwik again.*

CHAPTER 31

TAI

Strolling down the Safeway aisle, Tai carefully selected the ingredients to prepare a scrumptious dinner. Recently, although she loved cooking like a best friend, she had skimped on home-cooked meals. Nevada and Candace had encouraged her to launch a catering business and she had begun to contemplate bringing their idea to fruition. If she could determine a way to operate Next Phase of Life, her marriage and a second business, it would be heavenly. Sometimes she figured she would force too much on her plate, but her jack-of-all-trades personality and Gemini traits often took control. Since she enjoyed kitchen patrol to the utmost, why not add catering to her multiple streams of income?

Her cart contained organic boneless chicken breasts, fresh garlic, asparagus and cherry tomatoes. She stopped in the pasta section and perused the shelves. She noticed the flash of a person down the empty and lengthy aisle. When she looked up, no one was present. She picked up a box of pasta and was reading the nutrition label and thought she saw movement in the corner of her eye, this time on the opposite end of the aisle. Once again, she turned and didn't see anyone. She figured it was her imagination. The store was not busy as she'd left the office early today, so she could allow more time to prepare the meal. Marco had been truly sweet to her, she thought, and at least once this week she wanted to treat him with a new menu. She sighed, thinking perhaps her previous late night was causing her anxiety and illusion. After picking up the last few items to complete her meal, she headed toward the register and decided to do self-checkout. As she scanned her items and placed them on the runner, she sensed someone was staring at her. She cautiously turned around to slightly look over her shoulder. Besides a woman with a toddler girl and a man who looked like he was in a rush, she didn't see anyone in her lane. *Lack of sleep is really making me imagine things.*

She exhaled and finished her checkout, then packed her bags. After placing them inside the cart, she crept slowly toward her car while ensuring her guard was ready. The sun was setting and cast a pleasant glow over the lot. She loaded her bags in the trunk and wheeled the cart into the storage rack. She scoped throughout the area seeking solitude, and after satisfaction, she walked back to her car. After opening the door and hopping inside and quickly locking the door, she noticed a piece of paper on her windshield. She released the window and reached across the front window to pull off the paper. She rolled up the window and then opened the folded paper.

She attempted to read the scrawny lettering; it was intentionally to throw off the identity of the perpetrator's handwriting: *U lookin so sweeeet and deeeelicious. I can taste you now.* She cringed. *Who the hell?* She dropped the note on the passenger seat, turned on the car and gunned it off the lot. *I thought it was my imagination, but this is for* real. *And I can't be caught up in this game 'cause it could be dangerous.* She peeped in the rearview mirror and stared into blackness and distant headlights. Leery about a repeat of the night when she thought she was being followed, she nervously steered through the streets on her way home, constantly scoping her surroundings.

Tai pulled out all stops to set up her Italian dinner of chicken parmesan, pesto penne, creamy spinach and tossed salad. The candles were aglow and her bottle of Italian wine was chilled on ice. She'd brought out her special placemats and set the dining table formally. She was jittery as she served the salad with her homemade vinaigrette.

Marco beamed. "Mmm, you outdid yourself. This is simply a scrumptious-looking meal." He eyed her lovingly.

"Thanks," she responded like a shy schoolgirl. Her mind was obsessed with the earlier incident and note. She hadn't banked on it being suspense night. She'd coveted having a private night with her husband—one where she'd release all thoughts of business and family, and focus on him. She slowly bit her slice of garlic bread.

"You sure are quiet tonight. Not the usual 'talk till you drop' woman I adore," he shared honestly. One of his true attractions to Tai had been her bubbly personality and ambitious nature. "I figured we would talk about your idea to start catering professionally."

"Yeah, that's nice of you." She feigned a fake smile. "Of course, we can discuss, but this night is all about *you*." She jumped up. "Let me get course two." She headed to the kitchen and returned with two plates served with the main meal. She set them on the table on both placemats and then sat.

"You sure know how to spoil me." Marco thought about past relationships where some were hard pressed to fix a breezy breakfast. He understood that every woman wasn't a cook let alone a chef, and he'd found other talents. After all, he wasn't a cook either. He tasted his chicken. "Hmm, delicious, Tai. Yep, we need to talk about the catering thing."

"Okay, but not now. I'm not feeling that well." She dabbled at her meal and ate slowly.

"Oh, sorry, babe. Maybe I can do something to change that," he said seductively.

She smiled and raised her wineglass. He followed and they clinked their glasses, then sipped the wine.

"You truly have such fabulous taste."

"Okay, enough of the compliments," she said grudgingly. "Sorry, sweetie, I didn't mean to throw you shade. I'm not feeling myself." She held her stomach. "I'm having some weird pain," she lied.

"Don't overstuff yourself." He laughed. "But, seriously, if you're not feeling well, we can chill the rest of the night." He looked at her intently. "Want me to make you some tea?"

"No, that's okay, thanks. I'll be fine once I lay down." She looked into his eyes. "I apologize, sweetie. I wanted tonight to be special—"

"It is special...and delicious, just like you." He licked his lips.

She smiled. "And so are you."

Tai couldn't fathom who had left the note on her car. The wine effects were dizzying and she found it hard to concentrate on a conversation with Marco. They chatted as they finished their meal, although Tai remained steady with one-line responses. Suddenly, she envisioned with the wine sensation that the culprit was Hasan. *It's got to be him. Who else? He showed up at the masquerade party trying to get back with me. I thought he got the message. I don't appreciate him playing these games and I'm not going to let anyone or any damn thing interfere with my marriage.*

She wondered if she should call him—if he had the same cell number, or she could reach him at the gym if he were still a trainer. No, she thought, it would open a renewed line of communication. She pondered again. She decided, despite her resistance to be honest in the past, that the best option was to tell Marco about her affair with Hasan. His behavior was like an obsessed fan who wouldn't let their relationship dissolve. But now, not only her life could be in danger; Marco's could be threatened, too.

CHAPTER 32

TRISTA

"Trista, you know I always loved you. You were my ride-or-die chick. Yeah, sounds funny since you pushin' forty, but hey, you'll always be a pretty young thing to me," Dorian flattered her.

She smiled like a schoolgirl, enjoying the compliment. She nibbled on French toast that he'd prepared. "I see you honed some skills while in lockup."

Yeah, I guess you can't believe I actually cooked you breakfast. Seems like the real Trista showed up this morning. He recalled the unusual episode.

"I'm in fantasyland; this is a first. And it's yummy, too," she added, sampling the hash browns. "This omelet looks like it's from a restaurant menu."

Suddenly, she thought about her waitress job at Seacoast. "I guess I'd better call Miss Cynt and give her an update I'll be back at the end of the week."

Oh no, you won't be. Dorian cleared his throat and took a sip of orange juice. *Not when you hear my game plan.* "Listen, Trista, while I was laying in bed last night, I couldn't help but think about old times. I truly miss those days. I miss you. Maybe we can take another go at it."

"Okay, Dorian, just because I ran off the track for a minute and ended up here instead of on the train doesn't mean it was intended to be permanent."

"I got you," he said disappointingly. *Okay, let me try my plan B approach.* "You still got skills, baby, and you're letting them go to waste."

"Oh, you think I forgot how to be a top waitress?"

"Nah, that's not what I'm talking 'bout." He gazed in her eyes. "I'm referring to your dancing."

You don't know what the hell I've been doing. I was dancing in Hollywood. "I still like to dance."

"Well, I have an idea." He painted on his sweetest face ever. "What about you and the pole, Kat?" He winked, calling her by her stage name.

"No, you didn't go there. I retired my thong ages ago."

"Well, you can bring it out the closet, baby. You have no idea how many of your old fans are feening for you. Plus, you will get some new ones; the younger crew is old enough to experience it now."

"Hmm, that breakfast was the bomb. Thank you."

"You're avoiding my question."

"Well, it's kinda ridiculous. My age—"

"Let me stop you right there. Age is just a number. You are forty—almost—and fine."

"Okay, enough of the ego stroking. Of course you're going to say that."

"But I'm truthful." He sighed. "Okay, I'll back off, but do think about it. The money is quick and easy—"

"But that doesn't mean it's what I want with my life. It's going backward and I've been carving out a different lifestyle."

"Oh, I see you're trying to follow your sister."

"No, making wiser choices for *me*. Now don't get me wrong,

there's nothing wrong with stripping. I'm saying that at my age, I should move on. Leave it to the young-uns." She started reminiscing about her fans' favorite strip act to various songs. She snapped out of her thoughts and looked at him.

"Hey, it's a new day. You talking 'bout forty. Look at J.Lo. She's over forty and rockin' that new video 'Booty.' Now she's a fine forty, too."

"Okay, so now you want me to follow behind celebrities."

"Nope. Just saying don't let age hold back your *talent*. And remember the money is always on point."

She stared at Dorian, trying to determine if she should follow his advice. "Let me think about it."

He was relieved and sighed subtly. *If you don't go for it, I've got something that will make you think about it all right. Dollar bills, baby.* He started humming one of her theme songs in his head.

CHAPTER 33

TAI

Sitting nervously inside the intimate Aqua Cove, Tai toyed with the stem of her cocktail glass. She perused her surroundings to absorb all of the clientele on this evening. Now that she had concluded she was the victim of a stalker, her mind was filled with images of scenes from detective TV shows. She was careful though not to let such thoughts consume her mind and affect her everyday world.

"Did you want another drink?" The waitress startled her after noticing her glass was empty.

"Oh, no thanks. I'll wait till my husband arrives," she responded, offering a fake smile. *I need to keep my head level so I can deal with this conversation. I really hate I'm going to have to break it down to my baby this way. Or period. I tried so hard to keep my old days with Hasan under wraps. It's not like the sky is raining good men. Here I found one and have put his life in danger 'cause I wanted some side dick. But I must let him know the real deal.* She picked up her water glass and sipped. She stared out the window overlooking the peaceful setting on the Chesapeake Bay. She had selected the restaurant for its picturesque view, figuring it would help to ease any pain that she may deliver.

"Well, hello, aren't you looking lovely?" Marco's voice was comforting as he approached the table.

"Oh, hey, baby, that's sweet." She presented her best smile, soaking up his compliment of her dressy outfit.

"It's the truth. But then again, it's always true." He reached over and kissed her lips, then slid inside the booth opposite her.

"Thanks. You're full of compliments." She smiled. "I had planned to go home and change first, but it was busy at the office. I ran out of time, so I came straight here. And you don't look bad either, my hubby." She picked up the menu and opened it. "I've already had a drink so you need to catch up."

The waitress returned. "Hello, what would you like to drink?"

"Hennessy and Coke."

"Okay," she looked at Tai, "and I'll get you another Sidecar."

"Thanks."

"This is a nice spot." Marco picked up his menu. "Another one of your hideaways."

"No, I've discovered a lot of places that my clients have turned me on to."

They both flipped the menu pages. When the waitress set their drinks on the table, they ordered.

"This is good." He enjoyed his succulent shrimp dish.

She tasted her grilled trout. "So is mine. Good choice."

"Well, I got here as fast as I could. Like I said on the text, I had a new customer."

"That's okay. I understand how it is with clients."

"You sounded like it was urgent."

Tai started chewing slowly and placed her fork on her plate. She reached for her glass and sipped her drink and then again. She finally had drummed up the courage to tell him about Hasan—but there would be no specifics. Definitely she wouldn't reveal that she'd sexed him night after night following her personal training appointments at the gym. For a split-second, she guiltily had lusty thoughts recollecting their encounters.

"Marco, I love you so much. I am truly blessed to have you in my life," she started, staring him in the eyes while he also set his fork on the plate to focus exclusively on what she was saying. "I'm looking forward—"

"Excuse me, Ms. Moore, I'm sorry to interrupt you," the hostess who'd seated her said. "I had stepped away to seat some guests and when I returned to the station, I noticed this." She handed her an envelope, aware that Tai had provided her name to seat Marco when he arrived. "I didn't know if it was urgent."

"Tha-thanks." Tai frowned as she looked at the unfamiliar handwriting. Her full name was on the envelope. "No idea what this is or who it's from."

"Well, don't you want to open it?"

Not really. It may be another silly note from Hasan. "Okayyyyy." She slowly tore open the small white envelope. Her eyes glued to the paper, she silently read and her mouth gaped in disbelief.

Don't get too comfy in your marriage. He married your cash. I throw down between the sheets and he can't get enough of this juicy love. Hmmm. He's mine as much as he's yours. He's going to deny it, cause all men are cheats. You can believe him or me.

—Mansharer

Tai started sweating as she looked up at Marco. "Explain what the hell this is," she demanded, giving him a rare neck roll. "And who she is."

Puzzled, he reached over and took the paper from her hand and read. He dropped the note on the table.

"Exactly," she responded to his reaction. "I'm waiting," she expressed through clenched teeth, her arms folded.

"Damn."

"She already said you would deny it all." *But wait, I said* she. *Hold up, this is a woman. The note left on the car in the parking lot was from a man…so now I'm really confused. Are Hasan and a woman both messing with my mind? Maybe I'd better not mention Hasan—yet. It may not be him after all.*

She became bitter all over again. "I'm heading out." She grabbed the note off the table, along with the envelope, and tossed both inside of her purse.

"Wait, Tai. I have no idea who this person is or what she's talking about. I've been totally faithful to you and you should know that." He reached for her hands and she pulled back softly, trying not to create a scene. Besides the mystery people who had begun to be her shadow, she never knew when she may be in the presence of one of her clients or colleagues. She needed to preserve her public image.

"I'll see you at home." She started to stand but quickly realized it would be eerie leaving alone. Perhaps she'd at least walk out with Marco and he could follow her home. *Suppose this woman is in the lot or better yet inside the restaurant?* "Actually, I may need you to follow me in case she's lurking. And when we get home, you have some explaining to do."

He pounded the table with his fist lightly. "I told you I know nothing about this woman," he whispered, pleased that they were in a corner booth with privacy.

She gave him the side-eye and pursed her lips, forcing herself to maintain her composure although she felt like going crunk on him and letting another side release from her shell. She truly believed Marco, but the note seemed to be sincere. Maybe her mind was playing tricks on her again.

"Okay, I'll get the check." He motioned for the waitress who arrived with the bill. He reviewed the check and placed his card on the tray. She left and returned for his signature.

He signed the receipt and took his copy.

"Thank you and have a good night." The waitress took the bill and left.

They stood and walked toward the front. Tai kept her eyes focused on the door, holding her head high as she avoided eye contact with anyone. She could sense the hostess staring at her as she walked past the station.

Tai breathed heavily as Marco opened the door for her to exit. *Even if I don't talk about Hasan, after what went down tonight, I'd better tell him about the store incident. I'm going to wait until we get home before I get ghetto fabulous up in here—especially after these drinks.*

"Look, I'm not going to tell you again that I have no idea who the fool is!" Marco yelled, opposite his normally chilled-out demeanor. He paced back and forth in the living room.

"Why would someone go to the trouble of bringing a note to me at a restaurant?" she yelled back. "Who's the bitch?"

"Could be someone who's a hater, jealous of you, of us. Obviously, it's someone who's trying to throw you a curve ball, make you think something's up with me. But you know we don't have security issues, Tai." He stopped in his tracks and walked to where she was sitting. He placed his hands on her cheeks. "Tai, I love you and would never ever do anything to betray you, to hurt you."

She gazed in his eyes. "I love you, too." She sighed. "I don't understand any of this."

Marco sat in a nearby chair. "Any of what? You sound like it's more than tonight."

"Yes, I've been intending to tell you," she lied, "but I had another incident days ago. Remember the night I went to the store to cook a special dinner?"

"Yeah, that was Wednesday—"

"Right. Well, when I got to the car, there was a note—yes, another note—on my windshield. This time it was from a man."

"What?" He jumped up. "What man?"

"That's what I don't know."

"What did the note say?"

"That I was looking sweet and delicious," she shared, embarrassed.

"And you're just telling me about this? That's wild."

"I apologize, but I kinda brushed it off." Tai thought about how she didn't believe Hasan would harm her; he was attempting to win her back. But she wasn't positive that he wouldn't hurt Marco.

"Okay, so we've got two sneaky bastards playing a game. One's a woman who's trying to act like she and I are hooked up. The other's a guy who's diggin' on you apparently. And you have no clue?"

"Not one," she lied, positive that it was simply Hasan.

"Could be some fatal attraction-type shit. But you told me you hadn't dated in a long time before we met. You think it's—"

"No, absolutely not." She was definite that Austin was long gone from the picture with no return. There had been no sign of him since before he'd pulled a no-show at her fortieth birthday party. Suddenly, the memories caused a bitterness, then she jerked back to reality as she gazed at her loving, caring husband.

He sat down on the sofa. "Okay, we won't go there. So now we have two mystery folks. I'm not going to let this die. You've gotta be careful 'cause this is twice and they obviously are targeting you. Plus, these notes were delivered to you, so this means you're being followed, baby. You, no *we*, had better be careful."

Tai grimaced, closed her eyes and laid her head back on the chair pillow.

CHAPTER 34

MARCO

Digging deep into his desk drawer, Marco pulled out a piece of paper and stuffed it in his pants pocket. He walked downstairs and out the door to the outside, then opened his car door. Tai had already left for the office. Last night had been like a nightmare as he'd experienced a restless night with limited sleep. He yawned. Hesitantly, he looked at the number on the card and sighed. It had been at least two years since he'd last spoken to Crystal, his ex-girlfriend who had popped up at his place attempting to seduce him. She'd been drinking heavily and while he was tempted to give in to her wishes, he managed to refuse her, letting her sleep off the alcohol before forcing her leave to his house.

Man, I regret having to call this woman, but I'd better nip this shit in the bud. He had deleted her number from his cell, but had recalled that he'd kept the paper from when they'd first met. It was among a huge group of business cards that he'd collected over the years. He dialed the number and held his breath.

"Well, well, well," Crystal answered. "Who is this calling me—the 'stay out of my life forever' man?"

"Look, Crystal, I'm sure you're surprised just as much as I wasn't feeling calling you."

"Hmm, Mister Married Man—"

"How'd you know I got married?"

She smiled and sighed. "How do you think? Your moms."

"I'm sure…" *But why has she been in touch?* "Now, I'm only telling you once—"

"And how are you, too? Damn, where's your manners?"

"Look, Crystal, I ain't down with no bullshit from you."

"You calling me out the blue and jumping on me. For what?"

"You'd better leave my wife and me alone and stay outta our lives."

"What are you talking about? I don't even know who you're married to—well, maybe that's not true." She cleared her throat. "Her name is Tami, Tia, Tai, or something like that, right?"

"Correct."

"So, okay, explain to me what's up 'cause I sure don't understand what's going on. You rejected me when I was tryin' to get me a little something-something, so hey, I backed off. I've never made another move—and you know this."

"Well, I'm not so sure. Why in the hell did you leave that note for my wife at the restaurant last night?"

"Okay, I see you're delusional now for sure. What note? What restaurant? You got it twisted, buddy. I don't even know what your wife looks like, let alone where she hangs out."

"So you didn't leave her a note threatening her to stay away from me?"

"Hell to the no, Marco. You think you're all that—and I ain't gonna lie, I do miss all that—but I do respect you and you're married. When I fell up in your place that night, you weren't hooked up as far as a wedding." She smiled. "I'm not saying that I wouldn't fall for you again, though. So whenever—"

"Don't even go there. That's not why I called."

"Hmmm, sho' you right." She sipped on her cocktail, her third for the midday hour.

"You sound like you've been drinkin'."

"So what if I have?"

He realized that she was not a part of his life anymore. While he cared about her condition and suspected that she could have a drinking issue, he decided to keep on track. He recalled her intoxicated condition the last time he saw her. "Nothin', you do you."

"That's what I say. You certainly didn't give a damn about me. Lured me along thinking we were all tight and then dropped me like it's hot."

"Let's not go there, Crystal. Our relationship was not what you made it out to be. It was only a physical thing," he noted frankly.

"Wow, kick me some more, why don't you?"

"I'm trying to figure out if I should believe your ass. My wife is the sweetest woman, and she doesn't deserve any drama."

"Well, speaking of drama, that moms of yours…"

"What about my mom?"

"Oh, let me shut my mouth. Shame on me—"

"What are you talkin' about?"

"Look, I wasn't going to go there," she slurred, "but since you called..."

"Okay, I'm waiting. What's up?"

She'll kill me if she finds out I said anything. "I'm sure you're aware about how your moms feels about Tia, Thai, or whatever her name is. Anyway, she was tryin' to get me to sway you into having an affair." Crystal was enjoying the high she felt from teasing Marco and divulging his mother's vixen ways. "Bottom line is she doesn't care for her; thinks she's too old for ya. Actually, I agree—"

"Okay, it's time for me to go, when you start talkin' this dumb shit."

"No, your moms truly feels that your wifey isn't capable of having any kids. I hear she's over forty, right? Well, Moms was tryin' to get me to you know—"

"I've heard enough," he said angrily, disgusted with his mother's attempts to interfere with his marriage.

"Okay, I won't go there." She sipped on her Vodka on the rocks. "But remember, you didn't hear it from me," she slurred.

Marco was quiet, fuming about his mother's actions. She was constantly on a quest to have a grandchild, but this was off the chart. *Damn, Mom has lost it. She even went to Crystal to use her to get next to me. Wow, I love Moms, but I can't believe she's taken it to this level. She's always dissing Tai and ultimately it's probably because she wants a grandbaby, but it's below the belt to go to my ex.* "So you're telling me you had nothin' to do with a threatening note."

"Absolutely not, dear," she responded with a twang.

"Okay, I guess I believe you." *If she had, I'm sure this is when she'd admit the truth. I can see she's high and that's usually when the truth comes out.* "Crystal, have a nice life."

"Baby, if you ever—"

"Never." He sighed. "Listen, take care of yourself." He hung up. *She and Moms both need help.*

Puzzled, Crystal looked at her cell. She thought she would never hear Marco's voice again.

Marco seethed as he started the car and began to plow through the streets. He had an appointment with a prospective client and wanted to be on point once he arrived. He had a notion to call his mother and blast her for attempting to cause trouble in his marriage. While he didn't want to become even more upset, he hit his mother's key from his favorites contact list.

"Well, hello, dear, what a surprise to receive a call from you this early in the morning."

"Hi, Mom, how are you?"

"I'm fine, and you?"

Seconds away from cussing you out, he thought although he'd always treated his mother with respect and bit his tongue in times like this. "Not so good. I'm asking you again to stay out of my marriage," he spoke firmly.

"What's wrong?" she asked, hoping that all was not well in paradise.

"I see you've been up to your tricks. I talked to Crystal."

Oops. She grimaced. "And?"

"She says that you encouragin' her to throw some wrenches in the mix."

"I don't understand," she lied.

"Listen, Mom, I'm over the games. I don't have to go into details 'cause you know exactly what I'm talkin' about." He paused. "I don't get why you can't accept Tai for who she is—my soul mate and the woman I love."

"Well, I've tried—"

"Look, I've got to go. I'm on my way to an appointment."

"Okay, you are serious about your business, so I won't hold you." She paused. "And Marco, I love you."

"Love you, too, Mom," he expressed although pissed at her intentions. They hung up. *But I will never accept your negativity when it comes to Tai.* He focused on the streets. *I guess I should believe Crystal, but if it's not her, then who left the note?*

CHAPTER 35

TRISTA

"Why are you sweating what your sister thinks about your life? She wasn't ever concerned before." Dorian took a swig of his forty-ounce.

"Because I don't want her judging me."

"Damn, who gives a crap? It's your life and you almost forty effen years old."

"Hell yeah. You right about that." Her mind started swirling and she sipped her cocktail, made extra strong by Dorian.

"So what's the problem then? You scurred or somethin'?"

"No, I told you I like challenges, and if this will get me out of the hellhole I'm in, I'm willing to *try*. But if it don't work, I'm catching the first train to D.C." She was determined not to stick around. Her waitress tips at Seacoast were steady albeit considerably less than the dollar bills thrown onstage and tucked in her thong.

"Hey, Tai, you got it goin' on; you don't have to worry about a thing. It's goin' to be smooth." He reached over and placed his arms around her from behind. He pulled her close and rubbed his growing manhood on her hips. "You still get down between the sheets, so you definitely will kill 'em onstage."

She turned to face him and stepped back. "You think so, huh?"

"No doubt. I can't wait to see your first performance. In fact, why don't we go in the room and you practice. Sho' me what you workin' with."

"No, I want you to see my debut act when everyone else does. You've got to wait. I need to think of something new and fresh. If I'm making a comeback, then I want it to be a true comeback—not my old routines."

"Okay, no problem," he agreed, satisfied with what he considered a coup. Trista had been resistant to reentering her stripper world. He had to practically threaten to blackmail if she didn't adhere to his demand. After all, he was the sole person who was aware of her past. She'd been diagnosed with Borderline Personality Disorder after he'd been locked up. His cellmate had contacts at the local mental institution and had tipped him off. Learning her condition finally explained her odd and sometimes irrational behavior during the course of their relationship, which went back to high school. Sometimes she'd act violent and then suddenly become calm. Other times, she would engage in an imaginary conversation alone. After her recent outburst at the apartment, he wondered if her family and friends were aware of her condition.

Tai heard her cell phone ding to indicate she'd received a text. She walked across the bedroom and picked it up.

It was from Trista. *Hey. Decided not 2 come back. Gonna hang here for a few. Don't worry. I'm cool.*

She was too all consumed in her own distress and confusion that she was to pick up Trista from Union Station later. It appeared that she was extending her stay yet again as this was the second time she'd texted, cancelling her return to D.C. *Wonder why she's telling me this last minute? I have enough going on in my own life right now.*

She was convinced she would never figure out Trista's world. She texted, *K, sis. Keep me posted.* She figured Syndie was her closest friend who would look out for her. Plus, Trista would be company while her daughters were away at college. *That's cool. She needs her BFF. Maybe Syndie can help her get her life intact. She seems to be stable and responsible, family-oriented.* It seemed abrupt that Trista had decided to stay in N.C. but then again, she thought about how she breezily she arrived in D.C. from L.A. It was beginning to be her M.O. to appear and reappear in various locations. Her sister was approaching forty and she truly hoped that she could settle and conclude her fickle life journey. Suddenly, she remembered Trista's waitress job. *What about Seacoast? Quittin or breakin?*

Trista responded, *Takin break. Will call Miss Cynt.*

K. Take it easy. She thought about how her life had become difficult with the mystery man and woman who'd thrown her for a loop. She headed downstairs with her cell to the kitchen where she prepared a kettle of water and placed on the burner. She gazed out the back window and recalled when Marco had stripped off his shirt in the searing heat. It was the first time she'd looked at her landscaper lustfully. He had been her unlikely soul mate. Now someone was attempting to upset her connection.

The kettle whistled and she walked over to pour a cup of oolong tea. She grabbed the bag of multigrain bread and popped in two slices. After the toast was ready, she slathered on butter and set the plate and tea on the table. While enjoying her breakfast, she suddenly thought she could connect with Nevada and Candace. Now that she didn't have to go to the train station, perhaps today would be open. Lately, they'd been inconsistent with their monthly networking.

She started a group message to both friends and texted. *What u ladies up 2? Free to hang out later? Girls' day out?* She sipped her tea and was eager to bring her besties up-to-date about the crazy encounters. It was one thing to imagine being followed and wondering if her mind were playing tricks, but now it had become a reality—and the proof was on paper. Suddenly, a chill ran throughout her body. Hopefully, the daylight hours would work for both of them, she thought, as she sometimes felt creepy like she was in the *Texas Chainsaw Massacre.*

I'm game, Nevada responded.

I'm always ready. LOL, Candace confirmed.

Let's do it. Meet at 3 at Carolina Kitchen, Rhode Island Row.

CHAPTER 36

THE LADIES

"Aren't we always waiting on Candace?" Nevada shook her head. "Meanwhile, what's up? You lookin' well, but…" She refrained from commenting. Her keen detective sense alerted her that all was not on the up and up with Tai.

"But what?" Tai inquired.

"Nothing. So how's business?" Nevada quickly changed the subject.

"Girl, it's super. I've been a little tired, that's all, but my support team is fantastic as usual." Tai paused. "How's your business? Any interesting cases?"

"Hey, ladies, sorry I'm late." Candace approached in a turquoise wrap dress and black stilettos. "Fashionably late. Just kidding." She hugged Nevada and Tai before sitting at the table. "Thanks for inviting us, Tai. I don't know about you two, but I needed this break. I guess you both have been working hard, too. Whew! Thank goodness it's Saturday." She picked up the menu. "What kind of drink specials do they have? I'm ready."

"We hadn't looked." Tai picked up her menu and opened it. Nevada followed suit.

"This monster chocolate martini sounds wonderful." Candace closed her menu and reopened. "I'd better eat something, too."

The waitress approached. "My name is Gena and I'll be your server today. Can I start you ladies with a drink?"

"I'm going to try the Monster Chocolate," Candace blurted.

Nevada and Tai ordered Strawberry Bellinis. When she returned with the drinks, they ordered their entrees.

Tai twirled her necklace nervously, recalling during her last visit to a restaurant, she received the strange note from the hostess. She scoped out the scenery.

"Are you okay?" Nevada asked after noticing her disposition.

"I'm fine." Tai forced a phony smile while Nevada wasn't convinced of her status. *Chill, Nevada, you're reading me right, but I don't want to start off with my drama.*

"How's Trista?" Nevada figured her sister may be the thorn poking in her side.

"Oh, I guess I haven't spoken to you in a while. She went down South. Sadly, one of her closest friends from high school passed."

"Was it sudden or had she been ill?" Nevada's mind was always ticking.

"Apparently, it was a shock and she hadn't been sick."

"Wow, that's a sad note to start out on," Candace interjected. "That's life, though, and sorry to hear that."

"Yes, and in fact, she was supposed to be on the evening train today, but she texted this morning and said she was extending her visit. Going to call her boss, and I guess she either plans to tell the truth or say she's ill."

"Interesting. She just got back here from L.A., now gone again." Candace smiled. "She's sounding a little like yours truly."

"No, your traveling is different—for fun and entertainment. Sis is spontaneous, too, but she's still finding herself, her niche."

"I sure had hoped that dancing was going to be her thing. She seemed happy when she left here for La-La Land," Nevada shared.

"And she was excited and doing much better. But, it didn't work out," Tai remarked, unwilling to share that her sister's relationship had flopped and sent her packing back East.

"Hopefully, she'll get it together. It took me a minute to slow my roll," Candace chided.

"So, speaking of status, Candace, how you doing these days?" Nevada inquired. "You've been MIA for a minute."

Candace's bubbly persona turned sour. "To be honest, it's been a little crazy. Don," she lowered her head, "has been actin' standoffish."

"I told you—" Nevada interjected.

"Don't remind me." She looked upward. "Of course, the love and romance is still there, but he's not finding as much time for me. His schedule is busier with more and more flights, so I've had to take a backseat regrettably. He says he's going to make up for it."

And you believe him…I'm going to dig further about this Miss Chicago and Don, and I dare not tell her a word—yet. Nevada's mind temporarily flashed to the Chicago blues club scene described by her dad, noting that Don had appeared for concerts with an anonymous woman.

"Well, he's a pilot and may be in demand," Tai recognized.

More than you think. Nevada bit into her dish.

"I'm not giving up, though. He may not be around like he used to be, but I guess that was too good to be true. Having him twenty-four-seven got me spoiled."

"Now that wasn't new. You always getting spoiled or doing the spoiling," Nevada suggested.

She chuckled. "Hey, don't knock the hustle. But I did give up my playette membership, so I was thinking he would be under lock and key."

"What man wants that? Girl, you'd better let him breathe and not suffocate him. I tell you all the time, that's why Ryan and I are in sync—'cause we do our own thing and don't sweat each other constantly." Nevada advised, "You'll feel better if you give yourself some space."

"Well, he's done that *for* me, I'm afraid. Making time when he can, but the hookups are farther apart." She looked at her left hand and wiggled her fingers. "I'm still waiting, trying to be patient and not overbearing, but wondering why it's taking so long. But…I decided to back off from focusing so much on the ring but on our relationship."

"Wise move, Candace, and I'm not tryin' to be funny. Just keepin' it real. Ring time will be at the right time." *If at all, but keep the possibilities open. He's stringing you along, and I'm determined to step in and get to the bottom of this. He's not going to continue to run games on my girl and I sit here and act like I don't have cheating on my radar.* "Don's been around the block and besides the marital thing, he's aware you want a child. If he hasn't made a move yet, it's for a reason."

"I'm beginning to see what you've been telling me all along. It's hard to fathom after all these years, I finally meet Mister Right and he's coming off wrong. Ya'll know I'm hard to please—"

"You mean, you're picky," Tai interjected.

"I call it *selective*. I definitely have a type."

"Look, I'm not debating you." Tai sipped her cocktail.

Gena returned to the table. "Would you ladies like another round?"

"I could use another one, thanks. Tell the bartender to make it stiff," Nevada chipped in.

"Same here," Tai added.

Gena returned with a tray of drinks and set them on the table.

Tai had eased her way into sharing her recent chain of events. "I can't hold off any longer from telling you what's been happening."

"That you and Marco are doing fantastic and you're still celebrating your honeymoon," Candace teased.

"No, nothing like that, I'm afraid. Sorry, that didn't come out right. We're ecstatic and yes, still on cloud nine." Tai paused. "I'm being followed," she added frankly.

"Say what? A stalker?" Candace gushed in fear.

"I wouldn't call it that. I don't feel threatened, but it's scary that someone knows my road map; watching my steps and showing up at the same places."

"What do you mean?" Nevada raised a detective eye.

"I'll go back to the beginning. It started small…"

"Like the flowers. You never figured out who sent them to you, right?" Nevada recalled observing Tai in an intense discussion with the masked man at her party. She'd always pondered if he were the sender.

"You would've been the first to hear. No, not a clue. They're still in my office, though, dried up." She sipped her drink. "But it's much, *much* deeper. After that I started imagining someone was following me, particularly this one night I left a bar with Felicia. I dropped her off at the subway and then while I continued to drive home, I swore there was a car tracking behind me and took every turn and went through every light that I did. Suddenly, I looked in my rearview mirror and the car was gone. I thought maybe my mind was playing tricks on me."

"Hmmm…" Nevada had on her sleuth cap and listened intently, hanging on to Tai's every word.

"That sounds scary," Candace chided.

"You damn right. I've never had that feeling. I couldn't prove it, and since I'd had a few drinks, I wasn't positive that it wasn't the good ole alcohol.'"

Candace suggested, "Let's hope that's what it was."

"Well, after what happened next, I'm not so sure that was the case. I went to the store one evening and again, I thought maybe it was my nerves or I was hallucinating. I had planned to cook Marco a special dinner. When I walked down the aisles, I felt someone was watching me. Even at the checkout, I thought I had eyes peering behind me. But when I turned around, I didn't see anyone."

Nevada and Candace watched with focus.

"I shrugged it off, although I was creeped out going to the car. And when I got there, it was a damn note on the windshield."

"Well, what did it say?" Nevada inquired.

"It said I looked sweet and delicious."

"So you definitely have a secret admirer," Candace teased.

"If that's what you wanna call it."

"Flowers? Notes? That's how I'm reading this." Candace was assured.

"Maybe. Maybe not." Nevada asked, "So far, you feel it's friendly, nonthreatening?"

"Yes, up until that point." She paused. "But now, it happened again...this time I got a note from a woman."

"What the hell?" Candace asked.

"Yep, this is getting weirder even as I tell you."

"So, you remember I told you about," she looked around and whispered, "Hasan?"

"Ha-who?" Candace asked.

"Shhh, girl, my old trainer," Tai advised.

"Oh, of course, I remember. I would've loved to have been a fly in that gym," Candace teased.

Nevada gave her a this-is-not-a-time-for-jokes look.

"Hmmph, cute. Here's the deal: my secret admirer?" She recalled her encounter with him at her masquerade party and how she didn't share his presence with her friends. "Hasan left that note. He knows my car and definitely my license plate. He probably was in the store and made a beeline from the parking lot."

"Possibly," Nevada suggested, deep in thought.

"Okay, but here's the clincher. So I decided it was best to tell Marco about him—"

"Why, girl? What he doesn't know is all right," Candace advised casually.

"These folks out here are crazy. By keeping it quiet, I could be putting Marco's life in danger."

"Sounds like you could be playing with flames. I'd keep my mouth shut. Maybe you're overreacting," Nevada added.

"He always seemed harmless but you never know," Tai reflected.

"Could be an obsession," Candace suggested.

"Yeah, but this is out of the blue. I ended our thing a while back." Tai absorbed the feedback from her close friends. "Let me not get sidetracked. So I took Marco to one of my spots for dinner. So I could mellow him out before I broke the news. And you wouldn't believe the hostess comes to the table and hands me a note."

"Oh, from him again? He is checking for you, finding you." Candace's imagination kept running.

"No, this note was from a woman. So now I'm really losing my frickin' mind."

"What the hell?" Nevada was amazed.

"You lying? What did the note say?" Candace inquired eagerly.

"I'll show you." Tai opened her purse and dug inside for the note. She pulled it out of the envelope and handed it to Nevada as she and Candace read.

Nevada handed it back. "Well, I'll be damned."

"This is crazy. So any clue who it is?" Candace asked.

"I see the writing is whacked like it was done intentionally not to be recognizable," Nevada observed.

"I had no idea anyone was hating on me for being married to Marco."

"It may not have anything to do with Marco. It could simply be you," Nevada suggested, her mind going ninety miles per hour. "So the first note is from a man and the second from a woman. Hmmm, I need to think about this one."

"Detective's on the case here," Candace concluded, eyeing Nevada.

"Nevada, I would appreciate it if you could help me out," Tai stated.

"Yeah, no problem. This is some mad shit," Nevada declared.

"And it's beginning to make me mad crazy. It's hard to focus and act like everything's everything." Tai sighed. "So I definitely didn't enjoy my dinner and Marco wasn't feeling it either. We left without finishing our food. I was nervous enough getting ready to tell him I was being tracked by an ex... And then that happened and threw me for a loop, for real."

CHAPTER 37

TRISTA

"We're making a special announcement tonight," the deejay shouted. "Some of you old-school heads will remember her from Juicy. But now, we're pumped up that she's joined us here at Rumrock. Introducing the former Kat, now known as Seven!"

Trista strutted onstage in her five-inch black stilettos, a red glitter bra and matching thong, compliments of Dorian who'd shopped and paid for her debut outfit based on her request. The crowd roared while Rihanna's "Pour It On" triggered her seductive moves toward the pole. She ascended it with ease, threw her head downward, black wig cascading down her back, and slowly slinked her way upside down to the floor. Then she broke out in swirls, twirls, legs agape and worked her magic with the pole. The splits and acrobatics, honed during her cheerleading days, showcased her skills. After she mesmerized the onlookers, she collected the stream of bills and exited the stage on a mountainous high. *Not bad,* she thought, *for my first time back on the scene.*

"Now you see I was on point. You killed it!" Dorian kissed her forehead. He was curious how many dollar bills she had collected but dared not ask. *You're gonna make me a rich man.* With his criminal record, he had found it challenging to snag a position like he'd had when he met Trista. A white-collar job was elusive and for now he'd stick with his job stocking shelves at a family-owned convenience store. Now he needed to ensure Trista kept her—and his—pockets lined. His cellmate had planted the idea in his mind, suggesting if he possibly connected with her again, to lure her back in the business. Dorian had raved over her dancing skills.

"Well, if you say so...I didn't do too bad considering I'm rusty." *In fact, I pulled in a hell of some cash. So if this was my first time, I can only imagine. Hmm, maybe I should hang here for a minute. Then get the hell outta this camp. Hey, I know how Dorian thinks, but I'm gonna fool him. At least, I got a place to stay and he won't see me on the street. I'll make all the cash I can and then head back to D.C. I see through him like thin ice.*

"You were the bomb. And it'll only get better." Dorian continued to shower her with accolades to pump up her confidence. "You still got time in your career."

"Who said this was my career?" She was offended. "I can't dance forever."

"But you damn good enough to." He walked and put his arms around her waist. "My baby got skills. You work that thing."

I'm also smarter than you think. Take a chill pill, brother. Why are you so excited? It's not your damn money.

She headed to the bedroom to seek private mental space. She lay across the bed, leaving Dorian who'd switched the channel in the living room to sports. His roommate, Craig, didn't mind her resting across his bed when he wasn't home.

After D.C. and L.A. living, it would be challenging to return permanently to a small town, she thought. Her love and compassion for Dorian had long faded and he was no replacement for Kwik.

She tried to deny she still had feelings and longed to be in his arms again. Being with Dorian was a comfort zone as he wasn't a stranger; they went back to high school days, but she also felt it was strained, artificial. There was something about him that was shady, but she couldn't put her finger on it. For now, she would consider their relationship as no strings attached, but deep in her mind, she realized he was still pussy whipped. And she would use that to her advantage.

Dorian appeared in the doorway. "Hey, baby, I'm gonna make a run."

"Cool," she responded nonchalantly, relishing she would be alone.

"See ya when I get back. Maybe you'll have a little sumthin'-sumthin' poppin' on the stove."

I won't be havin' sh... "Okay, maybe, if I feel like getting up. I'm trying to cool out before the show tonight."

"Yeah, you do need all the energy you can get," he agreed. "After all, you're just gettin' back in the swing of things. So I'll grab us some food." He walked away and headed out the door.

"Yo, man, I'm on my way. Be there in fifteen." Dorian disconnected the call on his cell phone and crawled off the lot in his '95 Impala. "Won't be long till I'm cruising in a lux whip," he said out loud. He drove while brainstorming ideas clouded his mind until he arrived at Manny's where one could get anything from hot fried chicken in the kitchen to poontang in one of the back rooms. He parked and walked in, searching for Dembo. It wasn't long before he spotted the old-timer dressed in a flashy, lime-colored shirt and faded black jeans. His dark skin beamed in the low-lit room and they both took seats at the corner of the bar.

"Jack Daniels straight up," Dembo told the bartender. "And my man, here..."

"Hennessy on the rocks," Dorian requested.

"So, like I was saying, that gal of yours is nuthin' but the truth. She is truly a dimepiece. After what I saw last night, you definitely missin' out on some extra cash, bro." Dembo attempted to convince him that Trista was a prize worthy of graduating to another level than stripping. "You see," he winked toward a voluptuous woman in a blonde wig in the corner, "she's prime like that one over there." He nodded toward the woman.

Dorian eyed her and looked back at Dembo. "Man, Seven's got class. Lotta class and just 'cause she's knockin' 'em dead onstage doesn't mean she'd be willing to crack some beds."

Dembo chuckled. "I like that... crack some beds." He sipped his drink, then finished with a swallow. "Hey, she's fine and all that. A true stallion, but man, I'm tellin' ya, you can make some bank off that broad. For real, for real."

"I can tell you now she ain't goin' for that," Dorian professed.

"We can call her Redbone...naw, that ain't original. What about Peachez? Or Cinna—"

"Enough, man. I wanted to hear what 'proposition' you were talkin' 'bout you wanted to discuss. I thought it was one of your other streams of income." Dorian was disappointed.

"Nah, my man, I got enough runners. That's what the young-bloods like. I need some more girls as it's a vicious cycle—quite a turnover on this side of town. Some of 'em been doing a come-up lately and going to higher ground. I'm tellin' you, sistergirl is just what we need. Plus, some of the brothas be lookin' for city girls, thinkin' they can learn a little sumthin'-sumthin'. They're lookin' to get turned out." He laughed.

"City, country, it don't make a difference. Plus, she grew up not far from here. And, I shouldn't even tell ya this." He paused. "But my girl, or I should say *lady*, is going on the big four-oh," he added, lowering his voice.

"And the moon is red. Hell to the nah." Dembo was amazed.

"I'm telling you, it's true. No reason to lie, although she'd probably kill me for tellin' her age. Women *looove* to keep that under wraps."

"She don't look a day over thirty, bro." Dembo was impressed. "And that's on the high end. But hey, that's even better. In fact, I had a few brothas who were checkin' for her. She was the talk of town last night. That's why I called you right away."

"She's not that kinda woman. I assure you." Dorian finished his drink.

"Well, you seem ada-mite about that. I ain't gonna bug you but consider it some food for thought, hear?" He looked him in the eyes. "'Cause you could collect a mint on that one. She's more than eye candy. M&Ms, Butterfinger, Kitty Kat and I bet that's some potent kat—"

"Funny you said Kat 'cause that's her old stage name. But looka here, seriously, Dembo, you made your point. I'm not sure I can convince Seven. She's been up North with her sis. She's a successful entrepreneur, married, stable, living large. And when she left here to go there, I heard she was lookin' like a pauper. I was tipped off from some of my folks who had their eye on her while I was in lockup. But from what I can pick up—now, she's been on the down low since she stopped back here—she's been exposed to the sweet life." Dorian paused. "And you know, she only came this way 'cause her best friend died. She came for the funeral and I couldn't believe it when I saw her at the repast. I thought I'd never set eyes on her again 'cause she doesn't have family here anymore."

"Yeah, no kinfolk?"

"Man, her parents died in a murder-suicide. Moms had an affair and Pops found out and that was it. He shot her and then himself."

"Sorry to hear, that's sad, man."

"Yeah, the real deal." Dorian's thoughts drifted to the incident splashed on the front pages of the Salisbury paper and at the top of the TV news. "Well, I'd better get outta here. I promised I'd bring some grub."

"Yeah, I'm sure she don't wanna cook nothin' 'cause she needs to be ready to heat up that stage. Get it sizzlin' hot, uh-huh," the seventy-two-year-old expressed. "She'd better get that twang ready for tonight 'cause everybody and their daddy will be at Rumrock. That news went smokin' up the highway." He leaned closer toward Dorian. "Man, you one lucky brotha 'cause I know she puts it down between those sheets."

"Okay, man, you gettin' a little too personal now. Stay in your lane," he warned.

"Sorry, sorry, no problem." *Can't wait to see Seven's act tonight.*

"Check you later." Dorian swiveled his barstool and stood. "Thanks for the drink."

"You welcome, bro." *Maybe you'll come to your senses.*

CHAPTER 38

NEVADA

"Hey, hey, girlfriend. Is this *CSI* or *True Detective* or *Criminal Minds?* Or a combo of all three?" Sierra took off her sunglasses and placed them in her purse.

Nevada giggled. "You are crazy, girl. We need to hook up sometime and go have a drink." Her disposition turned to serious. "Thank you for stopping by. Have a seat." Nevada pointed to a chair in her office directly facing her huge, mahogany desk. It was full of clutter, a habit from her newsroom days when desks were a recycler's haven. "You been doin' okay?"

"Yeah, girl, just flying a lot. Steady trips and all." Sierra made herself comfortable in the cushiony, worn leather chair. "Nice office," she said, looking around. "I'm so proud of you, *Miss Detective.*"

"Thanks. Sleuths On Us. We're hangin' in here. It once was a field dominated by men, but more and more women are exploring the opportunity."

"Well, congratulations again." She crossed her legs. "So what can I do for you?" She laughed. "It must be pretty serious 'cause we normally only see each other for those fabulous ladies nights."

"Exactly." Nevada giggled. "Well, it's not so serious. No one's life is in danger or anything like that."

"I'm still proud of you for takin' down those bank robbers."

"Thanks. It was my intuition, but it was so clear when I focused on their descriptions on *America's Most Wanted*. I'm just glad my girls were out of danger," she said, referring to Candace and Trista who had double-dated the twin fugitives, Jansen and Jarrod, wanted for robberies in Florida. "And to think, they were some fine and I'm sayin', *fine* brothers, too. They could've modeled and made beaucoup money from their looks, not from holding up banks." She shook her head. "But guess they're enjoyin' life in the slammer now." She paused. "And Tai, Candace and I reaped the benefits of my reward money in the Bahamas. Their capture was right on time. We had a blast at Tai's bachelorette party."

"I heard. That was sweet of you." Sierra picked up a magazine off her desk and flipped through the pages. "So getting back—"

"Yes, the reason I called you here was I need your help." She sighed. "Candace is gung-ho about Don. He's her superhero, her everything, and she's patiently waiting on that ring." She shook her head. "I can't see my bestie getting caught up in some fantasy land, but it's been a minute and she's waiting and waiting and stressing and stressing."

"Yeah, I was glad I was able to introduce them and they hit it off. That's kinda rare these days. Whenever I talk to her, she's Don crazy."

"They connected, but her mission is marriage and child. She's totally focused on that. It's really a trip how she's been over the world and back but still hasn't heard a peep. Apparently, he's on his own mission and that's to fool her. She's hitting the big four-oh soon and talkin' family, but he's avoiding popping the question."

"I'm happy they've been keeping it steady. I don't talk to either much, but I've been doing quite a few charter flights with Don."

"Okay, I'm gonna put it on Front Street. You may not know that my dad is a musician who has gigs all over Chicago. Well, lately, he's been spotting Don at his shows at this blues joint called the

Back Room. At first, he wasn't sure it was definitely him, but then he compared who he saw in the audience to a photo I had texted him of Don and Candace."

"Oh, that's cool. I did hear that he loves jazz and blues."

"Hey, that's not all of it. He's been frequenting the place with a woman."

"Oh," Sierra realized. "Hmm. Okay, I get it, you want me to scope out the situation."

"Yeah, Candace is sweet and she's been waiting a long time for *the* Mister Right, like Tai who finally met hers. She thinks, dreams Don full time and I'd hate to see her hurt. Dad says he's up in there with this woman all the time."

"I notice he's been flying out of Chicago a lot lately." Sierra grimaced. "I hear where you're coming from. I'll put on my spy gear. I'm like you. I don't want to see my girl heartbroken."

"I didn't even give Dad an inkling that Candace is over the top about Don and patiently waiting on the diamonds. For all he knows, based on the photo, they could be casually dating. He's concerned because he was aware I'd know their status and if this other woman was an issue." She added, "He and Mom absolutely adore Candace so he's basically lookin' out."

"Okay, I'll see what I can find out." She looked at Ryan's framed photo. "I must say you and your boo make such a cute couple."

Nevada gazed at the picture. "Yeah, that's my babe. He's such a sweetie."

"You not trying to make it official, huh?"

"Naw, my baby and I are fine as single living together, and if we tie the knot, I'm not sure it will stay smooth. Even after fifteen years. Plus, we're not trying to have any babies, so this is cool by me."

"I hear ya. Well, Nevada, getting back to Don, I'll do my best and wear my nosey cap."

"Thanks, Sierra, and let me know if I can ever do you a favor."

"Hey, I will. No problem." She pushed back her chair from the desk, stood and walked out.

Nevada flicked on the local news, her usual routine at noon if she were not on a mission. It was as soothing as music to the detective. She also found it helpful to hear of any breaking news in Ryan's district. She portrayed a tough and fearless image, but internally, she worried about his duties as an officer.

After the newscaster led off with a national update, he announced a local suicide:

A woman was found in an apparent suicide in the seventeen-hundred block of Dorsey Street Northwest. Jolene Primrose, age seventy, allegedly took her own life, leaving behind a note. She stated that she had no reason to continue on this earth after her husband discovered she'd had an affair with a local pastor, whose name is not being disclosed for privacy concerns.

"Say what?" Nevada felt like an explosion had gone off inside her head. She walked to the sofa and collapsed. "No effen way." She immediately saw visions of the mild-mannered professor, Arthur. She'd never heard how he'd responded to his wife after she revealed the news of her cheating. Guilt pangs coursed throughout her body, but she resisted to give in. It was her job to track down cheaters and scandalous affairs when she was hired to do so. She was saddened of the news and could only pray for Arthur. She dropped her head and then placed her hand on her forehead. *You win some, you lose some.*

CHAPTER 39

FELICIA

Exhaling, Felicia rolled over. It had been another night of sexual bliss. She looked over at her partner and relished him from head to his baby toe. She'd managed to wrap him around her pinky like she sought to achieve with every man who crossed her threshold. It had been a couple of years now since her relationship had sprouted into full blossom. He was totally devoted to her, but she was feeling strained as they were forced to keep their union on the down low. But he was willing to cooperate and didn't seem to mind the secretive nature of their rendezvous.

He wasn't like the others who were merely play toys in her eyes, but she had started to develop feelings for Stan, a fictitious name she'd bestowed on him. By creating the name, it was easy to keep her from ever slipping out his real name when in conversation with her friends and family—all were yet to meet this mystery man. She was beginning to tire of the cover-up and wanted to pronounce her admiration for this man who lay beside her, sleeping peacefully. They'd rarely gone out except to a few private functions with strangers; not a soul present was in their pool of friends or acquaintances. Twice, they'd met up at the airport and flown to exotic locations for mini vacations. Otherwise, their usual love nest was where they lay at the moment—Felicia's home.

She sighed. Everyone had wondered whom she was seeing and

why she'd kept his identity exclusive. They'd guessed the gamut from "Stan" being a married man to her dating a coworker, perhaps considered unethical, to someone of disapproval status. One of her friends had even asked, "Is he you-gly or somethin'?" She had to laugh at that one.

For now, her anonymous lover would remain unknown much to her displeasure.

"Good morning, sweetie," she said once Stan started to stir.

He looked at her and smiled, adjusting his head on the pillow. "You truly know how to knock a man out." He turned toward the clock. "Wow, I didn't realize it was so late. I have an appointment."

I was aware, but hey, I didn't care. You can stay in my bed forever, she thought selfishly.

He leapt up and dashed to the bathroom.

"Guess I was still savoring last night. All that good lovin' you laid on me, I didn't even think about the time," she lied as it had crossed her mind. "Sorry..."

"No problem. I can still make it," he called out as he brushed his teeth. "Glad I showered last night before I crashed."

"That was good." She paused, directing her voice toward the bathroom. "Stan," she giggled, "I'm gettin' kinda tired of keepin' our relationship behind these closed doors."

He peeped his head out the door while brushing his hair. "Look, babe, the timing isn't right—not yet, okay?"

She grimaced. "If you say so..." She lay on the pillow and imagined what it would be like to walk in public with her "man" for the world to see. Her mind drifted to exactly why she was with the mystery man. She loved the idea that she'd seduced someone else's longtime lover. It gave her a sense of power. She often fought with feelings of jealousy and low self-esteem, and having a prize in her bed boosted her ego.

CHAPTER 40

TRISTA

Checking out her makeup in the mirror of her dressing room, Trista ensured every miniscule spot on her face was in place. It was time for her to appear onstage for the second consecutive night. She needed to repeat her performance for rave reviews. Top acts equaled top dollars. Dorian was right that she could reap benefits again from her dancing skills. This time, she thought, she would be wiser and actually save money instead of blowing every dime. Although her account was seized as a result of the embezzlement scheme, she'd made enough stripper cash that she never should have been practically penniless when she moved to D.C.

Life was going good, only after a night, but she felt guilty that she hadn't shared her revisited lifestyle with Syndie, who believed she had returned home to Tai. *Someday I'll spill the truth*, she thought. *But she'll definitely disapprove and tell me to get the hell outta this biz.* It would likely be only a matter of time before she was discovered as she was only on the outskirts of Salisbury, she thought. It wasn't far enough to elude anyone forever.

If all went well tonight, she would make the decision to remain in N.C., but not indefinitely with Dorian as she figured he was thinking. She'd also finally call Miss Cynt to inform her that her visit had turned into a staycation. She looked at the clock and ten more minutes and she'd be onstage. Jack, the owner, had pulled out all stops, providing her with a private dressing room and a bottle of champagne awaiting. Tonight, an added touch was a bouquet of yellow roses. She downed a shot of Absolut Cilantro vodka and chased it with a sip of ginger ale.

She entered the stage performing to Nelly's "Hot in Herre." She planned to thrill the audience by stepping up her game and including choreography she'd learned as a hip-hop dancer. As expected, the group was more raucous on this night and pumped up her act. She spun as a ballerina, kicked her heels like a tap dancer and swayed and gyrated with jazz moves, then topped it with some strenuous African dance movement. It was more than a traditional strip act and folks cheered her on as she teased in her black bra and thong, black fishnet hose and black stilettos. Tonight she used her wig as a prop as she tossed and turned her head, flipping and shaking it in rhythm.

Dembo had a prime seat in front where he tossed dollar bill after dollar bill onto the stage and then placed them in her thong when she circled the stage. He lustfully glued his eyes on her while licking his lips, imagining Trista as his personal piece where he would devour every ounce of her body. No matter what Dorian desired, he had his eyes on the prize and was determined she would become one of his stock.

"Man, I'm tellin' you that girl is nuthin' but the truth. Ooo-wee." Dembo pretended to make catcalls.

"I got this," Dorian responded. "Give me some time. I was barely able to convince her to strip again."

"You missin' out on a lot of cash, bro. These fools 'round here be lookin' for the new and fresh. You have it all at your fingertips and don't know what to do wit' it." He shook his head.

"Look, I've been dealing with Tris—Seven for a while." He caught himself from calling her by her birth name. "And I'm aware of how she rolls. She don't like anyone to push her into anything. She has to make up her *own* mind and in her *own* time. So ease back and let me do my own thing." Dorian had given some thought to Dembo's attempt to lure Trista into a side career of prostitution.

"Okay, apologies. Guess I'm too anxious, huh? I can't help myself." *But I ain't bad for a dirty old man. I still hold it down and I can't wait to get my lips on that piece of cinnamon mixed with a dab of honey. Mmm-mmm.*

"She's gotta be handled with a gentle approach." *You only know her from the outside, but I'm schooled on what's on the inside, too. And in fact, if I convince her to go that route, you, greedy fool, won't be benefiting like you think you'll be.*

Trista rolled over and dreaded that she had not closed the blinds last night. The sun peeped through the windows and after gazing at her cell, she realized she was awakened hours before she had wished. She yawned and stretched, recuperating from her show. Her clock ticking just northwest of forty reminded her that the exuberant exercise required for an over-the-top performance was draining. *I'm not twenty-five anymore, but I can hang—like I did in Hollywood. I was the oldest one in the bunch like I am now. But whoo, my body is feelin' it this morning.* She rubbed her aching leg and brushed it off as some needed time in the gym. She liked these mornings when Dorian was already out the door for his day job. Tonight would be her three-day run and then she'd be off for four days until Thursday. She didn't want to contemplate what she would do to occupy her time on off-days. Briefly, she pondered if she could double up and return to her waitress job as well. But thoughts of nosey Ginger at the Fork and Spoon Diner turned her off. Where she was chilling these days was far enough away from Salisbury that she could hide out and be at peace.

"How are you?" Trista asked as she lay on the pillow propped up on the bed.

"Hey, Trista, you must've known I was thinking about you. I said I was going to call and check on you and you beat me to it. How's D.C.?"

"Don't hate on me, Syndie." She ignored her question.

"What are you talking about? I'd never hate you. What a harsh word."

"Listen, I must confess. At first I didn't want to tell you the truth, but after so many guilt trips, I thought I should. We go waaay back and if I can't tell my BFF the real deal, who can I?"

Syndie patiently waited, unsure of what would follow the admittance of guilt. "Well, what's going on?" she asked hesitantly.

Trista cringed. "Girl, I'm not in D.C. and I didn't take Amtrak."

Syndie was stunned speechless. It had been about two weeks since she'd dropped her off at the station. She'd even texted her that she was back home safely. "Whaatt?"

"I'm here—but not in Salisbury..."

"Where are you? Who are you with? What's up?" She rattled off the questions with concern.

"First, I have to admit I'm with Dorian—"

"No way." She sighed. "He's a dangerous man."

"No, you got it wrong, sweetie. He's been so kind to me, showing me love," she defended.

"Huh, I bet, you and anyone else who falls for him. I have mixed feelings, even though I thought you could perhaps hook up with him again. I'm not your mom, but I didn't think you'd go through with it."

"But I did."

"So you left your stable job in D.C.?"

"Took a hiatus. It's open and waiting for me whenever I return. I told my boss I was taking a staycation. I needed this break."

"My mind is boggled. I don't get it. What made you stay here and you still haven't said where the hell are you?" She paced the living room floor. "My tummy dropped to my toes, girl. You got me worried."

"Well, I won't say exactly where I am 'cause Dorian is keeping a low profile. I promised him I wouldn't give out his address. Put it this way: I'm in a nearby town."

"Hmmm, I can't believe you. Not telling me you didn't leave here, then not telling me where you are." She shook her head. "Trista, is everything okay? That's not like you. We didn't keep secrets; we shared them." She probed further. "So, maybe you'll remember that after it sinks in. Well, I'm sure you told Tai your whereabouts."

"No, I didn't—yet. She actually thinks I'm here with you."

"No way. What if she had called me?"

"Remember she doesn't have your number. I never gave it to her. We only communicated between the two of us."

"So she thinks you are staying with me and we're doing the single ladies thing..."

"Tai knows you're responsible and the girls are in college. She figures you're on the up and up and I'm in good company. There's no need to worry about me."

"You need to come clean with her."

Okay, if I knew I was gonna be drilled, I never would've call you.

Only figured I'd tell you an inch and you want the whole mile. I'm a grown-ass woman and don't need a mother. "I will when I get ready."

"You've blown my mind. I'm speechless 'cause I was thinking you were back on your roll as a waitress."

I'm on a roll all right, all over the stage—up, down, and around that pole. Sis, I've been doing my thing. Turning it out and turned up. "Miss Cynt told me the door's always open, so if I get tired here, I'll have a place to go."

Syndie was dumbfounded, deciding to end the verbal questionnaire. Trista was in one of her weird funks, she surmised, and when she came to her senses, perhaps she would reveal it all. "Well, I appreciate the call, although you've got me stumped. If you find some time in all this, maybe we can meet someplace. I don't like talking on the phone. If you don't feel comfy, you can keep your whereabouts under wraps but we need the face-to-face action." She lied as there was nothing more important than knowing her exact location. She had to approach her a certain way or Trista wouldn't give up the 4-1-1.

"Yes, we'll see what happens." She paused. "Take care, Syndie."

"You do the same. Remember I've got your back no matter what."

CHAPTER 41

TAI

Marco eased away from Tai's glistening body, oiled with Wild Madagascar Vanilla fragrance. He dove in and licked her from head to toe before inserting his royal hardness into her queen bee nest. She clenched her walls to intake every inch while he stroked gently, then like a bullet he lodged inside her. It was truly a quickie and Tai lay unsatisfied, putting on her best I'm-pleased expression. Even being outfitted in her fuck-me pumps couldn't help amp up the feeling. He rolled over and propped his head on a pillow while stroking her breasts, lightly teasing her nipples. In his mind, he figured he'd better whip it out for a round two; his wife was lying dormant. He leaned over to kiss her before she put up her arm, guarding him.

"Baby, what's up? I'm ready for the finale, sweetie, and you must be, too. We can't stop now."

"Sorry, Marco, I'm not up to it," she alerted with a strained voice.

Marco sensed there was a mental block in the air, so he patiently pulled back and then laid his head on the pillow, looking at the ceiling. "You're not in the mood…"

"No, and," she turned to face him, "and it's not fair to you." She rose from the bed and headed to the bathroom to shower. "I'm going down to start breakfast. Nevada's stopping by this afternoon."

"And…?" Marco was perplexed by what Nevada visiting had to do with finishing their love session.

"We'll catch up another time."

"What the hell, Tai? You're talking to me like I'm some kind of stranger. Catch up? We're married, right? So don't be talking crazy like we don't live in the same house, sleep in the same bed. Catch up, huh?" he stated with aggravation.

"Maybe those weren't the right words." She stopped and turned around. "Okay, we'll *fuck* another time." She headed on to take her shower.

What's going on inside her head? he thought while he stretched and turned on the TV. He hadn't liked the communication lately between them. Something was amiss and it was more than identifying the sources of the notes. For now, ESPN would have to satisfy him.

"I appreciate you comin' over. Of course, I had to fix somethin'."

"I don't have to say a word 'bout how much I loooove your cookin'."

"Well, I didn't get to turn on the stove like that, 'cause Marco and I were doing our thing, or at least he was trying to." She left for the kitchen and returned with some turkey croissant sandwiches and baked potato chips on two plates. She set them on the coffee table. "I can't even concentrate to cherish all this good loving he pours on me."

"Yeah, we need to get you back on your grind," she agreed. "All I can do is try, but so far, I've been thinkin' hard and nothing's focusing yet on my radar." Nevada sampled her sandwich. "Delicious. Even the simple things you fix…you have some kind of secret condiment on this." She looked inside but didn't find a clue. "It's not your plain ole turkey taste."

"Well, you realize by now I don't share my secrets when it comes to food."

"Hey, I was tryin'. So, let's see. Back to my visit. You got flowers at the office from a secret admirer, then a note on your car at the grocery store from a man who apparently isn't a stranger because they knew the vehicle. Then a note arrived to your restaurant table and it's from a woman. You've ruled out it's anyone from Marco's past. You haven't completely ruled out it's the *ex*-personal trainer—I can never remember his name—and we don't know if it's someone new whom you may have met recently."

"You're right, all of the above," she agreed before tasting a chip.

"I'm brainstorming. Is there anyone that you've put on a blacklist lately or vice versa? Maybe one of your clients? One of their employees? You deal with a lot of folks on the regular. It could be someone you've offended in your business dealings."

"Nevada, I've thought about that, but I really don't think so. I truly work on providing the best service and keep it professional. I've never gotten involved with any of my clients or their employees." She cleared her throat. "Although I'm not saying I've never been hit on..."

"Hey, that comes with the territory. Plus, these men aren't blind; they consider you a good catch. Of course, now you've been caught." She smiled. "But seriously, we've got to figure this out." She chomped on her sandwich and chips. "Flowers, notes, flowers, notes." She gazed at the floral arrangement from Marco, now dried and still in place, adding to the room décor. "You brought them home from the office? You didn't mind the flowers from a stranger in your—"

"No, girl, those are from Marco. I wouldn't dare bring the ones from the 'secret admirer' to my house. They're still at the office, though."

Nevada stood and walked toward them, analyzing them intently.

"What's up? They're not from the stranger," Tai reemphasized.

"I...got...you. That's not what I'm looking at." She picked up the card and read the name of the floral shop. "You see this flower here?" She pointed to an unusual tall purple flower. "This can't be a common flower. Have you ever seen one before?"

"No, I haven't, now that you mention it. I was so excited that he was sweet to bring me flowers. Even though he works with them all the time, and makes his own arrangements, he specifically selected the bouquet. That meant a lot."

"Tai, I have a good recall memory, as you are aware, and girlfriend, this same flower is in the bouquet at your office."

"For real?"

"Yes, it's in there, only it's yellow, but it's the same."

"Girl, you do have a good memory. I guess I didn't bother to pay much attention since I wasn't interested in them. Only wanted to know who sent them and then I stuck them in the corner."

"Right and I remember the florist's name wasn't on the card." She reached into her pocket and pulled out her cell phone, then snapped a photo of the card to store the name of the floral shop. She then took a close-up of the floral arrangement, particularly quizzical about the brilliant odd flower.

"So what are you thinking?"

"Not exactly sure, but I'm taking this for evidence. It could be an important tip and lead me further." She joined Tai at the coffee table to finish her lunch.

"Well, I'm open to any ideas. You have keen instincts. I won't be able to sleep peacefully until this is a wrap. I can't stand the thought of being stalked."

"That may be a little dramatic, Tai."

"But it's how I feel. Somebody may not be stalking me at home, but someone—or some people—are definitely playing games with my mind."

"And I'm going to see to it that they lose." She paused. "So, Marco is acting kinda cool through this whole ordeal, huh? Doesn't seem concerned that you are in harm's way or anything, right?"

"Girl, he's always laid-back, so he's concerned, but not scared. To him, the notes seem harmless, not a threat. He probably thinks it's someone hatin' on me or crazy about me, but I'm not in danger. I keep going crazy 'cause after the second note, it's got to be two different people."

"Not necessarily," Nevada surmised.

"Why do you say that? It was clearly two types of notes—one from a man and another from a woman."

"Let me tell you, some of these folks out here are smooth operators. It could be only one. They intentionally are tryin' to throw you for a loop, keep you guessing."

"Hmmm, I never thought about it like that—one person trying to trick me into thinking it's two. Plus, the notes are totally different."

"Speaking of the notes, do you mind if I borrow them?"

"You don't have to ask." She stood and walked across the room and opened a book on the shelf. She pulled out the car note and the restaurant note still inside its envelope. "I decided to stash these away." She handed them to Nevada, who placed on a pair of plastic gloves from her purse before she accepted them. She then placed them inside a Ziploc bag, a staple in her purses.

"Thanks. I'm gonna take a closer look at these. Compare 'em. Maybe even check the DNA. I've got contacts at a lab. They may be able to expedite the process."

Tai sighed. "Anything…*anything* you can find would be helpful," she spoke slowly, placing her palm on her forehead.

CHAPTER 42

TRISTA

"It's crazy how these men be going off the chain. All I'm doing is dancing for their entertainment." She seductively crossed her legs. "But you say I'm damn good at it," she slurred, enjoying the taste of her Pineapple Cîroc.

"And they're lovin' every ounce of it." Dorian moved closer to Trista on the sofa. He caressed her hair, stroking it tenderly. "They see what I see. A beautiful woman with a ferocious body."

"Hell, it's not just my body; they love the way I dance," she teased, recalling the usual flurry of catcalls she received when leaving the stage. "Everybody and their daddy want to take me home," she added, attempting to make Dorian envious.

I bet they do. It's all good 'cause I'm workin' on you pleasin' 'em onstage and off. "I hear ya."

"You definitely be lookin' out for a sistah, though," she stated, acknowledging that he'd provided her outfits and transportation for her gigs.

Dorian glowed, relishing her rare compliment, and then cleared his throat. He clutched her right hand. "Well, Trista, I've been tryin' to tell ya. Some of them would do anything—everything—under the sun to get you in their corner. Which, brings to mind: what if—let's say they offered you a little sumthin'-sumthin'—like some cash—to throw down in private."

"Excuse me, what you mean, in private?"

"Dance for them on the side." Greedy thoughts rushed through his head with Dembo's voice in the background.

"No, what's the point? I make more on the stage at the club," she countered. "Look, I already went against my will to go back in this business. Now you're tryin' to push me even further." She jumped up. "What the hell you alluding to? Just come out and say it: you want me to give up my body to these triflin'-ass hood rats? No way. How dare you insult me like that! Do I look like I got 'fool' plastered on my forehead?" She was infuriated and stomped off to the bedroom.

Dorian followed her, realizing he'd better make a quick fix. He didn't want to lose her, his prospective retirement account—but he wanted plans to go his way. He'd let her down easy for now and keep collecting cash, at least in his mind, from Rumrock. He walked up behind her and put his arms around her waist. "Listen, baby—"

"Get away from me!" She pushed his arms off and moved toward the bed. "I can't believe you're tryin' to play me for a fool. Hey, some of the other girls are hookin' on the side, but I'm not going there. Now, go on about your business and let me chill out for tonight."

Dorian left the room and headed to the kitchen. He grabbed a beer from the fridge and walked to the living room. He looked around Craig's apartment: it was the bare minimum. He desired his own spot, and he'd wanted so much out of life before he'd ended up in lockup, and it was greed that put him there. Now greed still was at the forefront of his mind. Working menial jobs would never get him on another level. He'd heard a lot of buzz in prison about the prosperity in the pimping game, but he'd only dabbled in white collar crime. Dembo was known as the best mack in those parts, so he took his word as golden. Since Dembo thought that Trista had the potential of a casino jackpot, then he figured he would try every trick in his cards to allure her. He only needed to determine the best way to broach the subject—again. Dembo would ensure the johns as long as he ensured Trista was on point. Dembo had offered to split the profits. He couldn't afford to let this chance at easy money slip through his hands.

CHAPTER 43

NEVADA

"Hey, girl, will you be in the office today? And if so, how's your schedule looking?" Nevada had brainstormed about the potential culprits in Tai's mystery case. She'd developed a possible theory that she didn't plan to share with anyone.

"I'm wide open. No clients on my calendar. In fact, stop on by, I'm having a surprise birthday party for Noni. Sometimes you can tend to overlook the person at the front desk. They deserve accolades, too."

"Yep, you tell me she's a winner. Plus, a lot of time, the receptionist is the one who always has your back."

"Nevada, I agree. I don't know what I'd do without her. So we're having a little luncheon for her at one."

"Cool. I'll stop through. I wanna take another look in person at those flowers."

Tai looked in the far corner of her office at the dried arrangement. "They're still here. It's weird, but I don't want to get rid of 'em until I know the sender."

"I'm glad you didn't. I still have a hunch that the strange flower is a clue."

She gazed at the unusual-looking flower and admired Nevada's keen observation that it appeared in both bouquets. "I hope so. I'm still giving you props for noticing it, especially since it's a different color. Even if I had, I wouldn't have bothered to try to make a connection."

"Well, this is my lifeline. I love this kind of work. Gives me a chance to put the pieces together. Not like my frequent cheating hubby or wifey cases where you end up doing a lot of trailing. This one's a challenge. It's forcing me to think." She paused. "Should I bring anything for the party?"

"No, that's nice of you to offer, but thanks anyway."

Nevada immediately put on her detective cap and a flurry of ideas invaded her mind. A visit to check out the floral arrangement may offer more than one clue, she thought.

Once arriving at the office, Nevada bypassed Noni, putting on an innocent face so not to allude there was a party in the works. After being announced on Tai's intercom, Nevada headed to her office suite.

"She looks like she doesn't have any hint of a party," Nevada whispered once she entered.

"Yes, we've managed to keep it on the down low. Felicia and a couple of the staff are in the conference room setting up. They arrived earlier than usual to sneak in everything." She smiled.

"Cool." Nevada walked over to the corner and snapped a photo of the flowers to compare to the other arrangement. She fingered the odd flower. *Hmmm*, she thought, *these are rare. What are the chances that Tai received one twice?*

"I can't thank you all enough for making my birthday special. I still don't see how ya'll managed to pull this off without me finding out." Noni smiled, surrounded by coworkers sitting at the long conference table.

"We appreciate you, Noni." Tai raised a plastic glass of sparkling apple cider. "Cheers and may you celebrate many more." Everyone reached out and toasted with their plastic glasses. "Please take the rest of the cake home with you."

"It's yummy. Thank you."

"Okay, guess we'd better get back to work," Tai suggested after their extended lunch break.

"Not before I take a group photo of you to add to your Next Phase of Life collection," Nevada offered. The employees, along with Tai and Noni in the front, posed while Nevada snapped several shots from her cell phone camera. "You can get back on your grind and I'll do the cleanup."

"No way," Noni stated, accustomed to clearing the room after meetings. "I've got this."

"Absolutely not. You're the honoree. Enjoy the rest of your day." Nevada began picking up the plates as the staff, along with Tai, exited the room. She was anxious to clean as it offered a chance to snoop.

CHAPTER 44

TRISTA

Wooing the audience with her performance to an old-school medley, Trista worked magic with the pole in her dazzling emerald-green, two-piece thong set and clear peep-toe stilettos. In the mix were two observers of the opposite ends of the spectrum. Dembo had now become obsessed with the dancer on the verge of turning forty. To him, she possessed all the qualities and skills of a woman twenty years her junior. He was overly impressed and eager to add her to his roster. Dorian had failed him in persuading her to go a step further. He had johns lined up like concertgoers hyped to buy a coveted ticket. His patience was wearing thin and he'd decided he may make his own desperate move to win her over. He'd simply capture her—plain and simple, he thought. He was antsy in his front-row seat as he downed shot after shot of Jack.

Across the room in the farthest corner of the room sat Syndie. One of her neighborhood buddies, whose job was in the area, had casually remarked that he'd seen Trista at Rumrock, where he'd visited after work. Larry had raved over her dancing, presuming that Syndie was aware of her close friend's renewed reputation. Although she was performing in another town, news traveled swiftly among the neighboring counties. Plus, he recalled during Trista's previous dancer days, that she was popular and proud of her reputation; she was a fixture at Juicy.

Syndie had pretended she was not surprised of the news; she agreed that Trista was a hell of an act. Tonight, she'd decided to check on Trista in person. Larry had shared that the club was hidden in the backwoods. Syndie was disturbed that Trista had not been honest about her whereabouts or that she'd returned to dancing. She was forced to be brave going to the club alone, but she didn't hesitate once she found out her bestie was appearing. She'd called in advance to ensure she was on the schedule.

Wearing a long, black, curly wig and dressed in baggy jeans and a black T-shirt, she was disguised not to attract attention. Now that her daughters were off to college and she didn't have to listen to their critiques about her dressing youthful, she usually appeared in form-fitting clothes to accentuate her curves. But not tonight as she desired to be incognito. She sat in the dimly lit area and watched the engaged audience marvel over Trista. From Naughty by Nature's "Hip Hop Hooray" to Juvenile's "Back that Azz Up" to Cameo's "Candy," she took her routine to the zenith with her moves. Syndie thought back about how Trista was active in school musicals and on the cheerleading squad, so it was no surprise that she'd extended her talent to the stripper pole, then to Hollywood and now back to the club scene in an offbeat location. Her girl was a stunning act regardless of the location, she thought. Syndie watched how the men acted like hounds spellbound by her best friend. Suddenly, she felt overprotective, that she needed to look out for her welfare. Her hunches proved correct when she overheard a conversation.

Sitting near the restrooms, she tuned in as two men discussed Trista.

"Man, she'll be mine after tonight. I'm tired of waiting on Dorian's ass," one guy whispered in a raspy voice. "I've decided I'm just gonna take her, plain and simple."

"Say what?" another man asked.

"Damn right, I didn't stutter. She's gonna be mine, all mine," he bragged. "In fact, I don't care if she e'r dances here again. She can be my own *private* dancer. But hey, I got fellas ready and waitin', their pockets lined to spend some cash on this 'un," the raspy one continued. "Well, maybe I shouldna be selfish, huh?"

"So how you gonna pull this off?"

"Leave it to me. I got it alllll set. When sistergirl leaves stage after her second act, she's comin' wit' me. You hear me, bruh?"

"Naw, man, you can't do that. Dorian won't be playin' dat."

"Listen, let me handle this. All I need is for ya to be on the lookout." He smiled. "Actually, I gotta little sumthin' I plan to put in her bottle. You know she always tastes before she comes onstage. So I'll just slip this," he jiggled his jacket pocket, "into her flask back there." He chuckled. "Then I'll just whisk her away after she's relaaaxed," he added proudly, content with his ploy.

"Man, you ain't shit. Tryin' to steal Dorian's lady friend."

"Eff Dorian. I gave him a chance. I proposed my idea and he didn't make a move. Act like he scurred or sumthin'. Hell, she's definitely a moneymaker and if he ain't tryin' to go after them bucks, I am. He's supposed to recognize a dimepiece when he sees one. Man, there ain't too many opportunities like this one around these parts. You must admit."

"I hear ya, but I sho' don't want no parts of this. You on your own."

"That's fine. No problem, bruh." He stared at him intently. "Just make sure you keep yo' mouth shut. You know nothin'."

"Got it, Dembo," he agreed. "But I gotcha back."

Syndie had absorbed the conversation in the hallway unbeknownst to the two men. *Dembo? Who the hell is Dembo? Whoever he is, I've gotta get her outta here safely.* She put on her best superhero façade and realized she needed to help Trista escape any potential danger. She looked up and quickly down as Dembo and the other man walked past and back into the lounge area. She noted their physical features and attire, so she could recognize them later if needed in the future. She needed to think rapidly on her feet. She scoped out the huge space and spotted Dorian on the opposite side of the room. He surely wouldn't recognize her in disguise from such a distance, she thought. At least she hoped not. She was used to taking chances, but she was leery about making the daring move she needed to attempt. Once she produced the courage, she figured she could do anything to help her best friend avoid conflict and danger.

When Trista's act ended, she left for the dressing room to prepare for the second part of her performance. Syndie scoped out the space and when she ensured the audience was glued to the next dancer, she slickly left the lounge and walked back to find Trista. She followed the hallway and found her stage name posted on the door. She knocked.

"Who is it?" When there was no response, Trista stood, took a sip from her flask and opened the door.

"Ahhh, you scared me. Syndie? What the fu—"

"Am I doing here?"

"Yesss. How did you—" She barely recognized her in her disguise and was dumbfounded.

"Look, that's not important," she whispered. "You've gotta leave with me. Now!" she ordered.

"What do you mean? I can't leave before my next act," Trista demanded. "Where in the hell did you come from? I didn't tell you—"

"No, but somebody else did. Girl, you had me scared. And why didn't you tell me? Well, we don't have time for that." She was frantic and paranoid, hoping they wouldn't be seen by any of the other dancers.

"I'm sorry, Syndie. I couldn't." She was regretful she'd shown dishonesty.

"I figured Dorian wasn't any good for ya. He got you back into this lifestyle, I'm sure. No wonder you didn't tell me where you were, or what you were up to."

"Sorry—"

"It doesn't matter." She opened the door slightly and peeped into the hallway. "We've gotta get the hell outta here."

"Girl, do you know how much cash I'm making? If I skip this next act, I'll be losing a lot of dough."

"Dough, my ass. It doesn't matter, Trista. I wouldn't be back here with ya if I didn't think you were in danger. I heard a guy tellin' another one that he plans to take you."

"What?" She was puzzled. "Who would say somethin' like that?"

"Look, I'll tell ya later. But you'd better get on the next train steppin'. You can't stay here with Dorian, whoever. You gotta get back to D.C. away from this place."

"I'm not thinkin' too clearly, Syndie. I must admit, my mind is spinnin'." She pointed to the flask. "But you're my girl so I must believe you truly have my back."

"Definitely." She opened the door again and peeped into the hallway. "It looks like the coast is clear. How long before they expect you onstage?"

"Ohh, maybe fifteen or twenty."

"Okay, that's enough time for us to make a run for it."

She giggled. "You are too much."

"It's nothin' funny, so please, no jokes."

"Okay, got it." She grimaced, her head dizzying.

"Grab your purse—I guess that's all you've got here that's important—and we're gonna sneak out the back door. I'm in Miss Ella, so I'm prayin' the sucker's gonna start and won't be too loud," she advised, cringing.

"All I can do is trust my best friend. If anyone has my best interest, it's you."

"I'm tellin' ya, we've gotta get outta here. I heard these two men talkin' and one of 'em distinctly sounded like he was gonna kidnap ya."

"That's all you had to say again. I'm outta here."

"You can switch into your clothes later. And take off them heels."

She reached over for her purse and then stuffed her shoes and makeup bag inside a tote. She grabbed her outfit and wig, stuffed them inside the tote and then slipped on flip-flops. She looked at Syndie. "Let's go." She stuck her head out the door this time in case someone was outside. It wouldn't cause suspicion. She looked up and down the hall. "It's clear," she whispered.

The two stealthily walked out of her private dressing room and opened the back door, dashing through the parking lot toward Syndie's sometimes reliable hoopty. Syndie unlocked both doors manually with her key and they hopped inside. She pulled out of the graveled lot and gunned the pedal, coasting through the back roads until reaching I-85 North.

"This is surreal. I feel like I'm in some kinda Lifetime movie or something. You can tell me later how you found out where I was." Trista's mind raced with confusion. "We didn't even have time to discuss anything. But I believe everything happens for a reason, so I figure you were meant to be my savior. Rescue me, like in the movies. So, where are we headed?"

"Well, I don't think it's a good idea for you to go to my place. Even though Dorian doesn't know we've communicated, I'd likely be his first choice of where to look. Since this happened so fast and I surely didn't expect to be driving you away—I simply came to check you out—I'd better get you on the next train," she suggested. "I don't want to take you to my house. In fact, I'm going to take you past Salisbury. Once Dorian realizes you're missing, he may think the train station is the place to go…so I'll one up him and take you to another stop." She maneuvered along the dark stretch of highway, taking charge of ensuring her friend's safety. "You must get back to D.C. to Tai. She'll make sure you get on your feet. After overhearing that convo, I realize you're about to deal with some crazy and dangerous stuff down here. There's no way I'm gonna sit back and let that happen."

"One thing I can say about you, Syndie, you always sharp and on point." She paused. "I used to think you were a little overprotective with the girls, but I see that's your M.O. You were checkin' for me, too. And I appreciate you lookin' out."

For a fleeting moment, she started to regret leaving Dorian but was hit with reality. "It's all good. I'm not gonna get emotional."

"Emotional? My first mind was that Dorian wasn't any good for ya...sorry I encouraged it."

"Yeah, at first you didn't want me to hook up again. I didn't wanna tell you I was back in the lifestyle."

"Sucka," she charged. "I'm sure it wasn't only for you; he was planning to get a cut of the deal. He's a straight-up user."

Trista paused. She didn't want to believe that her old flame was not to be trusted. She didn't always agree on how he operated, but she had grown to care for him. Now she needed to deal with reality. "Maybe you can stop me someplace..."

"Just like a showgirl. We ain't in Vegas." She observed the signs on I-85. "We'll haveta see what's open this time of night. I got an idea. I'll pull off into one of the hotels and you can go in the lobby." She sighed. "No, girl, I'd better not. Suppose I stop and Miss Ella refuses to start?" She looked at Trista. "Hey, I'm sure you can work your magic and dress in the car."

"That'll work." She released her seatbelt, reached into her tote bag and pulled out her oversized top and jeans. Fortunately, the jeans were baggy and easy to slip on. Syndie ripped off her wig and handed it to Trista. "Here, put this on. It'll help keep you unrecognizable, although I don't expect anyone to see you. Guess I'm paranoid."

"Hey, I can wear my own."

"Nah, take mine. It's fuller, more locks." Trista placed the wig on as best as possible in the dark. While she completed changing her outfit, Syndie continued to zoom up the highway, constantly looking in her rearview mirror, but as time passed quickly, she figured she was far gone from the club. Dorian and Dembo wouldn't have a clue of what had happened to Trista. The bottom line was that she had escaped from a potential world of control.

Upon arriving at the station in Greensboro, Trista hopped out and walked inconspicuously into the practically deserted depot. Only a few passengers were present: a mother with two small boys and an older gentleman. The next train was scheduled to arrive within an hour. She purchased her one-way ticket and then returned to the car. Syndie had left it running to avoid a breakdown; she didn't take any chances on becoming stranded. Trista walked around to the driver's side where Syndie leaped out and they hugged.

"Thank you, Syndie, for looking out for me, helping me get away." Trista was now thinking clearly without the influence of alcohol. Her buzz had worn off and she realized that she truly was in danger. It was all surreal.

"You're welcome. What time does the train leave?"

"They expect in about an hour. Please don't wait on me. I'll be fine."

"You sure? Although I don't know if my gas will last that long. I'd better head back down the road. You keep in touch and text me when you get to Tai's."

"I will, I promise." She turned to walk toward the station, then turned around. "And Syndie, promise you'll bring the girls to visit. I'm going to get my own place someday."

"Sure. We can do a ladies weekend." She opened the door and gazed at Trista. "Take care of yourself." She hopped in the car, not sure when she'd ever see her bestie again, praying they both would make it safely to their destinations.

"Damn, where the hell is she? Tris—Seven, you here? They waitin' for ya ta come onstage!" Dorian frantically peeped inside the dressing room, then walked down the hall knocking on doors, angering some of the dancers who were concentrating on their upcoming acts and relishing their space. "You seen Seven?" he asked Rocket, a petite dancer known for her explosive act.

"Nope, not a peep," she responded. He closed her door quickly.

"Somebody had to have seen her," he said angrily and bug-eyed with dismay. He paced the hallway. "I don't know where the fuck she went," he spat out loud.

Dembo came up behind him, followed by an acquaintance. "Hey, man, what happened to your piece?" he inquired.

"Don't disrespect. You mean my *lady*," Dorian snapped.

"Well, the *lady* part is questionable," he chided.

"Man, you'd better get the hell away from me, bruh. This ain't no time to be jokin'." He pulled out his cell phone to see if Trista had called or texted him. The screen was blank.

"Listen, let me handle this. I know the plan you had in mind," Dorian stated, not aware that he truly had a different type of plan: kidnapping.

"What's there to handle? You obviously ain't equipped to control. I ain't never had this kinda issue with any of my girls," Dembo bragged, smiling at his partner and seeking support.

Dorian walked to the back door and opened it. The sky was pitch-black and eerie. He figured Trista hadn't braved walking in the woods—at least not solo. He tensed up and closed the door, spellbound that she'd pulled a fast one and left him hanging in the wind. "Damn, damn, damnit," he said furiously. He pulled his cell back out and sent her a text. *Where the f are u? Better get back here asap. Crew's waitin on ya.*

Dembo watched nosily over Dorian's shoulder, presuming he was attempting to contact Seven and checking if he would get a text response. He watched Dorian's face turn from hopeful to sour once the cell remained silent with no response. Dorian leaned against the wall and felt like sinking but managed to stand straight. He believed the link to future prosperity had slipped through his fingers and snapped.

CHAPTER 45

TAI

The text startled her from her peaceful sleep. Tonight, Tai had finally been able to doze off easily. She'd experienced a flurry of restless nights. There was so much on her mind that it had been a challenge. She'd managed to remain calm about her ordeal, having more faith since Nevada was now on the case. She heard the vibration again, realizing it wasn't a dream. She opened her eyes enough to see the time on the digital clock: 3:22. *Who is texting me this time of morning? Oh, no, hope it's not the mystery folks...* She slowly reached over to grab her cell phone off the nightstand. She looked at the message. *Hey, sis. On train. Back in morn. Sorry for late notice. No worries. Will take cab.* She jolted upward on her pillow. *What in the world is going on? Is she really coming this time? Twice she said she was and then she changed her mind abruptly. I'm getting tired of this roller-coaster ride. I wasn't expecting her back for a while. It's bad timing, especially with all this craziness going on. I don't need more drama.* She eyed Marco who was still sleeping and hadn't budged. *Get ready, baby. More changes on the way.* She stared at her loving husband and thought about how he'd been understanding, coping with such a rocky road that appeared as they entered their first year. She'd finally apologized to him for snapping when he'd tried to make love. She couldn't wait until life returned to some aspect of normalcy.

Tai lay back on the pillow and faced the ceiling. Now she truly wouldn't be able to sleep, she thought. She'd barely heard from Trista since her trip and suddenly, she was returning back to her home on the spur of the moment. Trista often proved as mysterious as the person stalking her. Sometimes conversing with Trista was like talking to a stone wall. And if she were lucky, she'd get a few pieces of 4-1-1 or none at all. For now, she couldn't afford to focus on her sister as it was an ongoing dilemma; she was on a mission of her own.

CHAPTER 46

THE SISTERS

Trista decided not to bother Tai about picking her up once the train pulled into the station. It was during the early morning and although it was Sunday, she respected her sister's quiet time. Perhaps she wanted to attend church or either rest. Since she had a wad of cash collected from the rainy stage, she could afford to pay for a taxi. It was a great feeling of independence that she'd returned with enough money to cover such expenses. She reached the curbside and hailed a cab, one of many lined up for passengers.

After arriving at the house, she inserted the key in the lock and breathed a sigh of relief. *I'm back in safe territory*, she thought. *There's nothing like family.* During the train ride, it allowed her time to reflect on her life journey: the ups and downs, pros and cons. She'd determined that she needed to bond with her older sister, but this time it would be straight no chaser. She would come clean with Tai about everything. She ascended the stairs, exhausted from the lengthy trip, hauling her faithful suitcase. She entered her room and plopped on the bed, falling asleep on the comforter.

Tai awoke to hear her footsteps. She was set to pick up Trista if she had called but relieved that she'd managed transportation on her own. After confirming she was safely inside, she drifted back to sleep. Marco had not budged and she chuckled to herself that if a stranger had entered their home, he would not be of any help as sound as he slept.

Tai encouraged Marco to spend the day with his friends as she needed some me time with Trista. He'd left early as he thought it was the best idea for the sisters to have one-on-one conversation. There was plenty of updating on Tai's end, and he presumed vice versa since Trista had extended her stay twice.

Tai rose to prepare a brunch where they could sit in the sunshine and catch up on the latest news. While whipping up her waffle batter, Trista entered the kitchen. Tai looked up, turned off the mixer and walked over to greet her with a hug. "Welcome back. You must be hungry. That's a long ride." She returned to her mixture.

"Yes, it was. I can't believe I slept so late."

"I can. Well, it's good to have you back," Tai stated with partial truth.

"And let me tell you, it's good to be back." She sat at the table.

"Want some coffee? I've already had a cup." Tai pulled a cup from the cabinet and then reached over to grab the pot before Trista could answer. "Sure you could use some."

"Yeah, I need a boost," Trista agreed. Her body was actually aching and all she could visualize was one of the massages Tai had treated her to in the past. She rolled her head around, attempting to unloosen her neck, which felt tight.

"We have a lot of catching up to do, sis. At first, I thought I'd take you to Sunday brunch at one of these places. But then, I thought, I can make my own brunch."

"You have that talent as a chef. I haven't had too many home-cooked meals—"

"Say what? I thought you said Syndie was a soul food aficionado. I was looking forward to meeting her and tasting some of that good cooking." Tai smiled.

"Well, it wasn't exactly that I ate all of my meals at her place."

"Oh, I see," she responded, sensing that Trista had details to divulge.

She sipped her coffee. "Exactly what I needed. Those hash browns are smelling some kind of sweet."

"We hope. Let me crank this up so we can eat."

After topping off the breakfast menu, Tai and Trista sat to eat at the kitchen table.

"Where do we start, sis?" Tai asked. "I've got a lot going on, and it's been insane."

"That makes two of us." Trista grimaced. "I decided I was going to come clean, Tai, and hold back no punches. I've been guilty of not being straight up with you. But you're my sister and if I should be honest with anyone, it's definitely you. For that short time, I learned a lot about trust and distrust and the experience was eye-opening. Even more so than my L.A. lessons on life."

"I'm all ears. So what happened there? I was confused because you kept saying you were on your way back, but then you texted you weren't. I figured it was some drama going on. I've never met Syndie, but she seems like a nice person."

"Oh, she's the best, and I truly mean that. You have your besties, Candace and Nevada. Well, Syndie is to me what they are to you." She paused after slicing her waffle. "Where do I start?" She sighed. "I wasn't honest with Syndie. She dropped me at Amtrak, I pretended I was hopping on, but actually, Dorian—yes, I said Dorian—picked me up."

"Dorian, your ex?"

"Yes, Dorian."

"Hold up! I thought he was in prison?" Tai looked puzzled.

"He was, but he got an early release. I never expected to see him, but he was at Venus' funeral. And I didn't realize he was back out until he approached me at the repast."

"I see. Interesting."

"So at first I was resisting him, which was always hard for me. He slipped me his number and I decided to call him. That's how we hooked up. Syndie dropped me off and he picked me up shortly after she left the parking lot. He had a proposition for me."

"Oh, really?" Tai said inquisitively.

"Yeah, sis, he encouraged me to go back to dancing."

"At Juicy?" She recalled the club's name from her visit to Salisbury.

"No, actually, he was holed up staying with a buddy outside town. There was a club called Rumrock. I'd gained a reputation so he thought it'd be a win-win."

Tai, surprisingly for Trista, showed no disdain for her stripper background. "So, how was it? I'm sure you were off the chain. After all, you were dancing for Dre Dyson."

"They loved me, yes; they loved my performances. I'll admit it was fun, and of course, I made a lotta cash in only three nights."

"Good for you, Trista. Make sure you save some of it."

"Oh, I will. I learned my lesson there, too," she agreed. "But here's the deal, I didn't feel comfortable telling Syndie. She would've persuaded me *not* to go back to the life."

"I'm sure she always looks out for you and wants the best for you."

"Most definitely." She sipped her coffee. "She saved my life, Tai."

Tai swallowed with a gulp. "Really? How so?"

"Dorian managed to convince me to strip, but then he came out of the blue alluding that I could get paid for more than dancing, if you get what I'm saying." Trista opened up, but she still didn't feel at ease with sharing the prostitution angle.

"No, he didn't go there!" Tai was disgusted. "I'm pissed he thought my sis would take it to that level."

"Yeah, I was never feeling that. Dancing was one thing; dealing with johns was another. That wasn't me."

"So what happened?"

"My girl, Syndie, found out I was dancing at Rumrock. Apparently, one of her guy friends had tipped her off. He worked in the area. And I'll tell you that I was sorry I wasn't honest with her from the get-go because she would've had my back." She exhaled. "She was on a mission. She showed up at the club. You should've seen her disguise."

"Halloween style or down low?"

"She was dressed down so not to draw attention. Turns out she happened to overhear two men talkin' about me. One of them said he was going to take me, as in kidnap. And he sounded serious. My guess is that he was in cahoots with Dorian. They were trying to set me up."

"Whew. That's a hell of a story. Kidnap? And believe every word of that. These fools out here are not to be trusted." Tai exhaled with relief. "Sis, I'm glad you made it out of there alive."

"Yes, so let me tell you. Syndie immediately slipped back into my dressing room and rescued me. Crazy like the movies. We escaped through the back door before I was to come back onstage for my second act. We got out of Dodge. She's a quick thinker so she decided to drive me to Greensboro to catch the train. She didn't want to take me to Salisbury, figuring Dorian could get wind of the ordeal. So she drove as far as she could, hoopty and all."

"Bless her heart. That's what I'm talking about; she was a true friend," Tai acknowledged. "Well, I'm definitely going to thank her."

Trista continued to eat her breakfast. "Tai, I must admit I missed this cooking. I stayed with Dorian most of the time, so I missed decent meals. A lot of microwave and takeout."

"Glad you're enjoying this." She slowly was getting the adrenaline to share her experience with Trista. She was tired of being standoffish, and while the two seemed to be worlds apart, they were still siblings. While she may never have been as close to Trista as she was to Nevada and Candace, she'd determined there was no reason not to include her in the mix. "Trista, I must tell you. It's been weird. I'm being stalked."

"Stalked?" she asked, frightened.

"No, not like that. I don't feel threatened like horror movie stuff."

"Whew." She held her chest. "Don't scare me like that."

"It's scary in that I don't know who the hell it is. First, I got flowers delivered to the office from a stranger, then a guy leaves a note on my car, and then a woman drops off a note at a restaurant where Marco and I are having dinner."

"Now that is strange."

"Yeah, and I have no clue, although Nevada's on the case now and she's investigating for clues."

"Good. It sounds like someone's hatin' on you, so you need to find out."

"I've got mixed emotions. The flowers and first note seemed like the guy adored me, but then the woman tried to say Marco was messing around on me." She sighed. "He says he wasn't, so I believe him. Hell, we've only been married a year."

"To tell you the truth, sis, I do think you've got a good one. And you'd better hold on to him." She frowned. "But you do need to find out who these folks are. I bet you can't even sleep at night, huh?"

"Barely. It's stressing me out, too." She stood to remove the dishes and place them in the dishwasher. "I'm fortunate Nevada's line of work is being a snoop. So hopefully, she'll figure it all out." She poured another cup of coffee and then walked to the table to pour one for Trista. She placed the pot back on the stand and sat down.

"I hope so, too. Whew, all I can say is we've both been going through hell."

A few hours later, Tai walked past Trista's bedroom door. She stopped in her tracks as she heard a strange sound. She stepped closer and leaned in, pressing her ear to the doorframe. *Hmmm, she's upset.* She determined that Trista must have been shedding tears, whimpering. Realizing they had bonded and mentally promised that they would be open and honest with each other, she didn't hesitate to knock on the door. "Trista?"

Trista froze and looked suspiciously around the room. "Yeah?"

"What's going on? You hear from Dorian or Syndie or someone?" she inquired, guessing the source of the disturbance.

"No, no one." She wiped her tears with a tissue and cleared her throat.

"I'm coming in—"

Before Trista could prevent Tai from opening the door, Tai was in her room. She walked toward her. "What's wrong, Trista?" Tai asked with compassion. She took a seat across from her on the bed. "Hey, we decided we're going to be straight up with each other. Tell me what's up."

Trista gazed at Tai, her fiery-red eyes blazing with sadness. She resisted sharing this type of information. She felt it was private and no one's concern.

Tai reached over and touched her arm. "Tell me, sis." Suddenly, she recalled another time when she heard loud noise coming from the room during the late night. When she texted Trista, she assured her that all was fine.

Trista stared at her, straining to share the facts. Voices in her head instructed her to trust her sister and reveal what she'd held under wraps. "I have an illness," she gushed.

Tai nodded as she still touched her arm, now stroking it for comfort.

"Sometimes I react in certain ways that are not the norm. I have trouble dealing with some situations and I can't handle it."

"Okay, I'm sorry to hear about this, Trista, but I'm glad you're telling me. You shouldn't have kept all this inside. Poor dear." She still gripped her arm and continued to rub it.

"And I hate being judged," Trista added, now displaying anger. "People act like I'm insane or something." She reminisced. "That Ginger told you about me being in that institution. She's a nosey bitch."

"Actually, it was Paul, the ex-sheriff."

"Oh, he's another one. Always poking his nose in other people's business."

"That was part of his job, to know what's going on in town," Tai defended.

"But she was so envious of the attention I got as a waitress that she tried to throw me under the bus. They spread word that I'd had a nervous breakdown."

"Okay, let's not go there. Don't focus on the negative aspects of your past," Tai spoke calmly. "So, what type of illness are you referring to? You were diagnosed?"

"Yes," she responded sadly. "It's called Borderline Personality Disorder."

"Hmm, I'm not familiar—"

"Most people probably aren't. I still don't know all the effects. I realize sometimes my actions don't seem to be conscientious. It's not like I do things intentionally." She sounded puzzled and stood. She faced Tai sitting on the bed. "You don't know the worst."

Tai cocked her head in disbelief. She'd revealed enough troublesome details.

"No one is aware but me, Tai. I saw Dad shoot Mom. I was there..."

Tai gasped and placed her hand over her mouth. Chills immediately penetrated her arms. She was speechless.

"I never wanted to tell anyone, Tai."

"So...so...we all thought you were at school like I was."

"I was at school, but you remember sometimes I was mischievous. I didn't feel well that day, so I decided—yes, at ten—that I was leaving school. I snuck away and walked home." She shook her head, now pacing the floor. "It was horrible."

The tears erupted and Tai stood, stopping her to embrace in a hug. "That's awful. How distressful. Poor baby. Who ever knew?" Tai gripped Trista tighter.

"Yes, I pretended I'd come home on the school bus. It was so eerie. I was in shock. That memory will never fade."

"Never. That's truly traumatic. I'm sorry I'm finding out so many years later. I wished I could've helped you somehow after witnessing that." She released the embrace, reflecting on their parents and how, in their eyes, they were exemplary, well educated, and loving. "You've had to deal with this all your life."

"And then when you were whisked away by Grandma, I was devastated. *Lonely* wasn't the word. Miss Laine was cool and all, but of course, after she died, I was shipped from foster home to foster home."

Tai felt a tinge of guilt, unable to relate to her sister's troubled upbringing. She led her back to the bed to sit. "I don't know what to say, Trista. You've been through this misery all alone. I feel badly. And you understand that if I'd known, I'd have done my best to bring you here long ago." With a tear-filled face, she wrapped her arm around Trista's shoulder to comfort her while they both dabbed their eyes.

When Tai returned to her room, leaving Trista in solitude, she locked her door and headed to her laptop. She logged on and Googled *BPD*. She'd never heard of the mental illness and was thirsty to learn as much as possible about her sister's diagnosis. After reading, she recognized some of the symptoms in Trista: emotional outbursts, impulsive behavior, inappropriate anger, and unstable close relationships. She was devastated that Trista had kept her illness hidden but she understood that it was a challenge to reveal. She would offer to assist Trista in seeking therapy. *She witnessed our parents' murder-suicide? Ten years old? That's lifelong devastation.* She cuddled up in her chaise, leaned her head back on the pillow and exhaled, grateful that Marco was nowhere in sight.

CHAPTER 47

CANDACE

"Isn't it gorgeous today?" Candace appeared at Farragut Square, a downtown park to meet Nevada and Sierra. "You ladies enjoying this lovely weather?"

She was chipper as she strolled in her cheetah dress and black thong sandals. She glowed as she joined them on the picnic bench, positioning her seat to watch the crowded streets at midday.

"Hi," they greeted in unison.

"Yep, nice day. You can't beat this weather in D.C. Not too hot or humid." Nevada pretended their conversation would be pleasant.

"So, you didn't ask me to meet you here for nothing. You both are always busy." She looked at Sierra. "I'm surprised you're not flying."

"I got in last night—from Chicago," Sierra advised.

"Oh…Chicago," Candace repeated, conjuring up images of Don.

"I'm trying to break this down easy—" Nevada started reluctantly.

Candace froze like she'd seen a ghost. "Whatttt?" she asked nervously.

Nevada and Sierra looked at each other, then turned to her.

"Don," they said in unison.

"What about Don? I haven't talked to him in a while. He keeps saying he'll be back here soon, but no show." Candace's look of disappointment made it harder for Nevada, but she had to deliver the news.

"Candace, Don's in another relationship—" Nevada shared.

She was in disbelief and immediately became defensive. "How do you know?"

"Well, Sierra and I both did some digging."

"And you found what you were looking for?"

"No, we were looking out for you. I always suggested for you not to dwell on Don and the whole marriage thing," Nevada advised. "Here's the deal. We're beating around the bush and I was trying not to be frank."

"Okaaay." Candace waited to hear more details, nervously twirling the shoulder strap of her purse on her lap.

"My parents love ya, and I had texted Dad a photo of you and Don, to show off how happy you were. He called me one day and said he thought he'd been seeing Don frequent the Back Room, where he's got his gig. Well, it turned out that he'd always be with this woman." Nevada paused to see how Candace would react. She remained quiet and calm, so she exhaled. "So, lil' detective me asked Sierra if she could do some snoopin'."

"Yes," Sierra continued the conversation, "and I'd been flying with Don on some of the chartered flights. I checked with some of the other flight attendants and they informed me he has a steady girlfriend and they've been hooked up for years."

"Say what?" Candace was shocked.

"And I apologize for the introduction because I surely never would've connected you. I thought he was an eligible bachelor. He seemed your type so I figured it was a good fit," Sierra explained. "That's not all, Candace, and I really hate to tell you this, but it's something you need to know." She looked at Nevada grudgingly and sighed. "Don's a dad..."

Candace's jaw dropped. "Dad?"

"Yes, it turns out the reason he's in Chicago so much now is that his son is two and old enough to miss him when he's not around."

"That bastard! Here all this time, I've been sweating getting married and always talking about how much I want a child. And he *never* said he was a father." Candace was hurt and furious. She stood and paced back and forth on the grass. "He absolutely had me fooled. All those wonderful trips, exciting places." *The fantabulous love.* She calmed and sat down. "But ladies, I'm going to take it to heart. He never planned to give me a ring. He never said he wanted to get married. It was all me. I guess I was so caught up because for once, I had found true romance. I never get so involved with any one man. It was so unlike me," she continued trying to rationalize her experience and ease what was now a painful revelation. She shook her head. "Well, he won't have to worry about me anymore. In fact, he needs to lose my number. I'll handle it."

"Listen, Candace, we didn't want to wait another day. That's why when Sierra got in last night and told me what she found out, I said we needed to meet you today."

"And although it's hurtful, I appreciate it, Nevada. If anyone had to break the news, I'm glad it was you."

"Yeah, sorry again, but we didn't want him to continue leading you on," Sierra expressed with empathy.

Candace remained on the bench after her friends left. She was somber and while disturbed at the news, she was pleased she'd discovered the truth about Don. She couldn't resist pulling out her cell and searching for his number. She sent a text: *Pls lose my number.* Even if she didn't mean the words in totality, she wanted him to feel her wrath without explanation. In actuality, she never wanted to see his face again. She pouted, stood, held her head high, and headed to the subway. She'd struck zero, but in her mind, she felt like a ten.

CHAPTER 48

NEVADA

Recuperating from bringing the sad but eye-opening news to Candace, Nevada had checked on her welfare several times. It was a crushing reality about Don, the man she overwhelmingly discussed in all of her conversations. Nevada was surprised to conclude that Candace appeared to be settling down and focusing on her career. In privacy, Nevada had told Tai, the other third of their trio. She, too, had placed calls to Candace and promised they would all connect soon for lunch. She and Nevada considered it best to allow her some space.

It had been two weeks and Nevada was inching closer to news for her other bestie. She had gained ground and it was a matter of time before she may solve Tai's mystery.

Tai checked the caller ID. It was Nevada. "Hey, girl, how you doing?"

"Well, I'm doing fine...I guess. We need to talk—immediately."

"Okay. You want to stop by? I'm here alone. Trista started back at Seacoast and Marco's working late tonight."

"Bet. I'll be there in twenty." They disconnected the call.

Tai walked downstairs to the kitchen to wait for Nevada. When she heard the doorbell, she opened the door to allow her inside. "Come on back."

Nevada trailed her to the kitchen, her head hanging low with an unusual shuffle.

Tai grabbed a wine bottle. "I've got one chilled—"

"No thanks. It's not that kind of party."

"Oh, please sit." She placed the bottle back on the counter, pulled out a chair and Nevada joined her at the table.

"Tai, you're not gonna believe what I found out."

She asked eagerly, "You solved my mystery?"

Nevada nodded, barely able to look her directly in the eyes. "Yes."

"You're usually so bubbly with your cases, but you're looking kinda scary. I hope I won't be too creeped out. I'm not in danger, am I?" she asked with concern.

"Nope." She sighed. "Let me break it down for you."

Tai jumped up to get two bottles of water from the fridge. She handed Nevada one and she twisted hers to open. Nevada sat hers on the table. "Thanks."

"I'm going to tell you the whole case first, not who. Okay?"

"That's fine." Tai attempted to remain calm although her nerves skyrocketed.

"Here's how it all evolved. Remember the flower. I kept saying it was unusual, so I went to Blooms in Northwest, the name of the shop on the card from Marco. Turns out the flower is called a Blazing Star. It's definitely unusual and the lady there said they specialize in a lot of exotic flowers and plants. This led me to suspect that since the arrangements both featured the same flower that it was possible they could have come from the same shop. So this was one clue. I followed my hunches.

"The office party for Noni," she continued. "You recall I volunteered to stay behind and clean up?"

"Oh, yes, of course, that was nice of you." Tai took a swig of water.

"Hmmm, I led everyone to believe I was simply helping out. I was actually on the case. Tai, I had deduced that sometimes we think of suspects as being total strangers when in fact, they could be someone right under your nose. So I wanted to rule that out. I threw away all the plates but when I arrived, I was equipped with a box of Ziploc bags. I put on gloves and placed each plastic cup in a separate bag, writing on the bag the person's name with a Sharpie."

"Wow, Nevada, you are smooth," Tai complimented, still unsure of the outcome and listening intently.

"I try to be but thanks," she acknowledged. "So I took them all to the lab for DNA processing. In addition, I'd dropped off both of the notes you'd given me to check DNA on those."

"Did you get results back?"

"I'm getting there. Back to the office party," she recalled, "you also may remember I took a group photo, right?"

"That's right."

"Tai, I don't like droppin' this bomb on you, but it's your girl… Felicia."

She jumped up in amazement. "What?! No way!" She sat back down and stared at Nevada to read her lips. "Come again."

"Fe-li-cia. It's Felicia." She shook her head. "When I went to Blooms, I also showed the woman—apparently she works there all the time, she's the owner's daughter—the group photo. I asked her if she recognized anyone in the photo who may have bought flowers at the shop. She pointed to Felicia. She also recalled that the bouquet she purchased with cash had a Blazing Star, just like the one in Marco's bouquet. The woman said Felicia paid for the delivery and insisted she not include a card identifying their shop and simply wanted the sender to be anonymous, a 'secret admirer.'"

Tai rose and walked to the cabinet for pain medicine. She returned to the table and downed a pill with the water. "I can't believe this. Felicia, huh? My right-hand woman, office manager, confidante, Miss On Point, all of that, but none of that. What a bitch!" She had been pitifully backstabbed, she thought.

"And Tai, here's the clincher. I really hate to deliver this news."

"Don't tell me there's more to this story. Naw, naw." She shook her head in disbelief. "Bring it on, Nevada. I don't think it could get worse."

"Well, brace yourself. After I realized she was the culprit, I decided to tail her a couple of times..."

"Hold up, speaking of tailing, I bet you she had someone follow me that night. I dropped her off at the subway—"

"Yeah, but she also could've jumped in someone's car and had them trail you. I can't speak on that incident, but we definitely know she's the one who placed the note on your car and left the note at the restaurant. She tried to throw you for a loop, for you to think that they were from male and female sources, but it was all her. Felicia."

"Wow, I can't believe it. I'm dumbfounded."

"Like I said, sometimes it's someone in your backyard, no pun intended, as you often describe Marco that way. But yeah, she's a sneaky bee-atch."

"You right about that. But I got you sidetracked. You were saying that you tailed her."

"Yes, twice. I used Ryan's sports car to ensure I'd be incognito. She's seen my SUV. So, I really don't...uh, I'm stalling. Okay, she's kickin' it with Austin." She sighed heavily.

"Austin? My ex, Austin?"

"Yes, your ex, Austin. I didn't want to tell you—"

"That bitch! You are lying, Nevada."

"I wish I was, but yep, she goes to his spot and he lays up at hers."

Tai stood and walked to the window. She looked out and then turned to face Nevada. "No wonder she never brings her *man* around. She simply calls him Stan. Stan, my ass. She's always saying she's got this wonderful lover but remains guarded about his identity, what he does for a living, where he lives, everything. She shares absolutely nothing about him. Now I can see why." She shook her head. "I truly thought she was my girl. I trusted her. And wow, she was so phony when I got the flowers, telling me how pretty they were and how it was cool a secret admirer had sent them. Huh, she was the damn admirer, all right. Or rather the hater. Here she was right under my nose.

"It's all so strange, though. What made her decide she wanted to play stalker and make me think I was losing my mind? Stressing me out. Dropping off notes. Following me. And now it makes sense, Nevada. She was at work when I left early to prepare dinner that day. She must've left out after me and followed me to the store. Then I'd told her the restaurant where I was taking Marco for dinner. She was using all of that info against me, to drive me insane," she reflected. "It's all coming into place now. I can't thank you enough. It hurts but at least I found out she's a ratchet hussy."

"What now?"

"For starters I'm firing her ass. I want to think of the best way to do this, make her look and feel like a fool." She brainstormed for options. "Hmmm, I'd like to have her come here."

"To your house? You sure?"

"Oh, right, bad idea. She's been here for the ladies nights. I should embarrass her in front of the crew. But no, I want to maintain my image. I do have my reputation to keep intact and don't need to bring myself to her level. I tell you what, can you come to the office in the morning? You can be in the office and I'll call her in."

"Cool. That'll work."

"I'd love to slap her ass, though, but again I won't go there. I'll do it with words."

"That's a bet."

Tai was eager to share the news with Marco and couldn't wait to see his reaction. He'd arrived sweaty from working all day in the heat so he jumped immediately in the shower. She'd brought a bottle of Hennessy from the bar downstairs. She poured two shot glasses and awaited on the bed. When Marco entered the bedroom, she handed him a glass.

"Wow, you're going strong tonight."

"Wait until I tell you what I found out, Marco," Tai stated, still in disbelief.

"I'd better sit down for this one." He sat beside her on the bed. They raised their glasses and clinked, swallowing the shots.

"Baby, Nevada stopped by today."

"She got results?"

"Oh, boy, did she ever. It was Felicia."

Marco gasped. "You've got to be kiddin' me. Felicia? The honest, loyal confidante Felicia?"

"Yes, it knocked me off my feet, too. Let me tell you the deal…"

He rose to pour another round of shots, taking both glasses to the table. "Hold up. I've gotta have another one…or two." He handed her the glass. They downed their second round. *"Felicia?"*

CHAPTER 49

TAI

"Here we go," Tai informed Nevada, sitting in a chair in her office. She buzzed the intercom in Felicia's office. In case trouble ensued, she'd already alerted the security guard in the lobby that she planned to terminate Felicia.

"Good morning, boss. What can I do for you?" Felicia inquired.

"Come to my office." Tai refused to be her usual courteous self, using "please" or "thanks."

"I'll be right there."

Felicia knocked on the door and opened. "Oh, hi, Nevada; I didn't realize you were here."

Nevada, seated in the corner, simply nodded, throwing darts with her eyes toward Felicia. She was steaming that she'd betrayed her friend and caused unwarranted drama in her life.

"Have a seat." Tai pointed to the empty chair in front of her desk. She wanted to look at her piercingly in the eyes. Felicia sat as instructed, beginning to feel a negative vibe. "So, do you have any idea why you're here?"

Felicia offered a fake smile and looked over her shoulder to check out Nevada. "No, I don't. What's happening?"

"You bitch," she charged forcefully. "You're a sneaky, backstabbing bitch. You see Nevada over there. She's a detective and her skills led her to find out you're the damn stalker. I don't even have to explain because you're aware of every single effin' thing you did to me," she stated, her voice elevating but careful not to attract attention from staffers. "The notes, the flowers, following me, stalking me."

"I... I..." Felicia couldn't find the words to respond. Her guilty expression spoke volumes.

"Yeah, 'I' is right, you selfish hussy." She smirked. "And oh, I also understand you're knockin' boots with my ex—the asshole."

She quickly straightened up in her chair, eager to talk. "I can tell you—"

"You have nooo shame in your game. You are scum," Tai spat with distaste. "I'd love to slap the shit out of you, but I won't go there. You're not worth being charged with assault."

"Look..."

"Go ahead, I'm listening, but I shouldn't give you the time of day."

"Austin, it was by accident."

"Oh, accident, huh? You go back and forth to each other's places by *accident*," Tai repeated sarcastically.

"No, I didn't mean that." Felicia looked in her lap and then held her head up, avoiding eye contact. "Austin and I were planning your birthday party at the hotel the night before. He'd asked me to meet him as he had some special touches and surprises. So I agreed. We met at the bar and one thing led to another. Blame it on the drinks. He got a room and it went from there. My drinks were strong that the bartender was hooking us with. We both woke up the next morning feeling guilty." She paused while Tai soaked up the scenario. She'd decided not to cut her off as her story was helping her to process why Austin pulled a no-show at the party. "The next day, Austin couldn't face you after what he'd done, cheating with me, so he didn't show up at the party."

"Right and I haven't seen him or talked to him since...but you have."

Felicia was speechless.

"Well, Miss Felicia, you can spend the rest of your life with him if you wish. The dawg. You two are good for each other and you'll have plenty of time. I'm officially terminating your position immediately with Next Phase of Life." She handed her a sealed envelope containing an official letter. "Get the hell out of my office and don't show your face anymore."

Felicia rose sullenly, her head dropped, and turned to head to the door. She'd betrayed Tai and as a result, she was now unemployed. She realized she had a sickness. In addition to "stealing" Austin, she'd hoped to someday steal Tai's status. Deep down, her desire was to drive Tai berserk so she couldn't focus on life. She had everything Felicia had ever wished for: a handsome husband, a thriving business, faithful friends, even exemplary cooking skills. Envy and bitterness had led her to such vicious behavior.

"By the way, we have boxes," Tai added, speaking to Felicia's back. "You'll find them in the conference room. And oh, one more thing, tell Austin he can kiss my entire black ass."

Felicia opened the door and walked out, closing the door behind her.

"Whew, you handled that, girlfriend. You handled that one." Nevada shook her head.

EPILOGUE

Six months later

CANDACE

Reverting back to her old ways, Candace was forever on the stroll for fresh romances, but this time, she vowed not to allow her feelings to become involved. Still seeking a ring someday, she'd decided not to rush into marriage, even if she met a prospect. After all, it wasn't always golden. For now, she'd relished the fun times with Don and their travel adventures and wouldn't dwell on his other family. She never heard from him after her final text. Recently, her latest was the handsome hunk Darrel, who owned a yacht docked in Annapolis. Their escapades on the water kept her occupied.

TRISTA

Miss Cynt and the Seacoast staff welcomed Trista back as a waitress. The seafood restaurant was truly her oasis where she was surrounded by support and appreciation. It had taken the stint in N.C. at Rumrock to help her realize that her heart was in the food industry. She didn't let her renewed dancing skills go to waste. She started teaching pole dancing classes to suburban housewives, twenty-something college students, and professionals who wanted to ease their tension after a day at work. Eventually, her goal was to save for her own apartment to establish independence. As promised, Tai helped her find a therapist and the office visits proved to help her manage her BPD. After the heartbreaking relationships with Kwik and Dorian, she'd taken a hiatus from romance, although she considered another ladies room adventure—no strings attached.

NEVADA

Ecstatic that she had solved the cases for both of her best friends, Nevada relished life as a detective. She'd thought about setting a goal to be an FBI agent. She and Ryan had discussed the idea, but she was leaning toward promoting Sleuths On Us. Her customer base continued to increase and after utilizing DNA to solve Tai's case, she also toyed with taking forensics courses. But neither idea proved to be feasible when she received news of her own. She was expecting a boy. Never in her dreams had she considered motherhood. She'd always denied she wanted to get married—that was still firm—but the pregnancy was truly a shock. Her parents were elated their first grandchild was on the way, and they couldn't wait to spoil him. Ryan was excited that he was going to be a dad. He'd already started buying infant-size sports T-shirts.

TAI

Tai had experienced happiness again after the turbulent period when she was stalked and betrayed. It was disappointing that Felicia and Austin had crossed her, and she was thankful Nevada had brought the truth to light. Her focus was on Marco, her adorable and loving husband, her lifelong supportive partner. They were close to celebrating their second year of marriage. Her personal relationships with her true friends were cherished. Next Phase of Life was flourishing and she'd promoted her true confidante, Noni, from receptionist to office manager, taking Felicia's position. After the ongoing encouragement from friends, she'd finally decided to launch a catering firm sometime in the future. And the most thrilling status was that she, too, was at the peak of her forty-something life: her belly was protruding, ironically along with Nevada's. She was expecting a girl in a few months. She had conceived after the storm and all was calm. Trista had helped her decorate the nursery and had already stated she wanted her niece to enroll in ballet, tap and jazz lessons. She was proud that she and Marco would soon be parents—and so was her mother-in-law.

Pieces of life had been under wrapped and now were revealed, she often thought.

ABOUT THE AUTHOR

Charmaine R. Parker is the author of *The Next Phase of Life* and *The Trophy Wives*. She is a former journalist who has worked as a reporter, copy editor, and managing editor. The publishing director for Strebor Books, she is the sister of *New York Times* bestselling author Zane. She received a bachelor's of fine arts in theater from Howard University and a master's in print journalism from the University of Southern California. Born in N.C. and raised in Washington, D.C., she started writing fiction during early childhood. She lives in Maryland with her husband and daughter. You may email her at charmainerparker@gmail.com. Visit the author on Facebook at Charmaine Roberts Parker, Twitter @Charmainebooks and Instagram at Charwrites.